GHOST ISLAND

K Patteson

ISBN: 1-7359525-0-5
ISBN-13: 978-1-7359525-0-5

To my Dad.

Who fostered my love of creepy old places
and what stories played out within their walls.

1

Winchester, Washington

Four Years Ago

"I said dig!" It was late, and it was raining. Eustice had woken his son, Gerald, by slapping him on the head and then ordered him to follow him out to the middle of the woods. Half stumbling out of bed, Gerald had put on the same clothes he had taken off before he'd gone to bed. As they walked through the kitchen and out the back door, Gerald had taken a look at the clock. Two in the morning. The rain was coming down in a steady shower. Eustice was not a man to answer questions, so Gerald had not asked any. Not even if he could go back to his room and get his rain jacket.

"You dig," Gerald said, refusing to take the shovel his father was handing him. It was a rare moment of extreme bravery. His father took one step and punched him in the face. The pain flaring under his eye, Gerald had been so focused on the human form wrapped in tarp, he hadn't seen it coming. His father tossed the shovel at his feet. "Dig," Eustice repeated, his lips curling as he said it. Gerald picked up the shovel, his eyes locked on the tarp. Whatever it was covering, Eustice wanted a grave dug for it. Maybe it was something other than a human. Maybe it just looked like a human. His father was a mean bastard, but murder? Gerald felt sick to his stomach at the thought. Looking again at his father, the question on his lips, he didn't dare ask. Eustice looked back at him and offered no answers. He looked once more at the wrapped form and mentally apologized to it, then he started to dig.

The punch to the face had cleared what was left of the fog of sleep, and Gerald's mind reeled with what had happened that night while his father had been on the mainland. Had he gotten in a fight? Eustice liked a fight, but only if he won, and he never fought fair. Had it gone too far? Gerald dug, the rain forgotten. Everything was forgotten but the person wrapped in the tarp. Gerald had never seen a dead body before, and he didn't know what he had expected, but it wasn't this. The tarp was wrapped around the body and duct taped to cinch it tight. Gerald could clearly see which end was the head and which was the feet. Where had Eustice gotten the tarp and the tape? Had he taken them with him? Had he planned on murdering someone? Cold rolled through Gerald, and his teeth began to chatter.

Eustice had killed someone. He snuck a look at his father when he tossed the shovel full of dirt. Eustice was standing in the rain, having the benefit of a rain slicker, and taking regular swigs from a whiskey bottle. 'He killed someone and I'm helping him cover it up.' Gerald thought to himself. 'If you keep digging, they will take you away with him.' But what was he to do?

"Keep going. I'll tell you when it's deep enough," his father said, seeing him pause. Gerald kept digging, the rain soaking through his clothes and running into his eyes. He wanted so badly to ask what had happened, who this person was, but his face still stung from the last punch. He worked in silence, shivering with the realization that his father had killed someone. Eustice was a bastard who loved nothing more than to hurt people. His mother knew that better than anyone, but murder? What had the poor creature suffered before Eustice let them go? How long before he found a reason to kill them? Himself, mother and sister. Gerald thought he was going to be sick and swallowed hard to hold it back.

"Stop." Eustice barked. Gerald stopped. He was shoulder deep in the sandy soil. "Get out." Gerald jumped out. "Grab that end." Gerald paused. He didn't want to touch it. "Grab it!" His father barked at him. Closing his eyes, he grabbed his end of the body and lifted. Whoever they had been, they had small ankles. Gerald almost dropped his end when he felt them. Any doubt that this was a human body, gone. "Don't be such a pansy ass." His father grunted. They counted to three and then threw the body into the grave. It landed with a wet thud. Gerlad stood there and watched the rain drops fall on the tarp, wondering if he should jump down and arrange the body in a more dignified position.

"Now fill it back in." His father snapped at him, turning and going back to the shelter of the trees. Gerald was tired, his back hurt, and his fear was turning to anger. He had a shovel in his hand. All he had to do was land one good hit to Eustice's head and all their problems would be over. But he didn't. He picked the shovel back up again and replaced all the dirt he had just removed from the hole. One shovel at a time, the tarp disappeared under the earth until it was no longer visible. By the time Gerald was tamping down the mound of dirt, Eustice was so drunk that he could not stand up without swaying and had to sit on a large rock. The bottle was empty and laid discarded next to Eustice's foot.

Maybe he could do it. Eustice was fast, but that was when he was sober. Maybe Gerald had a chance right now with him so drunk. He stopped working under the pretense of resting while he tried to figure out how hard he would have to swing the shovel to take care of it in one go. His hands tightening around the shovel, getting a good grip.

"Don't even think about it or I'll bury you next to her." Gerald looked over his shoulder. His father's glaring eyes were still visible in the night. Eustice was leaning heavily against a tree, but Gerald didn't like his chances and so went back to tamping. He tried not to think about what they were doing. Gerald tried to do the woman justice by making her grave look neat, which was hard to do with the rain. Using the handle of the shovel, he made a cross in the wet earth. Dawn was on its way. Gerald was shaking from the cold. He looked down on the fresh grave and hoped the woman would find some peace now.

"What was her name?"

"What the hell does it matter to you?" Eustice looked like he was going to hit him again.

"I'll make a name plate." Eustice got so close to him he could smell the whiskey on his breath.

"I don't know her name. It didn't come up in conversation. Now get back to the house." And Eustice pushed his son in that direction. Gerald walked quickly back to the house, happy to put distance between him and the scene. To his relief Eustice stayed behind at the graveside. The farther he got away from his father, the more he could feel the knot in his stomach loosen. By the time he reached the house, he was running, stopping at the back door to vomit before running up the stairs to his bedroom and locking the door behind him. Gerald broke out in uncontrollable shivers. Peeling his wet clothes off, he left them in a mound on the floor and wrapped himself in the blanket on his bed. He felt like he was going to be sick again. Taking deep breaths, he calmed himself, but fear was replaced with guilt. He should call someone, shouldn't he? Eustice had killed that woman. He had all but admitted it. The only phone in the house was downstairs. He was afraid to think what Eustice would do to him if he caught him on it. That was if it still worked. Eustice ripped it off the wall recently. His mother had managed to put it back, but no one had used it since. Finally warm, dry, and relatively safe, sleep pulled at Gerald. The sun was just making an appearance on the horizon when he finally let it take him.

When Gerald awoke late that morning, his first thought was, he had dreamt it. Then he saw the pile of wet clothes in the corner. He looked out his window which faced the back of the house and half expected to see a woman standing in the yard. It had not occurred to Gerald to make sure the person he had buried was, in fact, dead. He saw no one. He silently apologized to her again. His mother was making noise downstairs, and he could smell breakfast. If he didn't go downstairs soon, she would be up to check on him. 'You can't tell them, you can never tell them." He told himself. Not only would the beating from Eustice be tremendous, but he couldn't make his mother and sister live with the fear that was gripping him.

"What are you looking at?" His mother asked. Gerald was sitting at the table with a cup of coffee in his hand. His mother had put a plate of food in front of him and taken her seat across from him. Gerald hadn't noticed either. He could not take his eyes off the tree line at the back of the house. "Sorry." Gerald said out loud before he caught himself.

"You feeling okay Ger, you look like you've seen a ghost?" His mother asked from across the table. Gerald pushed his chair away and vomited.

2

For a whole month, life was close to normal. As the days and weeks had marched on, Gerald thought less and less about the woman buried in the woods. Though he still checked his bedroom window every night before he went to sleep and every morning when he woke up. Making sure she hadn't escaped her grave. Gerald was somewhat surprised and disappointed that no one from the mainland arrived to see what had happened to the woman they had buried. Every time he heard a boat engine, he looked to see if it was coming towards them. His father didn't speak of it, and neither did he. Then it rained again.

"Get up." His father woke him by smacking him in the head again. Gerald looked out the window and knew why he wanted him. His father had gone to the mainland that night. Eustice had not been to the mainland since he had brought home the body, and Gerald had wondered if he would be going soon. Eustice had been in an increasingly bad mood. When he left that night, Gerald had wondered if he would be coming back with another body. Now he had his answer.

Like the previous night, it was raining, and Eustice didn't

want to dig. Gerald said nothing this time. Clenching his jaw, he paid more attention to where in the woods they were going. When they got to a clearing, Gerald saw the mound of dirt from the last grave he had dug. Next to it was another body wrapped in a tarp. For one confusing moment, Gerald thought somehow the first body had escaped. Then he noticed this one was smaller than the other. Not by much, she had been shorter. Eustice told him where to dig. It was a little ways away from the other grave. Once again Eustice had already carried the body out to the clearing and gotten the shovel. He had gotten that far and then decided he didn't want to dig the grave. Gerald didn't wonder why he went through all the trouble of bringing the body out here before waking him to dig. He was just glad he didn't have to help carry it from the boat. He didn't want to touch them anymore than he had to. Gerald caught the shovel that was tossed at him and dug in silence. He had at least had the forethought of grabbing his rain jacket this time. Gerald apologized to the body once more, and once more, wondered where Eustice had gotten the tarp. Was he going to the mainland with the intention of killing? Eustice once again sat watching Gerald work and drank. Gerald had been digging for about an hour when his father broke the silence.

"Maybe next time I'll take you with me. About time you knew a woman." Gerald did his best to tune him out. He focused on the sound the shovel made when it went through the wet dirt. "I only do it when it's raining. Harder for them to find evidence when it's raining. Bet you didn't know that, did you? The rain washes everything away. As long as you do it on a rainy night, you can get away with murder." Eustice was a cunning man who mistook this for intelligence. He said the reason he hadn't gone to college was because there was nothing else for him to learn. "I wish there was a way for me to keep them around really. Such pretty little things. Then I could enjoy them whenever I wanted." This was what Eustice did. He would rile you up so you would fight back and then he would pound you. He liked it when you fought back.

There was a long enough pause that Gerald thought he was done talking. "Victoria's getting to be a pretty young thing, isn't she?" Gerald was out of the hole and had the handle of the shovel to Eustice's neck before he knew what he was doing. Eustice saw him coming and put his hands up, keeping the handle from strangling him, but he was grimacing with the effort to keep it off his throat. Gerald was a lean seventeen year old, Eustice was a hard drinking fifty-five. Gerald leaned into it with all his weight and saw fear in his father's eyes for an instant before the meanness returned. Bringing his foot up, Eustice kicked Gerald in the stomach. Gerald stumbled back and over the mound of dirt falling into the grave he had been digging. Eustice stood over him with a smile that was all too familiar. Gerald had seen it several times from the same perspective. Looking up at Eustice after being knocked and punched down, with Eustice grinning in triumph over him.

"Nice to know you have some fight in you. Too bad it's not enough. Now finish." And he tossed him the shovel again. Eustice didn't speak the rest of the evening though, other than to bark orders. The rage in Gerald's stomach kept him warm that night. He wouldn't have been surprised if there was steam coming off him. He promised himself two things that night. He would not let his sister out of his sight, and he would make sure Eustice fried for what he had done.

Having finished the grave, Gerald picked up his end of the body and they once again threw the body unceremoniously into the grave. Once again, Gerald watched as the tarp disappeared with every shovel full of dirt he tossed back into the hole. An apology sent with every splat of dirt.

Having tapped down the mud, Gerald did the same as with the other and made a cross in the wet earth and wished that she would find peace. He tried not to make it look like he was too eager to get back to the house when in truth he wanted to run. Eustice did not stay out in the woods that night, the evening was going from bad to worse. There was thunder off in the distance. He did not spend the rest of the evening with his trophies, but followed his son into the house. "Keep quiet." His father said grabbing the back of his shirt and pulling him close. Gerald quietly made his way up to his room. Waiting until he could no longer hear his father moving, Gerald flipped through one of his books, and finding an empty page, ripped it out. Using the stump of a pencil, he quickly wrote down the dates his father had gone out to the island and where the bodies were buried. His heart was beating quickly. There was no doubt in his mind if Eustice knew what he was doing, he would kill him. Gerald wrote at the bottom 'Please forgive me. I helped him bury the bodies. Not because I wanted to, he made me.'

  It was important that they not think he had anything to do with it.

Folding the paper up as small as he could, he hid it in the pages of a book. "It would be the last place he would look." Gerald thought to himself, and then took the first deep breath he had managed all night. He was too exhausted to think what he was going to do with the paper, but it seemed important that what was happening be written down. Like writing down would somehow alert someone and bring help. Gerald once again wrapped himself in the blanket from his bed and let the sleep that comes with exhaustion claim him. His sleep was restless though. His dreams disturbed by women crawling out from their fresh graves muddy and confused. Gasping for breath having been buried alive. Wandering through the woods to his backyard and looking up at his window, looking for the person who had buried them.

3

Winchester, Washington

Present Day

The breeze whipped through Evelyn's hair as Mark guided the boat towards their island home for the next two months. She was glad she had decided on the island house. It felt like they were leaving the rest of the world behind them and all the stress that it brought. Evelyn looked over her shoulder at her daughter, Julia. She would be starting high school in the fall. What a great summer it would be for them to connect before she, as the mother, was pushed aside for the all-important friends. It would be good to reconnect with Mark too. Looking at her husband, it struck her once again how he was getting better with age.

The past few months had thrown them in every direction it seemed, and there had been little time to talk about anything except immediate needs. As the trip neared, Evelyn had thought that two months on an island in the Northwest was a bit extreme, but now she agreed with herself that it was exactly what they needed as a family. They were just a short boat ride to the town. The island had plenty of space for Julia and Twain to explore. The golden retriever sat next to her, his face pushed into the wind like hers, letting the wind blow his thick golden hair back and sniffing the wind. Yes, this would be exactly what they needed so that when they went back to the hustle of 'normal' life they would be better equipped.

"Almost there." Mark yelled, pointing off in the distance. The boat had come with the rental of the house since it was the only way to and from the island. The island was visible from town, that's how close it was, but the house was now becoming clearer. The roof was peeking out over the tree tops at them. The gray shingle siding showed through the trees. Mark pulled the boat up alongside the dock with skill Evelyn did not know he had.

"Land Ho…" He said, turning off the engine.

"Let's get the food in first and then we can come back for the luggage." Julia ,wearing the standard teenage gear of headphones, sunglasses, and bored expression, picked up a single bag of groceries, threw her backpack over her shoulder, and made her way to the house. Twain followed obediently behind her. Evelyn and Mark exchanged looks.

"You okay with that bag honey? It's not too heavy?" Mark asked Julia who did not hear him over her head phones. This exact moment was one of the reasons they had agreed to come out into the middle of nowhere. They hoped that by removing her from everything teenager, she would see there was a world around her. Something she seemed not to notice anymore. Mark grabbed as many groceries as he could, and Evelyn pulled the cooler and carried the rest of the groceries in her other hand. Together they made their way to the house that would be their home for the next two months.

The house was bigger than they really needed. Three stories. But it was the remoteness they had wanted. The incline to the house was enough to take their breath. It had been nicely mulched with lights lining either side, so they would be able to find their way in the dark. Coming to the top of the hill, the path then wrapped around the side of the house to a small porch. Julia was standing on the front porch looking out when they came up.

"What do you think? Will this do?" Evelyn asked slightly out of breath from dragging everything up the hill. A shrug was the only response. At least there was a response this time. Usually Julia pretended she hadn't heard her. Evelyn dug the keys out of her pocket and opened the door. It was fantastic. The walls had been painted a light color to make the most of what sunlight managed to get through the trees surrounding the house. The furniture was of an older style, but it worked. The living room led to a large family kitchen, all the bedrooms were upstairs. The third- floor attic had been converted into a large bedroom for two with an ensuite.

"Go pick out your room, Honey, and then help get our things out of the boat." Julia went up the stairs and Evelyn and Mark dropped the groceries in the kitchen.

"I'm going to go check out the master." Mark said and left her to put the groceries away. It was fantastic. She could see them living here comfortably for the next few months.

Mark came downstairs a few moments later. "The bathroom is to die for. We have a great view of the water too."

"Where's Julia?"

"She has chosen the attic bedroom. Surprise. She was lying on the bed with her headphones on when I saw her."

"I hope she opens up here. I swear I spend most of my time these days keeping myself from ripping those headphones out of her ears."

"I think she's a little concerned about what to do out here in the middle of nowhere." Evelyn shrugged her shoulders.

"So am I, but won't it be nice to have to look for things to do instead of having too much to do?"

"I'm going to start hauling stuff up from the boat." Mark leaned over the counter and kissed her before making his way back down.

"I'll come down and help you when I get this stuff put away." Mark walked out the door and said, "What are you doing out here buddy?" He leaned down to scratch Twain's ears. "I think he's afraid of the new place." He called back to Evelyn. "Go on Twain. This is home." And taking the dog by the collar, he led him into the house. Twain half crawled into the house and then went under the coffee table and hunkered down. Mark and Evelyn exchanged looks. "I guess he doesn't like being in a new place." Mark said.

"He'll be fine once we settle in." Evelyn put the groceries in their place while she examined the house around her. It felt like a home, a proper home, and she couldn't figure out what made it feel different from the other rental houses she had stayed in. The house had been advertised as originating on the island in the 1920's as a fishing post and had been a place of rest for fishermen for many years. Whoever had decorated it had obviously kept this in mind when renovating. The lamp next to the sofa was a fish with the top of the lamp coming out of its tail. She leaned over the sink to get a better look at a panoramic picture of fishermen lined up in front of a building, holding their nets. There had to be twenty of them. She could just see the porch behind them, the same one they had just walked across.

Julia lumbered down the stairs. "Did you choose your room?" Evelyn asked. She had gotten used to the fact that her daughter always looked bored these days no matter what was going on.

"Yeah, used to be the attic. What's the Wifi password?"

"It's in that paperwork in my purse. You can look. The agent did warn me that while they have Wifi out here, it can be spotty, so don't throw a fit if you can't get online."

"Whatever." Evelyn had also gotten used to that word, which was good because it seemed to have replaced most other words in her daughter's vocabulary. "Where's Dad?"

"Getting the rest of our stuff out of the boat. Why don't you go help him? He's gonna need it with all those books you brought. Why didn't you just put them on your e-reader?" This elicited an eye roll so large Julia's eyes almost rolled back in her head.

"I told you, some of them I already had, but I want to re-read them. There wasn't any point in buying them again just to put them on the e-reader." With this Julia put her ear buds back in her ears and slapped the screen door open whistling to Twain as she did so. Like a shot, the golden retriever was up and out the door before it could close behind them. Evelyn shook her head. Julia was a good kid. She knew she was. She had a good head on her shoulders, didn't take anyone's crap, and loved her dog. Like her parents, she seemed to prefer the company of books to people and luckily had found a group of friends who felt the same way. It was for this reason that Julia had not thrown a fit when Evelyn and Mark had floated the idea for this trip. Julia had a stack of books she had been wanting to read but had not been able to because of school and the rest of what had been happening in their lives. From what she had been able to gleam from Julia's Instagram account and what few conversations she had with her in recent months, there were new books out from a few different book series Julia and her friends followed, and they had all promised to read them together over the summer break. 'Together' meaning at the same time, in different places, and then talking about it over Instagram and text all summer.

Evelyn, having put all the perishables in the fridge, now started on the dry goods. They had bought enough for a week since they were planning on going to town at least weekly, if not more. She sometimes worried about Julia's ability to socialize, and they had talked about the fact that secluding themselves on an island for two months would do nothing to help Julia's naturally anti-social tendencies.

"We were the same when we were that age, and we turned out alright." Mark had told her. And it was true. The world finds ways of making you deal with other people. Even she, a writer who spent most of her time in her office with no one around, was not socially inept. Though she could think of a few of her distinguished colleagues who were. When she had met Mark, she had definitely been the more social out of the two of them, and now he spoke in front of classrooms of disinterested college students daily. Evelyn shrugged her shoulders at her own thoughts. 'That's what mothers do isn't it? We worry. If I wasn't worried she wasn't social enough, I would be worried she was too social. Actually, out of the two options, I think I like things better the way they are."

Her thoughts were interrupted by the screen door banging open and Mark stammering through pushing one large suitcase in front of him while pulling a second one behind him.

"Julia, you could have gotten the door." Mark yelled.

"I told you to hold on. I'm coming." Julia was several steps behind him, struggling up the hill under the weight of the suitcase with her books inside.

"Hold on, I'm coming." Evelyn came out from around the kitchen counter and relieved Mark of the suitcase he had been pushing, freeing a hand to push the screen door back and pulled the second case through. Normally a patient man, Mark did not like being out of breath and sweating. "They could have told us we would have to hike half a mile up a damned hill to get to the house. We may not have brought as much with us." He half flung the case into the room.

"You could have brought one up at a time and waited for me to come help you." Evelyn politely informed him.

"When's dinner?" Was his answer. Julia came through the door. She was also out of breath and looking a little red in the cheeks. She dropped her bag on the floor and collapsed onto the sofa. Evelyn looked at her watch. It was already seven, and if she was perfectly honest with herself, did not feel like cooking.

"Do you feel like driving back to town? Maybe get something there?" Mark nodded his head. "You might have to drive back because I'm having a beer."

"Alright, let's go back the way we came." They grabbed their stuff and headed back out the door.

"What about Twain?" Julia asked as they went down the steps of the front porch. He was looking rather sad laying under a rocking chair on the front porch.

"Well, I'm not sure we are going to be able to take him into a restaurant with us."

"Moooom, we can't leave him here. It's our first night."
Evelyn had to admit it seemed like a mean thing to do.

"Okay, we'll figure it out." The words were no sooner out of
her mouth than Twain shot out from under the rocker and flew
past them down the hill. He was sitting at the front of the boat,
tongue hanging out and looking very pleased when they
managed to catch up with him. "Move over skipper, I'm
driving." Twain bounced into the seat next to Mark, and they
went back to town with Twain as the co-captain.

4

The only place they could find that was open and had outside seating for Twain was the pizza place, which was fine. The waitress came up and asked them if they knew what they wanted.

"Yeah, I think we are just going to go with the peperoni." Evelyn said. She always ordered. Not because she loved it particularly, but because her husband froze at the thought of ordering from a stranger, and Julia was a teenager. Evelyn thought it made her look overbearing to order for the whole table, but if the waitress didn't speak in blank stares and eye rolls, they would never order.

"I don't think I've seen you all around. Are you visiting?" Her name tag said 'Becky', as she took their menus.

"It's our first night here." Evelyn answered.

"Well, welcome to Winchester. Are you staying at the lodge?"

"No, the house on the island actually. We'll be here for the summer."

"The island right out here? Sea Island?" Becky pointed in the general direction of the island. Evelyn couldn't tell if the look on her face was one of concern or confusion.

"That's it."

"I didn't realize they were letting people live out there. I mean, that they were renting the place." Becky opened her mouth like she was going to say something else but turned it into a smile and walked away to put in their order.

"Weird." Julia offered, not taking her eyes off the book she had propped up on the condiments rack. Evelyn took it as nothing more than a local not being thrilled that such a prominent house was being used as a vacation rental.

"So, what are we going to do tomorrow? Our first full day of vacation."

Mark shrugged his shoulders. "What do you want to do?"

"I think just go out and explore…"

"There's a book store between here and the harbor." Julia piped up. Her parents looked at her somewhat in surprise as they had not thought she was paying attention on the walk through the town. "I saw it when we were walking up the street here. It's closed, or I would ask to go tonight. It looks kinda neat."

"Didn't you bring enough books with you?" Mark asked. Julia rolled her eyes.

"Honey, you know there is no such thing." Evelyn joked. "I think it was a used bookstore wasn't it? Maybe Julia can trade some of the books she's read for new ones. We are going to be here long enough. I wouldn't mind looking around the town more myself. It looks like most of the stores are closed for tonight. So, we will get up when we get up tomorrow, and when we are ready, we'll make our way back over here and have a look around. Sound like a plan?"

"While you too are in the bookstore, I can check out the bait and tackle shop." Mark had decided he was going to fish on this trip. Something he hadn't done in over twenty years. He had even brought his horrible, floppy fishing hat along just for the occasion.

They ate their pizza, and by the time they were done, the sun was hanging very low in the sky, so they decided to make their way back to the island. Neither Evelyn nor Mark was familiar enough with the island to find the dock in the dark. Evelyn went in to pay the tab.

"It was nice meeting you." Becky said. "Hopefully we'll see you again soon."

"I'm sure you will, thank you." Becky held onto her receipt when Evelyn went to take it from her, and Evelyn looked up at her with that same concerned look.

"You be careful out there on the island." She released the receipt and went back into the kitchen. Evelyn shrugged it off at the time, but when they had gone to bed that night she found she couldn't stop thinking about it. After reading the same page in her book three times without taking any of it in, and said, "The waitress at the restaurant tonight told me to be careful out here on the island."

"What's strange about that?"

"It was how she said it, like she was trying to warn me about something."

"There's nothing out here. What would she be warning you about?"

"I don't know. It was just strange."

"Probably just hazing the tourists. Don't worry about it."

"I hope so.

5

When Evelyn woke up the next morning, way later than she normally woke, she had completely forgotten about the waitress's strange warning. She lay there for a moment enjoying the luxury of not having to rush out of bed and then made her way downstairs. Mark was in the shower, and it sounded like Julia was up because she could hear something moving on the floor above her. She went downstairs and started pulling out food for breakfast.

"What time is it?" Mark said coming down the stairs.

"I have no idea. Isn't it wonderful?"

"What's for breakfast?"

"Eggs and sausage, and coffee is going over there. Oh my goodness, this is brunch, not breakfast." She said, looking at the clock. They had slept until ten. She couldn't remember the last time she had done that. "I guess we will eat and then make out way over to the island, probably plan on eating dinner over there."

Having heard her parents moving around, Julia lumbered down the stairs, eyes still glazed from sleep. Twain followed closely behind her.

"How did you sleep dear?"

"Aagh, fine I guess. Didn't go to bed until two."

"Couldn't sleep in a new place?" Mark asked.

"No, finishing a book. I'm going to take it with us today so I can trade it." Evelyn smiled. Julia was a teenager with all that went with it, but she loved her books and that made her mother's heart proud.

Coffee drunk, teeth brushed, and breakfast eaten, they piled into the boat and once again headed over to town. With Twain, of course. He had not waited to be invited this time but ran for the boat when he saw they were leaving. Evelyn had a thought as she watched the house grow smaller. The house was clearly built in the early part of the century, so maybe this used book store would have some history on it. It would be fun to see what kind of life it had before it was a rental property. Why was it built on an island with no other houses? She thought about the picture of the men standing in front of the porch and who they were. Maybe she would find out why the waitress last night was so concerned. Was there a legend around the island that only natives to the town knew about? She shrugged her shoulders to herself. Who knew, there might even be a book in it. You said you wouldn't think about work. She told herself. That doesn't mean you should ignore a good story if you find one. She answered herself.

They pulled up to the dock, and Julia almost jumped out of the boat. Twain jumping out after her, tongue flying out of his mouth. "Twain." Mark had yelled after him, but Twain paid no attention. He ran straight to Julia who had stopped and picked up Twain's trailing leash. With Twain, Julia then turned and started for the bookstore. Evelyn was still getting out of the boat.

"Julia! Wait for the rest of us!" Her mother yelled after her.

"Well, hurry up." Julia did not run back, but instead stood still, impatiently waiting for her parents to catch up.

"What are you in such a hurry for? It's not going anywhere." Her father said as they got closer. Julia shrugged her shoulders, "I can't help it if you guys are slow." Together as a family, they made their way up the same high street they had walked up the night before.

"Are you going to look for your book?" Her husband teased, tugging at her hand. Of course she was. Any author of any book looked for their book when they entered a book shop. It didn't matter what kind of bookstore it was.

"Please, people don't get rid of my books." She joked back. Evelyn had just finished her third book of fiction before they came out on vacation. It would be published in the fall, and though she knew writing and publishing three books in a lifetime was more than most authors accomplish, for the first time in her life she didn't know what she was going to write about next. It was said that everyone had one good book in them, and she had written three. While they may not stand up to the test of time, they had sold well. But she didn't like the idea that she would never write anything worthwhile again.

They found Julia and Twain standing in front of the store. Julia looking impatient and Twain's tail wagging. "I'll take him while you too have a look around." Julia handed over the leash. "Don't spend too much money." Evelyn gave him a peck on the cheek before following Julia through the door of the bookstore.

The door hit a bell above it as they entered, and Evelyn was instantly hit with the smell of aging paper that so epitomized old bookstores. The place was like stepping back in time. The décor had not been changed for at least one hundred years. Every available inch was covered in books; it would be impossible to search every title in a day. Where there was a table, there were books stacked on top of it as well as below it. Bookshelves had categories, but they were still so over-stuffed with books going every which direction it was hard to find where one category ended and the other began. A kindly woman in her fifties lifted her head from the book she was reading and, pulling down her reading glasses, letting them fall on the chain around her neck said, "Hello, can I help you find anything?" Evelyn wondered honestly if she could. She thought about asking for a title just to see if the woman would be able to locate it.

"Yes, do you buy books?" Julia piped up and practically leapt towards the counter.

"Of course." Evelyn followed her daughter over to the counter while still looking around her and admiring how any available space had been put to use. The woman took Julia's book and turned it over in her hand.

"Does five dollars work?"

"Sure," Julia answered. The woman went to open the till and Evelyn stopped her. "She is planning on buying something, so you can just put it towards that if you want." The woman closed the till, "That works for me if it works for you. Let me know if you need anything." Julia nodded her head and then went off into the stacks like an explorer into the jungle.

"Well, that's her gone for the afternoon." Evelyn remarked.

"My name's Meg. Are you guys new to the area?" Evelyn was getting the idea this area didn't see a lot of tourists.

"Evelyn, we are staying here for the summer."

"Visiting?" Meg had a natural air about her, and Evelyn had

the impression that if they sat down and talked, they would become friends.

"Just vacationing. Hiding away from life for a while."

"That's fantastic that you are able to do that. Where are you staying?"

"Out on the island." Meg's expression immediately changed, and she looked down the aisle where Julia had disappeared.

"The house on Ghost Island?"

"I thought the name was Sea Island?" Evelyn's look of concern was greeted with Meg's smiling face and a nod. As far as she knew, there was only one island out there.

"Locals call it Ghost Island. When the weather rolls in, fog often comes with it. On the island for some reason the fog moves through the trees and gets stuck…looks like ghosts. That and people think the place is haunted."

"Is there a reason people think it's haunted?" This time it was Evelyn who almost leapt towards the counter. She was not alarmed by the idea that the house might be haunted. In her travels, she had stayed in haunted hotels and B&B's, and had taken many haunted tours. Never yet had she seen a ghost. The stories were an interesting way of finding out local history though, and her author spidey-sense was sensing a story.

"The fog is the biggest reason. Rumor has it a few sailors came to a violent end out there on drunken nights." Evelyn got the impression Meg wasn't telling her everything, but she didn't push it.

"I was actually going to look for some information on the place, do you have any?" Meg's face went back to business.

"I'm sure we have something in our local history section." She came off her stool and around the counter, and Evelyn followed her down one of the aisles. Meg kept looking over her shoulder like she was going to say something, but then thought better of it. Evelyn remembered the waitress from the night before and wondered why it was striking people as strange that they were staying on the island.

"If we have it, it should be here," she said, stopping in front of a bookshelf towards the back of the store. The Local History section was possibly the smallest section in the entire store, taking up only two shelves. "Thank you, this will be great." Evelyn started looking through titles for ones of interest. Meg did not go back to her counter. She continued to stand next to Evelyn like there was something else. The tension reaching a certain point, Evelyn decided to take the direct approach.

"Have you lived here a long time?" Evelyn asked.

"All my life." Meg answered.

"Maybe you can help me with something else."

"Of course."

"People keep reacting in a strange way when we tell them we are staying on the island. Why is that?"

Meg shrugged her shoulders. "People are probably surprised to find someone is staying out there. We've all been watching while work was being done on the house, but I don't think anyone thought that people would want to stay there."

"Why not?" Evelyn was a dog with a bone now. She could smell there was a story that Meg was trying not to tell her.

"Again, local legends."

"Well, I'm interested, you have me intrigued." Sensing she wasn't going to get out of this gracefully, Meg gave in.

"Several years back, there was a family that lived out there. They were pretty messed up as it turns out, and it all came to a violent end. People avoided the island even before then, but very few would step foot on it now."

"How messed up?" Evelyn knew without Meg saying another word that this was her next book .

"Serial killer messed up. The town hasn't seen anything like it before or since, thankfully."

"Is there anything about it in these books?"

"I wouldn't think so. Most of this stuff is going to be farther back than that. Back when the town was using the island to house rowdy fishermen. The newspaper would have archived articles about it. As you can imagine, it was big news at the time. Or you could get it straight from the horse's mouth. The sheriff was there when it all went down, so he might be willing to tell you. Is this going to be your next book?"

"How did you know I was a writer?"

"I recognize you from your book jacket."

"Do you like mysteries?"

Meg waived her hand around the room. "I like everything."

"Evelyn Cunningham, author of three books and desperately looking for her fourth." Meg smiled broadly.

"Three books? I only knew about the two."

"It won't be out until the fall, just finished it. If I get an advanced copy while I'm here, I'll bring it by for you." This got a very wide smile out of Meg. "That would be fantastic, thank you. Your books sell very well here." Meg said.

"I'm sorry to hear that actually. I was just joking with my husband that my readers never got rid of my books."

Meg left Evelyn to look through the stacks of local books. Julia swung by briefly, three books in her hands.

"Remember all the books you brought with you ." Evelyn reminded her.

"I'm trying for a book and a half a week, Mom, and at that rate, I'm going to run out in two months." Julia said as she passed. Evelyn's phone buzzed. Text message from Mark.

```
Mark: How much longer?  Twain is going nuts.

Evelyn: We are both heavy in the stacks,
        at least another half an hour.

Mark: Going for a walk then,
      will catch up with u later.
      Luv u

Evelyn: xoxo
```

Evelyn looked down at her watch. It was already two in the afternoon. She could see them spending a decent amount of time here and then they would be ready for dinner after walking around the town a little more. She went back to looking through the stacks. Meg had been right. They were mostly about the island's fishing days, but they may answer why there was only one house built and expose any secrets from the early days. That being said, she kept a firm eye out for anything having to do with the killings that Meg had mentioned. Evelyn was seriously thinking about getting in touch with the sheriff and seeing if he would talk to her.

Having chosen the books she thought useful for the time being, Evelyn made her way to the front of the shop. Julia was there picking through the paperbacks on the floor.

"Julia, we'll be back dear."

"I know." She said reluctantly getting up off the floor.

"Come on. Dad texted Twain is going nuts without you around." Meg had taken up her book behind the counter again and closed it as they approached.

"I got to thinking." Meg said. "I know you are on vacation

and so feel free to say no, but we don't get authors here very often and I would regret not at least asking. Would you be willing to do a reading for us? Maybe in a week or so?"

"Do you think anyone would be interested?" Evelyn could feel Julia rolling her eyes, she did so every time her mother mentioned being an author out in public.

"I can think of a handful that would show up, maybe more. Nothing too grand."

"I would love to." Evelyn pulled out a card from her purse. "E-mail me when you are thinking of doing it." Meg put their books in two bags and said, "Books are on the house then." This got a reaction out of Julia. "Really!"

"Absolutely. If you don't want those books on local history when you leave, just bring them back. Same goes for you. Just bring those books back and exchange them for new ones if you find yourself running out of reading material."

6

They were barely out in the street when Julia said, "Do you think that's why Twain doesn't like the house?"

Evelyn spun her head around. "What?"

"Because of what she said. The house and the island being haunted. Maybe he can sense it, ya know?"

"You heard that?" Julia shrugged her shoulders. "I have no idea why Twain doesn't like the house. It is probably because it is new and smells different from home. As for the house being haunted, I don't really believe in all that. Do you?"

Julia shrugged again, "It's kind of old and creepy out there on that island."

"Well hopefully, after reading these, we will have a better understanding of our vacation home and why it is out there on an island by itself. I can almost guarantee it has nothing to do with ghosts. " Evelyn looked at her phone. "We better get moving. Your father says he and Twain have found a park but he's not sure how long he's going to be able to keep Twain from looking for you." Evelyn messaged Mark that they were on their way. Heading in the direction of the park Julia said, "Are you going to go speak with the sheriff?" Evelyn stopped walking and looked at her daughter.

"How much of the conversation did you hear?"

"Almost all of it. It's not a big shop."

"Are you worried about something, Honey?" Julia shrugged again.

"The house is kind of weird. Don't you think?"

"I don't know, hadn't really thought about it. Weird how?"

"It's like it's empty and not empty all at the same time."

"Are you uncomfortable?"

"No, not really, just seemed strange that an empty house doesn't feel empty when you walk into it. It felt like there were people there who had left the room just as we walked in. Like they were in the other room or something." Evelyn did not put much into this. It was an old house, and what Evelyn interpreted as character, Julia was interpreting as creepy. After a few days in the house, it wouldn't feel so creepy anymore.

"You can help me with my research if you want. It'll be fun." Changing the subject.

"Maybe." Well, it wasn't a 'no'.

They found Twain running around off leash in the park. Mark had found a suitable throwing stick, and Twain ran back to them with the small tree limb hanging out of either side of his mouth. He looked very pleased with himself.

"Well, I see you both found something to interest you." Mark said, taking note of their bags. "Was it everything you hoped it would be?" To Julia. A half smile lit up her face and she said, "It's so cool. There are books everywhere, and the woman, Meg, is letting us just borrow the books."

"An interesting way to run a business." Mark lifted an eyebrow.

"I agreed to do a reading while we are here, from one of my books. I was interested in some local history books, and since she knew I probably wouldn't have any interest once we left to go home, she told me I could bring them back when I was done. I think she took one look at Julia and knew she would be a repeat customer." Julia had taken up the job of throwing the stick. Twain didn't seem to be running at his full speed.

"How long have you been out here?" Evelyn asked.

"Since you two went into the shop practically. No matter where we went, Twain kept trying to pull me back there. This was the only thing that distracted him." Julia having moved a safe distance away, she brought up what she had learned in the shop.

"Julia thinks Twain doesn't like the house because of something Meg told me."

"The bookstore owner? What did she tell you?"

"Well, she kept giving me the same response the waitress did last night, so I finally asked her point blank what the deal was. She said that something happened on the island a while back. She didn't go into a lot of detail, but she told me I could go talk to the sheriff if I needed more. He was a deputy when it happened."

"You thinking of using this for a book?" Evelyn shrugged her shoulders.

"I don't know. I don't know if there is anything to write about, but it's something to keep me entertained for the summer anyway. I have a bag full of books on local history to sort through."

"What did she say happened on the island?"

"Murder."

7

She watched him walk down the hill to the boat, and with every step he took, she could feel herself relax a little more. She hated the sight of him. She would leave, but she didn't know how to take the kids with her without him catching them. He had made it clear more than once that if she ever tried to leave, he would kill her, and she believed him. She had seen the look in his eye when he said it. There was no one she could ask for help. She never went to town when he wasn't with her, and then he was the perfect gentleman and loving husband. Who would believe her? Her family had all died years ago.

Gerald's heavy feet were making their way down the stairs. He had no doubt seen his father leaving and decided it was safe to come down.

"He's gone for the night, again? Nice clear night." Gerald said, coming to stand next to his mother. They could no longer see Eustice. The trees blocked their view, but they would continue to watch until they saw the boat moving towards the mainland.

"Going out more and more these days," she said, holding her own arms so tight her nails were leaving imprints.

"Are you complaining?"

"No, just wondering what he's up to over there." Gerald did not look at her.

"That's their problem." Gerald shrugged his shoulders. His mother looked at him sideways. It was unlike Gerald to speak this way. He had been acting strange in other ways as well. Sleeping until lunch time and not speaking much even when she spoke to him. It was like he was hiding something, and it hurt her feelings a little. It had always been them against Eustice. She hoped her son wasn't starting to turn out like his father.

They heard the boat motor start, but they continued to stand in silence for a little bit, keeping an eye on the part in the trees where they would be able to see the boat moving away from them. "Do you still love him?" Gerald asked not looking at her.

"What?"

"Do you still love him?"

"What would make you ask a question like that?"

"I was just wondering. We are both standing here, ready for him to be gone for the night so we can be ourselves. If you don't love him, what are we still doing here?" She reached out and rubbed his back.

"Because there is only one way off this island, son, and he just drove off in it. Believe me, if I could figure out another way, we would be gone by now."

"We could take the boat at night, when he's asleep."

"And do what when we get to the mainland? We have no car. We have no money. Eustice still has enough friends on the mainland. If we leave by boat, we are going farther than the mainland where no one would know who we are or who we are running from."

"I could swim over there and get us a boat, come back for

the two of you."

"If your father found you missing and even suspected what you were doing, you would be met on the dock by him and his shotgun, and I'm not so sure he wouldn't use it on you."

"So, you would really leave if I could figure out a way?"

"If you can find a safe way for us to get out of here, I would gladly leave. But the only way I can think of is to fly away, and I can't grow wings."

Something had been bothering her, nagging at the back of her mind, and now she wondered if Gerald hadn't picked up on it as well. She thought about asking him but didn't want to plant the idea in his head if it wasn't already there. They already lived in enough fear as it was. She thought she knew what Eustice was doing on the mainland, and Gerald was old enough he might have noticed as well.

Eustice didn't like her reading the paper, didn't like her having any contact with the world really, but with him gone more, she had been able to read the paper in relative peace from time to time. He was arrogant enough to think she still wouldn't read it when he was gone simply because he had told her not to.

The boat sped off in the distance, and Gerald went off into the living room to watch TV in peace. For some reason, this evening, the nagging in her mind would not stop. Gerald was right, what did she care what he was doing over on the mainland? The important thing was he wasn't here. But she had been reading the paper about the missing girls. She knew for a fact that Eustice was on the mainland on the dates they went missing. She went into the living room and grabbed yesterday's paper that was sitting next to Eustice's chair.

* * *

The search continues for the three missing women of Winchester. Yesterday a group of volunteers met in one of the nearby parks to search for any clues. A line of women and men walked from one end of the park to the other not knowing exactly what they were looking for but hoping to find something, anything that may give a clue in what has so far been a clueless case.

"We encourage women to be vigilant and walk with someone. If you don't have anyone to walk with, please call us, and one of my deputies would be more than happy to walk you to your car or back to your house. It doesn't matter how far or how short the distance," the sheriff said when asked what advice he had for residents.

"All we know about this person is they are obviously targeting women and in every single case the women left somewhere alone late at night and haven't been seen since."

"I think it's ridiculous," said Betty Hymer, a volunteer who has helped with every search party so far. "The sheriff should have called in the State Police by now. I mean I don't want to criticize since he is doing his best, but things like this don't happen here, do they? I've talked to most of the police force now, and none of them has ever worked on a case like this. We need help. We need and deserve to have police here who know what they are dealing with and how to handle it. I mean when the first girl went missing, that was bad enough, but after the second one, he should have called the state, and now there are three missing, and he still hasn't reached out. Single women are starting to spend the night at each other's houses because they are so afraid to be alone. I mean imagine there is a target on your back. Oh, I know whoever it is isn't after me, I mean none of these women has been over thirty, but still. I'm afraid of the dark and I'm sixty-five years old. It's ridiculous."

There have been other calls for the sheriff to hand the case over to more senior authorities. "My men went through the same training those officers did. I know these aren't muscles we get to flex around here a whole lot, thankfully, but I assure the public we are just as capable of handling this case as anyone else." The sheriff answered.

She skimmed the page for dates. In every paper they had listed the pictures of the missing women when they went missing and where they were last seen. The last couple of times Eustice had gone out, she had written down the date. If he found out she was keeping tabs on him, she would pay for it, so she never let the notes out of sight. The pictures took up the entire second page of the paper now. Pulling the piece of paper out of her pocket, she compared the dates. All three of them were a match. She looked at Gerald, her hand beginning to shake. What do you want to bet another girl was about to go missing tonight? Eustice was many things, but she never thought he would go so far as to kill. Her, maybe. But some stranger? She wanted to tell someone, warn them that he was heading for town, but who would she call? The police? What would she tell them? Eustice could be charming, he could be damned charming. He had been charming all the time they were dating. It wasn't until they were married and living out here on the island that things changed. The first time he hit her and knocked her to the ground, she had been shocked. All the more shocked because he didn't apologize, just walked over her like she was a piece of trash. It was so different from the man she had fallen in love with, the one who had held her hand and whispered lovely things in her ear. She thought for a crazy moment that she had married the wrong man.

She stood there with her hands shaking, wondering what

she was going to do? Without realizing it, she had moved back into the kitchen and was standing in front of the phone. She stared at it, and her heart beat faster. She didn't even know if it worked. She raised a shaky hand to the receiver. *"They all think you're crazy. That you won't leave the island anymore no matter how much I beg you."* Eustice's voice screamed in her ear. *"Told them you were gone. Went to go visit your mother and never came back. No one would know if you went missing."* This was his new threat. Her hand was really shaking now. They wouldn't believe her. She was Eustice's crazy wife. *Maybe the dates will be enough? A lot of people were out on those nights. Evidence: call the sheriff once you have evidence. You get them evidence, it won't matter how charming he is. They will have to arrest him.* The mental image of Eustice being taken away in handcuffs was enough to make her hands stop shaking.

She looked over at Gerald. *Maybe he could help me.* But she had meant what she had said earlier. It was no longer impossible to imagine Eustice shooting his own son if Gerald threatened him in any way. She had been worried about her daughter being alone with Eustice long before the missing girls. There had been a look in his eye more than once when he looked at his daughter, a look that made her uneasy. She didn't think Victoria had noticed, but the poor thing stayed locked in her room most of the time afraid to come out. No, it wouldn't be fair to involve the children. It would have to be her.

If Eustice was out tonight, it was entirely possible that he would come home with a victim. It would be tonight then. She grabbed Gerald's arm. "Keep an eye on your sister."

"What?"

"I want you to keep an eye on your sister. Don't leave her alone with him, you understand me?"

"What's wrong?"

"Just promise me baby. I can't tell you what I'm thinking right now, but I'm worried what might happen if he gets Victoria alone, so promise me you won't let that happen."

"I promise."

"That's a good boy." She kissed him on his head and went back into the kitchen to figure out what to do next.

8

The house was silent. Gerald and Victoria had gone to bed hours ago. She sat waiting in the dark kitchen in her pajamas. A completely unsensible outfit for what she had in mind, but if Eustice didn't come home with a victim, she would have to quickly run upstairs and pretend to be asleep. A flashlight sat ready on the counter next to her. Just the thought of doing something Eustice would not approve of was enough to make her nervous, much less Eustice being a murderer. She looked at the clock again. it was almost one in the morning. Many times, she thought about going to bed. What did it matter if he was the murderer? Why did she have to be the one to catch him? The sheriff would catch him eventually.   Eustice's cockiness would catch up with him, and she would still get to see him being taken away in handcuffs. But how long would that take? How many young women would have to die before the sheriff figured out the man he was looking for was right across the water? Would he kill her and the children before they found him? No, tonight was the night. Before it went any further, before he hurt anyone else. She thought about Betty Hymer on the mainland locking her door tonight and looking out her

42

window for the man who was stealing away the town's women. Pictured Eustice calmly sitting at a bar drinking and picking tonight's victim. Did he follow them? Did he wait for them in the dark shadows and attic them? She couldn't imagine they went with him willingly. He was good looking in his day, but he was past his prime now and wore that ridiculous hat wherever he went.

Once again, she imagined in her mind's eye what it would look like when the sheriff's boat pulled up to the docks. Eustice's face when he realized he had been caught, when they had figured it out and came for him. What it would feel like when they took him away and she would be free. Free to live her life without fear with her children. The surprise on his face when he realized it was she that had told them. His own wife, who he thought too scared of him to do anything. Had found out what he was doing and gotten enough evidence together to get the sheriff out. That was why she was still sitting there at one in the morning in her nightgown. So, she could see that look on his face when the time came.

A light on the water brought her attention back to the present. Eustice was heading home. It was strange how it seemed to take forever for him to leave, but no time at all before he was back at the docks. She looked around quickly to make sure there was no light that might give her away, and then tucked herself to the side of the window. The moon was full and shone brightly off the water. It highlighted the white sheet Eustice was carrying very well. She squinted to try to see better. She could not see Eustice, just the white sheet bobbing up and down as he walked down the dock and began to walk up the hill towards the house. He disappeared behind the trees again, and she knew he wouldn't appear until he cleared the trees at the bottom of the hill just below the house.

Somehow, he seemed closer than he normally did when he cleared the trees. Her heart was pumping so hard she thought she would pass out. The white sheet was wrapped around something long and limp. She could make out a shape but no definition. From the way Eustice was walking, it appeared to be somewhat heavy, grunting as he came to the top of the hill. For a moment, she thought he was going to walk into the house, and panic set in. She didn't know where she would hide. But he turned at the last minute and followed the path around the house. She tucked to the side of the window so he couldn't see her, peaking out after he passed. Eustice was heading towards the tree line behind the house. The white sheet bobbed, and she tried to make out the shape of what was underneath it. A hand fell out. Its white skin glowing in the moonlight and swinging with every step Eustice took.

Grabbing the flashlight she had ready and waiting on the kitchen counter, she moved to the back door and waited until Eustice had gotten far enough away to not hear her when she started to follow him. His arrogance irritated her. He had not even looked around to see if anyone was watching him. She was surprised that he had even bothered to cover the body in a sheet. Opening the door slowly, she went down the three steps to the back yard. Eustice was almost to the tree line, and now she was out in the open. If he turned around, there was no place to hide. Flashlight firmly clenched in her hand, she took off in the night after him, hyper aware of every sound her boots made on the wet ground. She covered the distance between the house and the tree line as quickly and as quietly as she could, worried she would lose him once he was beyond the trees. Eustice followed a wildlife trail into the woods which made it a little easier for her to follow him.

Pausing at the opening of the wildlife trail where Eustice had disappeared, she took another deep breath. What if he had seen her? She had been out in the open with no place to hide for a while, and the moon was bright. What if he had seen her and was waiting for her in the woods? You could go back to the house now and call the sheriff. Maybe they would catch him in the act if they hurry. She thought to herself. The island isn't big, but if Eustice finds out the sheriff is on the island looking for him, he could hide himself away for weeks. If you can find out where he hides the bodies, you could tell the sheriff. If the sheriff finds all the bodies, Eustice will fry for sure. She took a deep breath and stepped onto the trail. Thankfully, Eustice wasn't there. She couldn't see him anywhere.

Continuing down the trail, the white sheet once again came into view. Hiding behind trees where she could, she managed to keep Eustice just in view until he came to a clearing where he stopped walking. She thought he was just pausing. He had been carrying a body some distance at this point, but then he unceremoniously dropped the body to the ground with a thud. She ventured closer, hiding behind a tree and a thin bush that was growing next to it. It was not a very wide clearing, but a decent size. Eustice bent over and picked up a shovel that he had stashed among the trees and started digging. She looked around for any sign of the other victims. The moon was shining off rocks standing in the clearing. It took a minute for her to realize the stones were lining the outer edge of the clearing and were placed in a circular pattern. They were evenly spaced and the same distance from the trees. Headstones. There were also three of them with this evening's victim being the fourth.

A cold chill ran through her like a winter wind. Eustice had killed them, all of them. But why? And why hadn't he killed her or the kids? You think of a killer as being someone who kills blindly, but he obviously hadn't. He could have killed his entire family, and it would have been months, even years, before anyone knew anything of it. What would he do if he couldn't go to the mainland to kill? Would he start killing at home? He seemed to be favoring young women, so would he go for Victoria? She backed up to go back to the house. She would call the sheriff and, hopefully, he would be here before Eustice was done burying the body.

"Where are you going?" Eustice said. It was the first thing he had said since coming off the boat. She wasn't sure he was talking to her, but then who would he be talking to? She turned slowly towards him. Sure enough, he had stopped digging and was looking at her, his arm casually resting on the handle of the shovel. She thought about not answering. Maybe he couldn't see her. Maybe he was thinking she was there but wasn't sure. Maybe she could make a run for it. No, that always made it worse. If history was any indication, he would catch up with her and whatever he was planning would be worse because she ran.

"At least stay for the rest of the show. You've gone through so much trouble." The look on his face was familiar, and it was the part of him she hated the most. Why make it sound like it was a choice when they both knew it wasn't? She put one shaky foot in front of the other and stepped into the clearing. It was creepy. They were all there, all those missing women, and who was the poor soul he brought here tonight lying helpless under the sheet? It felt like they were screaming at her for help and all she could do was shake.

"What have you done?" she managed to say, though it came

out sounding weaker than she would have liked. Eustice liked when she was afraid, so he was smiling now.

"None of your damned business. I'll deal with you later, just sit down and shut up. I want to finish this as soon as possible."

"Why Eustice?"

"I said shut up." He went back to digging, but she didn't sit down. She looked at the graves of the three women and the one yet to be buried and knew that there was nothing keeping him from doing the same to her and her children. If she sat there and waited for him to finish like he had told her to, what was going to happen? They would go back to the house and act like everything was normal? Doubtful. She was next, and then what would happen to the children? He was so sure she would do what he asked, he hadn't bothered to look at her again. She gripped the flashlight tighter in her hand. The arrogant bastard could think again if he thought she was going to politely sit there and wait to be killed.

Quickly, she turned and ran as fast as she could in her rain boots down the path. She heard Eustice's heavy feet coming after her. She could see the break in the trees, and after that she would have to cross the long back yard. If she could keep her distance from him, it would work. She broke through the trees, and the back door of the house was visible. The house shone like a beacon in the moonlight. She thought she could make it and smiled to herself. It was going to work. Turning back to see how far away Eustice was, she saw the flash of silver metal before it made contact with her head. It came with such force, she fell forward hard, knocking the wind out of her. She couldn't make herself move. Her vision wouldn't focus, she felt sick, the coolness of the earth felt good on her face. It didn't hurt, it should hurt, he had hit her hard, but her head was numb. She did feel something warm falling down the side of her face. She tried to move her arms so she could wipe it away and keep it from going into her eyes, but her arms wouldn't move. The darkness was beginning to surround her. Fight she yelled to herself. Fight. But she was just so tired. The darkness came up and swallowed her in a warm blanket. She was vaguely aware of being pulled through the grass before she slipped into the darkness completely.

"Stupid bitch."

9

Gerald was awakened by the sound of his father calling up the stairs for his sister. Every time he called out, another threat was added. If Victoria was smart, she would stay where she was. Gerald jumped out of bed and threw yesterday's clothes on. He opened his bedroom door just as his father was yelling another round of threats up the stairs.

"I'm coming." Gerald informed him. Eustice looked him up and down, like he always did and said, "What's wrong with your sister? Is she deaf?"

"She's not feeling well."

"Come make me coffee." And Eustice stormed off to the living room to sit his lazy ass down while everyone else in the house did his bidding. Gerald wanted to ask where his mother was. She had always made the coffee and cooked his breakfast. With her gone, the privilege had fallen to Victoria. He looked at her bedroom door. It was shut. It wouldn't matter who was sick, his father would still expect his coffee served piping hot.

Gerald went down the stairs and got the coffee going and then started on the breakfast. He didn't need to be told what to make because it was always the same thing every morning. If he ever got off this damned island, he had vowed he would never eat scrambled eggs and country ham. Every single morning for as far back as he could remember, Eustice had eggs for breakfast with a slice of country ham on the side. The smell was enough to make his stomach turn.

Gerald took Eustice his breakfast which was acknowledged with a grunt. After cleaning the kitchen, Gerald went to take Victoria her breakfast and something to drink. She was sitting white faced in her room.

"What did he want?" Victoria was more afraid of their father than anyone else, and with good reason. Both their mother and Gerald had noticed Eustice paying unusual attention to Victoria, and she had started staying in her room most days unless Gerald was around to protect her.

"Someone to wait on him. Something's not right." Gerald had put her breakfast on the dresser and was standing in front of the window where there was the smell of a fire. Eustice was standing over a drum, smoke coming out the top.

"What do you think it is?" Gerald watched, his heart sinking as he watched Eustice throw a box full of his mother's belongings into the fire.

"I think Mom is gone."

"What do you mean gone?" Panic rose in Victoria's voice.

"I mean gone Vic. She's not here. She's gone off the island."

"She would have taken us with her." A tear rolled down Gerald's cheek. Victoria stared at him with desperation, her lower lip starting to quiver. It felt like their protection was gone along with their hope of ever leaving.

"I don't think she had a choice." In truth, he wasn't sure what had happened to his mother, but he was sure that she was gone. He was also sure Eustice had something to do with it. The possibilities ran through his mind as he watched Eustice put a piece of his mother's dress into the fire. Had he somehow heard them talking and decided to force her to leave the island? Had he made her swim to the mainland? Had he knocked her out and thrown her in the water? He had considered that his father had killed his mother, but he couldn't let himself believe it. That she was gone and not coming back for them. Without her, they had no hope of getting out of here. He prefered to think she had escaped, and was figuring out how to come back for them.

Rage was building in Gerald as he stormed out of Victoria's room.

"Where are you going?"

"To find out what the hell he did to our mother." Victoria didn't want him to. With everything in her, she didn't want him to. It would only make Eustice angry and then there would be no peace in the house. Gerald's shoulders were set when he turned away from the window and stormed out of the room. She turned back to the window and took a bite of the toast Gerald had brought her. It was most likely going to be the only food she got today.

Gerald stormed downstairs, ignoring the warning voices in his head that reminded him of what angering his father would lead to. He stormed through the kitchen and opened the back door screen with such force that it hit the wall and swung back on him. Eustice looked up from the fire as a familiar sliver of fear ran through Gerald.

"Where is she?" he said before he let common sense get the better of him.

"Who?" His father calmly poked the fire.

"Mom. What have you done with her?"

"She's gone."

"Gone where?"

"None of your damned business. Get back inside the house."

"Where did she go? She wouldn't have left without us." He wanted to hear it from Eustice. It happened so quickly, Gerald didn't see Eustice move away from the fire, and before he could flinch, Eustice had his hand around his son's neck and was running a red hot stick down the side of Gerald's face. The hot ember burned, but when Gerald tried to move his face away, the grip on his neck got tighter.

"Now listen to me, stupid." His father was so close to him, he could smell last night's beer on his breath. "I said she is gone and that is all you need to know. She left and she isn't coming back. Now get back in the house and mind your own goddamned business." He pushed Gerald back so hard, he stumbled and fell. The smoking stick still in Eustice's hand, he looked down on his son with a sneer on his face, but the sneer turned to laughter when he saw Gerald's tears.

Gerald was so ashamed of the tears, he scrambled to his feet and ran back to the house. Just once he would love to punch his father. To see the surprised look on his face when Gerald hit back, but today wasn't that day. Stomping back upstairs, he sat on the end of Victoria's bed and cried.

"Gerald?"

"She's gone Vic. I think he killed her." But that was only part of the reason he was sobbing and she knew it.

"You okay?"

"I want to hit him. I want to hit him so bad. Why can't I?" Victoria came up behind him and wrapped her arms around him.

"Because you are nothing like him, Ger Bear."

"I think he killed our mother, and I still can't bring myself to hit him."

"It wouldn't do any good if you did, Ger."

"It would make him think twice before hitting us again."

"No, it wouldn't. Eustice doesn't think before he hits anything. He just knows it makes him mad and therefore it must be punished."

"I think Mom knew something was going on. She was strange last night, kept looking at the paper and told me I have to protect you."

"You always protect me, don't you?"

"What are we going to do with Mom gone?" He wasn't crying as hard anymore, but his body still shook with the sobs. Victoria came around and sat next to him on the bed.

"I love Mom, but to be honest, Ger, she wasn't really able to protect us from Eustice, was she? I mean she would take the beatings for us, but often that was just delaying the inevitable."

"I'm not going to be very good. I can't even bring myself to hit back."

"Maybe you don't have to hit him to beat him. Maybe we can out smart him."

"What do you mean?"

"Mother was keeping tabs on when he was leaving the island and those girls who were going missing on the mainland." Gerald froze. How had they known?

"How do you know that?"

"I found the paper she was writing all the details on in the pocket of her dress when I was hanging it up to dry. I hid it in my pocket so Eustice wouldn't find it."

"I think it was fairly safe on the clothesline. He's never done honest work in his life. How did you know what it was?"

"I saw her do it one night. And I've been sneaking the papers Eustice throws away. For something different to read." She looked at the burn on the side of his face. Red and angry. She went to get a cold washcloth out of the bathroom.

"That was risky Vic, what if he found out?"

"I left most of the paper, just took the top couple of pages. I don't care for sports and all that." She came back and put the cold washcloth on the burn, Gerald winced.

"So, Mom thought he was killing those girls on the mainland?" Gerald said, slightly surprised. He wondered if she also knew Eustice had made him bury two of them. He had been extremely relieved when he found out Eustice had brought one back and buried her himself. The relief had been so great, he was ashamed of it.

"I think he is too. The dates match up in every instance. They weren't sure until recently that the girls were murdered. They hadn't found a body until last week. She was found behind the dumpster of the place she worked." So, they all knew Eustice was killing. He and his mother had been keeping tabs on him. Was that where she had gone? To tell someone what was going on? Gerald felt hope for the first time in a long time. He brushed Vic's hand away and got up off the bed and went to the window. Eustice was still standing over the fire. Quickly and softly, he told Victoria where the papers in his room were hidden. That Eustice had him bury a few of the bodies, and he knew where they were. He had proof. Victoria's cheeks flushed. "We have to get to the mainland. We have to tell them."

Gerald did his best to keep his father happy. He made his breakfast, lunch and dinner. Did the laundry and all the housework. Victoria would often feel ill in the morning, and he worried about her. Most mornings she was only able to keep down toast. In the afternoons, Eustice would watch TV or go off into the woods. This is when they would plot their escape. They were going to get off the island and watch while the police dragged their father away in cuffs. For the first time in a long time they had hope of getting off the island. Days passed into weeks with them spending their days like this. Hopeful that soon they would be off the island, out of this house and away from the man who had tormented them their entire lives.

10

The house was so quiet, the only sound was the clock ticking on the wall. Julia looked at it and watched the minute hand make its way around the face. Her eyes were growing heavy the farther it got. No doubt her friends would find this a strange way for a family to spend the evening. All three of them were absorbed in a book. Her father was reading one of his autobiographies. Occasionally, he would get her interested in one, but for the most part she found them extremely boring. Her mother was pouring over the history books she had gotten that day and making notes. If she wasn't going to work while she was on vacation, why did she bring a notebook? Authors. Always looking for the next book idea. Julia yawned so deeply it made her eyes water. Looking at the hour on the clock this time, she realized what time it was. "Goodnight you two. I'm going to go take a shower and go to bed." Julia lifted herself off the couch where she had been reading her book and, kissing them both good night, headed for the stairs.

"Don't use all the hot water because a shower sounds nice, I might take one before I go to bed." Evelyn said to her back. Julia waved as a response and disappeared up the stairs. Twain lifted his head and thought about following her, but then laid his head back down again. The groaning of pipes was heard a short time later, being forced into action after a long vacation.

The bathroom attached to Julia's room was tiny. The slanted roof on one side making it feel even smaller. There was hardly room to turn around because the claw foot tub took up so much space. At home, Julia was used to a modern looking shower and personally didn't get the charm of these tubs with only a thin shower curtain around you. Thankfully, the water was hot, really hot, and had decent water pressure. After listening to the pipes groan when she turned on the water, she wasn't expecting much, but the hot water hit her skin, and she felt the grime of the previous day wash away. Once she had her shower, Julia was planning on hopping into bed and getting on Instagram. She had a date with her friends to discuss the book they were all reading. She had wanted to start the next book in the series but was now contemplating starting one of the books she got at the bookstore that day. Her friends would also want to hear about the awesome bookshop she found and what she heard the shopkeeper telling her mother about the house they were staying in.

"You can't just watch them whenever you want. It's creepy." He told her. They had not been around living people. Not since they died. He could feel the energy flowing through him like never before, and he knew that the living were the source of it. His first reaction had been to hide. Victoria's had been the opposite. She had gotten so close to them, he was sure they would feel them, see them. Somehow know they were there.

"I just want to see her."

"She's in the shower."

"She can't see me." She sounded like the petulant teenager she

was. Victoria disappeared into the bathroom, but he didn't follow.

The woman in the bookstore had been talking to her mom about murder on the island. Julia had caught the waitress's strange response to their being on the island as well and wondered what exactly had happened here and how long it had been. The woman in the bookstore made it sound like it wasn't all that long ago, which was a bit concerning. The woman had said people had been killed here. Could you still see the blood stains? The more she thought about it, the more uneasy she felt. She opened her eyes and looked around. It felt like someone was sitting on the toilet watching her. So much so, that she refused to look in that direction for fear of seeing a form there. Maybe it's Mom or Dad. She tried to comfort herself, but she hadn't heard either of her parents come in, and they surely would have announced themselves. Maybe it was Twain. It wouldn't be the first time the dog had freaked her out by sneaking into the bathroom. Convincing herself she would turn around and see the shadow of the dog, Julia looked around, but saw no one through the thin shower curtain. Julia found the opening in the curtain and opened it just enough to see if someone was there. There was no one. She was alone in the bathroom, but she still felt the eyes on her. No longer wanting to enjoy the hot water, Julia picked up the shampoo. It was time to get this shower over with and get out.

She was smiling to herself. She wanted to talk to her, to somehow let her know that she was there, but she didn't have the strength to make herself visible yet, and she didn't need her brother to tell her that a disembodied voice would scare the girl. So, she thought of another way of making her presence known.

Julia finished washing her hair, and after giving her legs a very quick once over with the razor, she turned the water off.

Standing there for a moment, she 'felt' the room. She no longer felt like someone was watching her and thought she had let the old house get to her for a moment. *'Mom's talk at dinner is just getting in my head,'* she thought to herself. Still, she opened the curtain just a tiny bit as if expecting someone to be there before she pulled it back completely and grabbed the towel. It was while she was wrapping the towel around herself that she looked ahead of her and saw what was written in the steam of the mirror. *HELLO.* Julia froze. She blinked to make sure it was really there, and then ran from the bathroom, down the stairs to her parents.

"MOM, DAD!" Twain was barking at the bottom of the stairs, and Julia couldn't take the stairs fast enough. She had made so much noise coming down that both of her parents were standing at the bottom of the stairs with questioning looks on their faces.

"What in the world is the matter?" Her Mother asked her. Julia tried to find the words to explain. But all she could come up with was, "It's written on the mirror."

"What is dear?"

"Hello." Mark gave his wife a curious look and then went upstairs, Evelyn and Julia following him. Mark entered the bathroom, humidity still thick in the air and looked at the mirror. "What was written here?"

"Hello." Julia said, confused as to why he was asking since he was looking right at the mirror. She pulled away from her mother and stood next to her father in looking at the mirror that was no longer covered in steam. The word no longer visible.

"What's going on, Sweetheart?" Her father asked. He could tell from the look on her face at the moment that she had fully expected something to be written on the mirror.

"It was there, when I got out of the shower. I thought someone was watching me. It was really creepy, so I hurried up and finished my shower. When I got out, the word 'Hello' was written in the steam on the mirror."

"You felt like someone was watching you?" Her mother had completely skipped over the phantom words on the mirror and gone straight to that.

"Yeah, I looked but there was no one. I thought it was just what you said at dinner and the creepy house getting to me."

"Mark, check for cameras." And she started looking around the part of the bathroom she was standing in. "You hear about these things, don't you? Rental properties where someone has installed hidden cameras so they can spy on the guests."

"Eeww." Julia said. She did not think it was a camera. It had felt like the person was standing right on the other side of the shower curtain.

"That wouldn't explain the word on the mirror." Mark pointed out.

"Probably the housekeeping having fun. I saw a program once where they tried to scare the guests by doing something like that. It's a product they put on the mirror. They write out the word with this chemical which doesn't fog over with the steam, so it looks like someone has written something on the mirror while you were in the shower." She came over and hugged her daughter who was now shivering because she had not grabbed a towel for her head. "Don't worry, Honey. I'll clean the mirror in the morning, and you'll see, it won't happen again."

What her mother said made sense. Made complete logical sense. No doubt that was someone's idea of a joke. But something made Julia think that it wasn't as simple as housekeeping playing a joke on them. Despite the fact that the scenario her mother had suggested made much more sense than the house being haunted, Julia could not shake that feeling of being watched. A shiver went down her back just thinking about it. Julia was not entirely sure they were alone in this house.

"I didn't mean to." Was all she said to him.

"I know." Was the only thing he could think to say. They didn't know what to do with their power, and to be honest, he thought maybe it would be better if the living left. They weren't the only ones gaining strength now that there were living people on the island. Victoria stayed there watching the girl and her parents. They seemed like normal parents. Parents who loved their kid. How did it hurt to watch them when he was dead? He went outside and looked towards the woods. They weren't the only ones getting stronger the longer the living stayed.

11

Gerald walked up the beach, with the full moon lighting the docks and the town on the other side of the water. He looked back tentatively at the house but saw no movement there. The piece of paper was folded up tightly in his jacket pocket. The list of how many bodies, and where they were buried. He had to do something to make it stop. Gerald had not been to town in the three months since the bodies started showing up, so he did not know about the wanted posters, the search parties and prayer visuals that had dominated the town where girls were going missing at an alarming rate. Unlike his sister and mother, he did not steal glances at the papers his father brought home. It wasn't worth the beatings.

He did know that a list of bodies and where they were buried on their small, little island would get someone's attention. But how to get it over there? As he walked, he hoped that inspiration would strike him. He stopped walking and studied the water. Though summer was approaching, he knew the water would still be frigid, so he wasn't sure he would be able to swim it. *But I would only have to swim it one way.* He thought to himself. *I would come back on a boat with the police.*

A heavy weight hit him from behind and Gerald let out a grunt as he fell forward on the ground. He was rolled over, and before he could see what was happening, a punch across his left cheek informed him that his father knew he was out of the house. Eustice was sitting on Gerald's legs, his hands now gripped his jacket. Gerald worried about the paper in his pocket.

"What the hell are you doing sneaking around out here? And don't tell me 'nothing'."

"Was thinking about swimming to the mainland."

"What the hell for?" Gerald wasn't scared. The scene was too familiar to bring fear with it any more. This was often how he and his father had conversations. Eustice didn't seem to think his children would tell him the truth without the immediate threat of physical violence.

"Haven't been off the island in months. I'm bored." Gerald could tell from the loosening of his father's grip on his jacket that he had bought it. Eustice didn't get up though.

"Why do you want to go over there?"

"Just to see something different. I've seen every tree and rock around here a thousand times." Eustice smacked him.

"If you kept your mind on your work, you wouldn't be bored." Gerald didn't say what he wanted to, which was that there wasn't any work to do. It had gone for the winter and hadn't come back yet. Eustice paid his bills by repairing fishing nets. Or rather bringing them home so that he could drink beer and watch TV while his children repaired fishing nets. Victoria was particularly good at it.

"Yes, sir." Was what he said instead. Eustice got off of him and pulled Gerald up by the collar of his jacket. Gerald was worried about the paper in his pocket again but didn't dare reach for it. He thought he had managed to calm his father's paranoia and at the moment that was all he could afford to worry about. "Now get to bed. If I see you out again, I'll shoot you and tell them I thought you were trespassing." Gerald walked quickly back to the house. He knew why his father wasn't following him. Eustice was going to stay and look to see if his son had hidden anything on the beach.

His cheek throbbed. He would have a bruise tomorrow, but he was glad he hadn't tried to send the paper. His hand touched the outside of his jacket, and he relaxed when he felt the stiffness of the folded paper there. Gerald knew he had been lucky tonight. He didn't even dare think about what would have happened to him and Victoria if Eustice knew what he had really been doing. Gerald got to his room and quickly put the folded paper back in it's hiding spot before his father got back to the house, and then he sat on his bed and buried his head in his shaking hands. Eustice would kill him if he found him out there again, of that he had no doubt. He had managed to convince him tonight that he was up to nothing, but if he was found again, there would be no convincing him. *But there will be more, and he will make you dig their graves.*

Gerald hugged himself and bit his lip. Not for the first time, he wished his mother was there. He didn't know where she had gone . He hoped she was happy there and didn't think less of her for leaving him and Victoria behind. It would have been almost impossible to get all of them away from Eustice at the same time. Victoria wanted to wait, convinced that she would come back for them, but Gerald couldn't wait any longer. Eustice was killing people for fun now, and he wasn't sure what would stop him from killing Victoria and himself. He had to do it. He had to reach the town somehow. *If you die, they will still find the paper when they fish you out of the water.*

Gerald leaned back in his bed. He wondered if he would be okay with dying. He pictured them fishing him out of the water, searching his body for identification, and finding the folded paper protected from the water by a plastic bag. Their faces as they opened it and the horror that would cross their faces as they read what was written there. The sheriff would get all his men together and the shock on Eustice's face when he saw the sheriff's boat coming across. He wasn't sure if his father would resist or go willingly, convinced that he would be able to talk his way out of it (he had seen him in the town when he was charming). There was an equal chance that he would stand and fight. Either way, Victoria would be free and there would be no more bodies.

Gerald got into his pajamas and laid back down in the bed. Rolling over, he could see the full moon out of his window. He would try it again when there was no moon. Eustice would be more vigilant for a while, so he would have to be careful. Gerald hoped that by the time the moon waned, Eustice would have forgotten about tonight, and Gerald would be in town or at least far enough out in the water that Eustice wouldn't be able to catch up to him. He would have to warn Victoria before he left. She would have to spend the night in the woods where Eustice wouldn't be able to find her, but it could be done. For the first time in a long time, Gerald had hope of leaving this island and living free from Eustice. But then Victoria got sick. Really sick.

12

The sheriff flicked the papers in his hand and read what they
had been waiting for, the fingerprint report from the duct tape
that had been cut off of Marcy Gray's wrist. There were three
photos of missing girls on the white board behind him and not a
shred of evidence leading to the killer. The duct tape had been
used as makeshift handcuffs. Her body had been found just two
days ago behind a dumpster at the Bait N' Fish where she
worked. One of her co-workers had found her when they
showed up to open in the morning. The sheriff had sent it off to
the lab with a request to rush it and had been waiting for the
results. He still hadn't expected it this morning when he got in.
He looked around the office for someone to share the news with,
but there was no one. They were all out. A fourth girl had been
reported missing two days ago. Reports were coming in so fast
now his department was hardly able to keep up. A waitress at
one of the local bars had left work in the early hours of the
morning. Her mother had reported her missing two hours later
having sat up to wait for her, a common thing for mothers to do
these days. Uniform was still out making sure it was legitimate,
but it would be. Everything about it matched this guy's MO.

The girl was the right age, and all the victims had worked late night shifts in a restaurant or bar. Soon, there would be a fourth picture on the white board behind him.

'Maybe we can get the bastard today.' He thought to himself. *'Maybe I'll be sheriff here a bit longer after all.'* He was up for re-election in a few months. With this hanging over his head, he could feel his supporters slipping away, and his opponent had been making hay out of it. A car pulled up outside and his deputy Henry got out. *'Just the man.'*

"Henry, get over here," he yelled. "They got one, a good one too,"he said, waving the print report in the air. "They ran it through the state system and looked at who they came back with." He handed his deputy the paper and watched for his reaction. As Henry scanned the page, his eyes lit up when he saw the name.

"Makes sense when you think about it. He'd have the perfect place to hide the bodies. What do you want to do?"

They had not had one lead. It was like this guy was a ghost. No one had seen or heard a thing. An offer of a reward had turned up nothing. There had been a huge storm over the summer, and the sheriff had been sure it would have uncovered something: a shallow grave, a body, clothing, anything, but there had been nothing. Not one damned thing. In the meantime, the mayor was breathing down his neck, as well as every panicked woman in town. This could end today. Hell, maybe he hadn't killed the missing girl yet. In his mind he briefly envisioned himself rescuing the poor girl from murderous hands. The sheriff grabbed the paper back from his deputy and slapped his hand with it. Nothing was going to happen while they sat here.

"Grab your stuff; I'm gonna call the judge and get a warrant. I know Eustice is going to ask if we have one before he lets us search the property, so we'll have one in hand." The deputy went to put on his bullet-proof vest and grab the shot guns. Eustice Thompson was a hermit for lack of a better word. He lived on Sea Island, just himself and his two kids now that the wife had left. He came to town to get supplies and drink the night away in the bars, but that was about it. Anyone who ventured out to the island was met by Eustice or his son, Gerald, and a shotgun. His nickname in town was 'The Mad Hatter' because he always wore the same old-fashioned fedora that was so weathered, it no longer resembled anything other than a wet piece of leather laid across his head.

Henry was loading the truck up with the guns and the sheriff's vest when the sheriff walked out of the court-house grinning.

"Did ya get it?"

"Easiest warrant I've ever gotten in twenty years on the force," the sheriff said, waving the warrant in the air. Taking his hat off, he hopped into the seat of the truck and they drove to the docks.

They transferred the guns and themselves to the police boat and set off for Sea Island. If Henry was honest, the closer they got to the island, the more he thought they should have brought back-up. He could tell from looking at the sheriff that he was nervous as well. They said nothing as they guided the police boat the short ten-minutes over to Sea Island, but there was no telling what they would meet when they got there. Eustice would be able to see them coming; hell, he was probably already grabbing his gun. They were within view of the house already. The island was nothing more than a hill with the house sitting on top, surrounded by thick pine trees. Eustice would have the advantage when they pulled up to the small dock on the eastern side of the island. They would not be able to see Eustice approach before he emerged from the tree line, but he would be able to see them the whole way down the hill. Henry had his hand on the shotgun and had taken the safety off his handgun. With the sheriff driving the boat, if Eustice opened fire, it would be up to Henry to provide cover.

They pulled up to the dock. Henry watched the tree line and what he could see of the path leading up to the house while the sheriff concentrated on parking the boat. They say in the academy that when it happens, you won't have time to act. You will have to rely on your training, and that is exactly what happened when the shot hit the dock next to them. The sheriff grabbed his arm, hit by either wood or buckshot. Henry brought up the rifle and just saw Eustice break the tree line walking calmly and holding his shotgun. "Police! Drop your weapon," Henry yelled. He thought for a second that maybe Eustice hadn't realized who it was. Henry hoped Eustice would drop his weapon, but he didn't. Henry saw him start to raise it again and quickly fired a shot.

It didn't hit him; the shot went into the ground in front of Eustice's feet. Eustice ducked behind a tree. "PUT THE GUN DOWN EUSTICE," Henry yelled, moving over to the sheriff who had drawn his handgun and was positioned behind the windscreen on the boat. Henry ducked behind the seat opposite. "Keep an eye out for the kids." The sheriff warned. The sheriff put his weapon in his injured arm, which was clearly shaking from the strain, and radioed for back-up with his good arm. They both knew it would not be soon in coming. It was a small town, and they had only one police boat. Volunteer boats would have to be contacted before anyone arrived. They were on their own for a while. "GET OFF MY LAND" Eustice barked from the trees.

"WE NEED TO ASK YOU A FEW QUESTIONS ABOUT THE MISSING GIRLS. WE HAVE A WARRANT," the sheriff yelled. He had no sooner gotten the words 'warrant' out of his mouth than the gun fire started again. Eustice was out from behind his tree and firing at them. One bullet hit the front of the boat; the second one almost found its mark, hitting the wind screen in front of the sheriff. Eustice had paused to reload and that is when Henry stood up and opened fire. While Eustice was loading the cartridge in the gun, Henry lifted his gun, took a deep breath and fired. Eustice went down. The sheriff tried to radio in 'shots fired' but the radio had taken a hit when Eustice shot the wind screen.

"You okay?" Henry asked the sheriff. He nodded. Henry got out of the boat and cautiously made his way toward Eustice. He had just cleared the dock when he heard yelling and saw someone running down the hill. He couldn't tell what the kid was yelling, but Henry saw the barrel of a shotgun and yelled, "FREEZE!" Henry had never seen Eustice's son; he assumed that's who this was. The young man was yelling loudly as he ran down the hill, but Henry couldn't understand what he was saying. There was the crack of gun fire, and the young man went down. Henry couldn't tell where the gun fire had come from but looked instinctively back at the sheriff who was lowering his gun. Looking back at the son, Henry saw a leg move. He was still alive.

"Call for help. He's still alive." The sheriff pulled out his cell phone and climbed out of the boat. With his weapon ready, Henry checked to make sure there was no one else who was going to run out at them. Since both men had come from the house, he focused his gun in that direction. He got to Eustice and kicked his gun away. Eustice didn't move, so Henry knelt down to make sure he was dead and no longer a threat. The sheriff passed him at a fast walk. Blood ran down his limp arm. He was heading straight for the boy. Henry raised his gun to give him cover, but nothing happened, so he too made his way toward the boy, scanning the tree line as he went. If he remembered correctly, Eustice had two children.

The boy was in the process of leaving this world. He had been shot in the stomach, some of the buckshot hitting his chest. Blood covered his neck and chin. The sheriff dropped his gun and applied pressure to the wound, but he and Henry both knew it was pointless.

"Don't worry son, help is on the way." The boy's face was white. His eyes wide with fear and pain.

"Is he dead?" The boy's voice was surprisingly normal considering. They got the impression his father being dead would not be bad news to him.

"Yes."

The boy's breathing got slower, and he was shuddering, but his eyes were still wide and looking firmly at the sheriff. His bloody hand reached up and grabbed the sheriff's vest. "I didn't want to. I…I didn't want to."

"I know son. I know you didn't."

"The papers….my room." The boy was almost pulling the sheriff down on top of him. "Get them, they are in my room. They explain…"

"Stay calm now." The boy's eyes grew heavy, and with another big shudder, he grew still. The grip that had held onto the sheriff's vest with urgency, hung limply and all the light left his eyes. The sheriff did not let go of him. He sat back and simply stared at the boy who was just that. A boy. He couldn't have been more than sixteen or seventeen.

"I saw the gun. I saw the gun and thought he was coming for us." The sheriff said.

"Sir, isn't there a daughter?" Henry had not yet holstered his weapon. The sheriff looked around them. "Yeah, Victoria. She must be in the house." Then they were sitting targets. The sheriff gently removed the boy's hand from his vest and laid it across his chest. He picked up his weapon, and the two men carefully made their way up to the house, keeping an eye on the windows for any sign of movement.

Their backs flat to the slats of the house, they made their way to the front of the house and onto the front porch. Henry kicked the door in, and they went room to room securing the house. There was nothing. The house was silent and   empty. The downstairs secured, Henry took the lead going up the stairs. "Police, come out with your hands up," Henry yelled, but there was no response. No sound of movement. They opened the door right in front of them at the top of the stairs. It was an empty bathroom . They went to their right and opened the door to a bedroom. The bed clothes were pulled back and it smelled stale. Dirty jeans and shirts thrown over the floor.

There were two rooms on the other side of the hallway. They went to the first one and opened the door, and were met with the still form of a girl laying on the bed. At first, she looked asleep, but she was too still. Lowering their weapons, they approached. Whoever had laid her out had taken great care. Her long blond hair was combed and laid out to the right of her. She was wearing a clean dress, and her arms lay next to her. Henry placed his fingers at her neck to check for a pulse, but the cold flesh told him she was dead. There was no visible sign of struggle; she did not appear to have suffered any violence.

There was a deadbolt on the back of her door. What had that been for? Had Eustice killed his own daughter? The two men looked at each other in confusion.

"The coroner will figure it out," the sheriff answered the unspoken question between them. They moved onto the next and last room, but they did not bother to raise their weapons. All occupants of the island were now confirmed dead. This had been Gerald's room. There was a deadbolt like the one found on his sister's door. Henry thought it was very tidy for a teenage boy's room. The bed was made with a book open and lying face down on the nightstand. Henry could almost picture him sitting here reading only a few moments ago. Why had he followed his father down to the dock with a gun? The sheriff was leafing through books looking for the papers the boy had mentioned. Henry opened and looked through drawers. A small square of paper fell out of the book the sheriff was holding. Picking it up, he opened it and stood there reading it for a moment before saying, "I'll be damned."

"What is it?"

"All the evidence we would need to convict him. The boy wrote down the dates his father brought the bodies back to the island and where he buried them. Read what he wrote at the bottom." The sheriff handed Henry the paper but didn't look at him.

'Please forgive me. I helped him bury the bodies. Not because I wanted to, but he made me. Hopefully, this will help you lock him up forever and we can be free. If there is a punishment for what I have done, I will pay it. I am sorry I was not able to stop him.' Jesus Christ. He forced the boy to help him bury the bodies." Henry pulled an evidence bag out of his pocket and placed the letter inside.

"The boy wasn't coming after us. He was coming after his father." The sheriff's shoulders were slumped, and tears rolled down his face. "I shot an innocent kid." A shaking hand ran through his hair.

"We didn't know that, Sir. You saw someone running down a hill with a gun screaming. That looks like a threat, and you eliminated the threat."

There was a sound of people arriving at the dock which ended the conversation. Henry realized how well the sound from the water travelled up to the house. Eustice would have had plenty of time to grab his gun and get down to the water. So would the son, so why had he been so far behind his father? Hearing their backup arriving, the two men made their way back downstairs to greet them.

The sheriff's face was pale now, and the sleeve of his uniform completely soaked in blood. They made their way down the hill to the dock. They could see through the trees multiple boats tied to the dock and officers starting to cautiously make their way up the hill.

"Police," someone yelled from the beach, seeing them through the trees.

"Sheriff," the sheriff answered. Guns were lowered, and the lead officer approached. "Scene is secure. Eustice came after us as we came up to the dock. The boy came running down the hill with the gun. We found the girl in the house already deceased." The officer nodded.

"We need to get you to the hospital, Sir." The sheriff reached into his vest and pulled out a folded piece of paper, blood on one corner of it.

"We were here to execute a search warrant. Eustice's fingerprints were lifted from the duct tape found on Marcy

Grey." He handed the paper over to Henry. "Have them search the property. Get the cadaver dogs out here. If those girls are here, I want them found. This all ends today." Henry nodded, and the sheriff let himself be led to the boat.

"You heard the man," Henry said to the men standing around him. The other officers broke apart and went about the job of finding the missing girls. The sheriff allowed himself to be ushered back to the boat. He would be back as soon as they had stopped the bleeding, though. Henry was sure of it. Henry walked with the sheriff to the boat as the man continued to bark orders at him. As they passed the boy's body, the sheriff stopped. "I thought he was going to shoot you Henry."

"I know, Sir."

The sheriff went to go and then turned back, taking his jacket off, he placed it over the boy's body. The crime scene people were going to hate that, but they would get over it. Seeing the sheriff off Henry grabbed the first officer that passed him. "Have the men search the woods for a clearing. Specifically a ring of stones in a clearing. Radio for cadaver dogs and when they get here, have them search the woods and any clearing you find." The boy's letter had mentioned a clearing and that Eustice had him place stones at the top of each grave. He just hoped there wasn't more than one clearing on the island.

13

Julia got into bed, the stack of books she had gotten from the bookstore on the nightstand next to her. Her parents had offered to have her sleep in their room, but she was a big girl, and would have been mortified. She positioned her pillow behind her back, pulled the covers over herself, and patted the bed. Having waited for the signal, Twain jumped up, and the bed undulated under his weight. Julia waited while he made two circles and then laid down with a grunt. Pulling the first book off of the stack next to her, she opened the front flap. It had been a library book, probably bought in a sale. It still had the plastic covering over it and the library stamp in the inside flap. It was listed as 'Teen Fiction,' a title which Julia disliked. In her opinion, fiction was either good or bad. Which age group it was targeted towards should have no bearing.

"I'm sorry, Julia." Victoria stood on the other side of the door feeling bad for having scared the girl.

Her feet under Twain's warm belly and propped up in her bed, Julia gladly settled in for a long night of reading. Mom and Dad were still downstairs, her mother cracking open the books she had gotten shortly after dinner. No doubt both of them would be reading themselves to sleep tonight. The house was quiet, outside her window she could hear an owl hooting. It did not take long for Julia to become absorbed in the plot. The story was gripping, and Julia had no idea what time it was when she heard her mother's voice whisper 'Julia' from behind her door. Julia wondered why she didn't just come in like she normally did.

"Yes?" Nothing happened. Twain, who had been sleeping so soundly he had been snoring, softly jumped up and stared intently at the door, making Julia think someone was there. "Mom?" Still no answer. Julia got herself out from under the covers and went to her door. The hairs on the back of her neck stood up. Looking over her shoulder, Twain was still looking at the door with full attention, and she realized he wasn't wagging his tail like he normally did when Mom and Dad were around. Twain looked serious about whoever was behind the door, and it made Julia wonder who it might be. Who else would be in the house? Staying a safe distance from the door, Julia said, "Mom." again. Her voice came out more as a whisper.

"She heard me." She thought the dog could actually see her, and she reached out her hand to pet him. He barked. Nevermind.

Twain barked at whoever it was. Julia stood there, in the middle of her bedroom, frozen to the spot, and listening for any clue as to what was happening. Surely, her mother would call out again. Or had her mother called her from downstairs? But the house was completely silent. She looked at the clock on her night stand. It was one in the morning. Would her parents still be up this late? They were like her when it came to a good book, so it wouldn't be impossible for them to have gotten wrapped up in what they were reading and lose track of time like herself. She didn't think her mother would then risk waking her up by calling her name. Had she been checking on her? Julia wanted to open the door and see what was going on, but she was also afraid of what was on the other side of it.

Julia walked slowly up to the door. Twain still standing at attention next to her. Placing her hand on the door, she leaned in to see if she heard anything from the other side of the door. Letting out a breath, Julia saw her breath form a cloud in front of her and confusion added to the mix of emotions.

"I'm sorry." Whispered a voice from the other side of the door. Julia leapt back so quickly she fell to the ground and scurried backwards on all fours until she hit the wall on the other side of her room.

"What is Twain barking at?" Evelyn asked sitting up in bed.

"Twain!" Mark yelled from his side of the bed, but the retriever did not stop, and there was something in his bark that Evelyn didn't like. She got out of bed and put her robe on. Knowing he was expected to join her, Mark also got out of bed, where he had just been falling asleep, and followed his wife up the stairs.

Evelyn paused at the top of the stairs because she sensed an odd feeling. Like something had just happened there and they were too late to see it. Thinking something had happened to Julia, Evelyn ran the short distance to the door and opened it. Twain barked and then backed up to where Julia was sitting on the floor shivering. Twain whimpered. Mark had been pretty sure the dog had been barking at a mouse or something on the same level of significance until he entered the room and saw his daughter on the floor. Evelyn ran and knelt down next to her daughter.

"What happened, Jules?" Evelyn was holding her and stroking her hair.

"Someone said my name." The parents exchanged looks.

"Someone said your name?" Mark asked.

"I thought it was Mom but then she didn't answer. It whispered it was 'sorry'."

"Come on dear, let's get you out of here." Evelyn didn't know what the hell was going on, but it was clear that there was not going to be any sleep in the house as long as Julia was in this room. "Get your stuff and come on." They stood up and Julia retrieved her books, headphones, phone. Twain wagged his tail and followed behind them. Mark, not having a clue what was going on, left Evelyn to settle Julia down while he and Twain checked the house from top to bottom. He was a little embarrassed to admit that after the night they had, he was glad for the retriever's company and was reassured by the dog's wagging tail.

"The house is locked up tight." Mark announced coming back into the bedroom. Running past him, Twain jumped onto the bed and quickly settled himself at Julia's feets who was already in bed and looking comfortable with a book propped up in front of her. Evelyn laying next to her looking very similar with her own book. It was clear there was not enough room in their bed for all four of them, so Mark retrieved extra pillows and blankets from the cupboard and made a pallet on the floor. While Mark had been searching the house, Evelyn had asked Julia one more time what had happened and got the same answer. It was not enough to explain what had happened though. It was now two in the morning and they were all exhausted. There would be time to figure out what happened in the morning. Evelyn stayed awake until she saw Julia's book slump next to her. She could hear Mark snoring lightly from the floor, Twain making much the same noises at her feet. It had been a long time since they had all slept in the same room together. Julia had been about six at the time. Back then they had all fit in the bed. Evelyn put her own book down, and having made sure her family was safe and asleep, turned over and herself went to sleep.

'I told you it wouldn't help.' He said to her in his best big brother tone. It annoyed her as much in death as it had in life.

'I didn't mean to scare her.'

"Maybe they will leave now.' This did get a reaction out of her.

'I didn't mean for them to leave, I like them.'

"I went out to the woods last night." They never went to the woods. They never left the house.

"Why?"

"I wanted to check something. If they are making us stronger, they are making him stronger too."

"He's all the way out in the woods."

"It doesn't seem to matter. He's getting stronger too." She knew what that meant. It wasn't safe for the living to be here anymore. It wasn't safe for anyone to be here.

14

Needless to say, they all woke late the next morning. Evelyn got her family fed and set about their day. Mark checked his emails and then went out on the porch to read his book. Julia had slept in more than the rest of them, which was expected, ate a tiny breakfast, and then headed to the beach with Twain to throw his stick and read her book. As soon as she thought they were preoccupied, Evelyn pulled out her computer and searched the island and the town. History was great, but she wanted answers about the night before and all she could think about was the recent murders Meg at the bookstore had mentioned.

Lovely things about the island popped up, but further down the page, she found what she was looking for. The missing girls had been big news in the area while they were happening and several news items popped up regarding the research teams and vigils that were held for the victims. The disappearances went the entire length of the summer. The fourth of July celebrations were cancelled that year for fear that whoever the murderer was would take advantage of the crowd. Single women had sleepovers thinking there was safety in numbers.

There were pictures of the victims. They were all so young.

Not much older than Julia really, which hit her with a pang. Evelyn had already decided she was going to call the sheriff and arrange a meeting. She made notes on her pad, two pages worth of questions to ask him. They had not been in the town long, and she was having a hard time equating the peaceful village-like atmosphere to the fearful chaos she was reading about. From what she was reading, the town had a hard time coming to terms with it as well.

The details of how the bodies were found were thin. There had not appeared to be a trial of any sort. Or at least not one she could find a record of. Evelyn did find pictures that had been posted of the funeral for the four women. The whole town had shut down, including the schools, so that everyone could attend the services. Four coffins were laid out next to each other, lovely flowers laid on each one. Their respective families standing, crying, in front of them. Evelyn studied the picture. One person had done this. One person had taken these people's lives and stolen them. Look how many people it had affected. Not just the families of those four people, but the entire town had been in fear. Mourned the lives lost, and wondered what they could have done to stop it.

"Who the hell was the bastard that did this? Why did he do it, and what did he get from it?" Evelyn thought to herself. There had been mention of the murderer, but not much, which she had found odd.

Looking up from the computer, she had been staring at the screen for three hours, and her eyes were feeling the pain of it. She got up from her chair and went out to the porch where Mark was. Starting to tell him what she was doing, she found he was asleep. Evelyn went down the path a bit to find where Julia was. Having worn Twain out with fetching the stick, they had both moved to the dock where Julia was sunbathing and reading her book. Twain, not needing a tan, had found a shady spot in the trees not too far away and was having a very active nap from what Evelyn could see. His feet were switching in his sleep.

'This would have been the perfect place to hide the bodies.' Evelyn thought to herself. The need to know more about what happened was like an itch now, and there would be no rest until she was able to scratch it. She watched her daughter and thought of the four young women who had been pictured. Her thoughts went back to the night before. Evelyn wasn't sure what had happened, but something strange had, and she couldn't help but wonder if it was somehow connected to the island's recent history. If she was thinking that, though, it meant she believed in ghosts. Which she didn't.

"Did you put sunscreen on?" Evelyn yelled out to her daughter. Julia sent her back a thumbs up. Evelyn stood there for a minute longer taking in the view and then went back to her computer. Determining that she would not find out much more without looking in the local archives, she gave up searching for the day. Organizing her notes and adding a few questions, she put everything back in her bag. Grabbing a towel and her own book, Evelyn went down to the docks to join her daughter in some sunbathing. She would call the sheriff tomorrow to see about meeting. What was the rush? They were here for two months, she might as well enjoy the sunshine .

15

Henry stood in the clearing looking around at the scene. The place Eustice had chosen to bury his victims. While the island had been a great place to hide his crimes, Henry no longer thought that was why Eustice brought them back here. The crime scene guys were still all over the place. They had now been working the scene for three days. They would start with the first light and not stop until after dark. Henry had been here the whole time. He had put himself in charge of supervising the removal of the victims' bodies. The sheriff and his team were working the house.

"You don't have to do that Henry." The sheriff had told him. "No one should have to see the body of their murdered sister removed from its grave." Henry had shaken his head.

"I'm not going to know which one is hers anyway, they are all wrapped in tarps. I want to be there. I need to be there." The sheriff had let him get on with it. As Henry stood in the clearing, the morning sun just starting to peak over the trees and the dew still heavy on the ground, he was surrounded by the now empty graves of Eustice's victims. The bodies had all been removed and were being looked over by the coroner at that very minute. The notes left by the son had painted a picture for Henry, and he tried to imagine the boy and Eustice in this clearing. Eustice watching the boy dig the graves.

"Where did you want us to look?" The guys with the radar had made their way to the island. It had taken a lot to get them out here. Henry snapped out of his imaginings and gave them his full attention. What they found today may answer a question he had been asking himself since all this started.

"All throughout the clearing please. We are looking for any unmarked graves." Henry had gotten them out here at great expense with the argument that there may be more victims buried in the clearing. That Eustice may have been burying victims here for longer than they had any idea and for whatever reason had not marked the graves. What he was really wanting to know was, where was the wife? He had gone through the house, and there was not a scrap of clothing, not one item left in the house to let anyone know that Eustice had ever been married. To Henry, it didn't look like a woman who had left, as the sheriff had suggested. To Henry, it looked like the woman had been completely erased.

The guy with the ground radar set about his task and Henry decided to get out of the way. Leaving the teams to get to work, Henry went into the house to see if he could be of use there. Entering through the back door, he walked into the kitchen. The crime scene team was all over the house, but he knew where he would find the sheriff. Going up the stairs two at a time, Henry found the sheriff in the bedrooms of the children. Gerald's room had offered so much information already, the sheriff had been hopeful they would find more clues as to what had been happening in the mind of Eustice.

"Look at this." The sheriff said, seeing Henry come up the

stairs. "Crime scene guys found it. Says it looks like someone trying to force the lock." Henry knelt down face to face with the door knob. There were scratches around the keyhole. There were more scratches and chipped paint around the door frame.

"Someone trying to force their way in?" Henry asked. The sheriff odded.

"It certainly looks like it. They have also found blood splatter in almost every room of the house." Henry stood up and looked at the sheriff.

"You think he killed in the house?"

"Not enough blood for that." The sheriff said, shaking his head. "But like he beat the shit out of someone. So far they have found fingernail tracks on the wallpaper along the hallway, multiple places of blood splatter, and locks on the inside of both kids' bedrooms." Henry looked around him. He so desperately wanted to know what had happened here. What made Eustice go from a cranky weirdo on an island to being the monster that had killed his baby sister. There was no one around to give him the answers. Just a house full of clues that would all need to be put together to paint the full picture.

"What room is this? The one with the forced lock."

"The daughter's." The sheriff answered.

"Similar marks on the son's door?" The sheriff shook his head. Neither one of them needed to ask why Eustice would want to get into the daughter's room but not the son's. Henry ran his hand through his hair. "This place just keeps getting better and better doesn't it?"

The sheriff leaned against the wall. His arm still in a sling from where he was shot. "The ground guys out there?"

"Yeah. They said it will take a few hours."

"You think they are going to find more?"

"I wouldn't be surprised." In a rare moment, the sheriff leaned his head back and showed the weight of all of it.

"Jesus Christ, Henry. Why didn't we know what was happening out here? Why didn't any of them say anything, reach out? Why didn't we guess when we hadn't seen any of them in months? I should have known something was up, hell the way the guy grinned at me whenever he saw me should have clued me into something."

"In your worst nightmares, would you have thought this was going on?" Henry answered. The sheriff didn't answer him, but shook his head. He had felt it too. It killed him to know that Eustice was torturing his family not ten minutes away and Henry hadn't done anything to stop it. To know that Eustice had killed girls practically across the street from the station and they hadn't heard a peep. How much suffering they could have prevented if they had only known.

"Any more clues in the kids' rooms?" Henry broke the silence, getting back to the work at hand.

"No. The girl was a reader. There are bits of newspaper stashed all over her room, but nothing pertaining to the murders."

"Any clue about the wife?" Henry knew this was shaky ground. The sheriff was of the mind that she had left of her own free will years ago. Henry did not.

"No, nothing. You better get back out there in case they find something." Henry nodded and went back down the stairs. A crime scene guy was spraying the ceiling and then running a black light over it. There was blood on the ceiling. *How damned hard had he hit her*? Henry thought to himself. The coroner had not released his official findings on the children yet, but he had said enough to Henry to know that the boy had suffered injuries far beyond his years. He wondered what the report on Eustice's wife would show. If they ever found her.

"Find anything?" Henry said, coming into the clearing.

"Over there." The guy operating the sonar said, pointing to a flag in the ground in line with the other graves.

"A body?" He almost whispered.

"No, but close. Here, I saved the image. He walked over to a table he had set up with a computer on it and pulled up the image. "See there?"

"I see black and white lines."

"See how those lines look different from the ones around it?"

"Yeah."

"That means the ground was recently disturbed."

"But no body?"

"I don't think there is a body down there, but worth a look. Maybe he was getting the ground ready to bury another one." Henry let out a deep breath. With all the focus on the ones they hadn't been able to help, he had forgotten the ones that would never happen now. So Eustice had dug a grave, getting it ready for the next victim. Henry thanked the guy and let him get back to his scanning. There wasn't much more of the clearing to do, they would be done in another hour. They would investigate the 'disturbed ground' tomorrow. Making sure everyone was busy with their jobs, Henry went into the woods and cried.

16

Henry and the sheriff stood there shoulder to shoulder, dressed in their dress uniforms, hats off out of respect for the dead. Two open graves in front of them, the coffins hovering over ground. There were chairs there, but the two men preferred to stand. Every accommodation had been taken for there to be more people, which somehow made it worse that they were the only two in attendance.

The minister said his words over the caskets. They were rather generic words, Henry thought, as the minister mentioned life being cut short and God having a plan for them. Seeing as how no one living knew much about Eustice's children Gerald and Victoria, the minister didn't have much of a choice in being generic . The town had been out in force the week before for the funeral of the victims. It looked like no one had come out for Eustice's children. The sheriff's arm was still in a sling. His jaw clenched tight. Henry had told him he was happy to attend the funeral by himself, but the sheriff had insisted.

The Sheriff had been the law and order of the town for twenty-two years. He had never killed anyone before. The fact that he had killed a seventeen year old boy had aged him in the past week. For some reason, it seemed important to the sheriff to make sure the boy knew how sorry he was. It had become more clear in the investigation after the shooting, that the boy had not intended to harm them, but to make sure his father didn't escape. Henry knew as well as the Sheriff, and everyone else who stepped into that house, that the children had been as much a victim of Eustice as the bodies buried in the clearing. Living on the island with him must have been living hell.

"I killed a kid, Henry. Never fired my gun in anger before and when I do, I kill a kid." The sheriff's voice quivered. The minister had stopped talking and they were now lowering the coffins into the ground. Henry didn't look at him.

"He was running at me with a gun, Sir."

"I know, but the more I think about it, knowing what we know now. I think that boy saw us coming and knew what his father was going to do. I think that boy was trying to help us. Imagine living on that island with a man like Eustice for a father and the law shows up to take him away. I shot him before he had a chance to live."

"There was no way for you to know."

"I could have waited a bit longer to find out."

"And what if he hadn't been trying to help us? What if he was doing exactly what it looked like he was doing and had every intention of helping his father get rid of us? You know as well as I do there was just as good of a chance we both could have died out there." Henry didn't feel good about what had happened out there either, but what had happened had happened, and he wasn't sure if the scenario played out again it would have turned out any different.

The men went quiet and watched the dirt spill over the caskets. A thought had been brewing in Henry's mind since they had left the island that day. Where was the mother?

"Did a runner years ago. Went to go visit her mother and never came back. Can you blame her?" The sheriff ad told Henry when he had asked. But as it turned out, Eustice had been the source of that information. Henry had been researching the wife and found the death record for her mother. She had died several years ago, so had the father. It looked like Eustice's wife had no family to speak of. Henry knew a man like Eustice would have loved that. Abusers often like women who have no support system. Nowhere to run. A picture was forming in his mind, and he was all but certain that the wife had not left the island voluntarily. If she had left it at all.

Henry and the sheriff stayed while the grounds crew continued to cover the graves. It didn't take as long as Henry thought it would since they used a backhoe. For some reason, he had thought they would use shovels. They waited until the diggers were done and the sheriff laid flowers on the grave of the boy. Henry laid flowers on the grave of the girl. Henry wasn't sure which one of them had suffered more at the hands of their father, but from what the coroner had found, Victoria had suffered a great deal.

It was not until they had left the graves and were walking back to the car that he brought up the mother again.

"Sir, I would like permission to open a formal investigation into the whereabouts of Eustice's wife."

"I told you, she ran off years ago." The sheriff answered not looking at him.

"Then why hasn't she come back?"

"Everyone is dead, why would she come back?"

"To see her children be buried." The sheriff shrugged his good shoulder. "I've looked into it a little and the mother she supposedly went to go live with died several years ago. Before the wife went missing."

"So she went to go live with some other relative." Henry couldn't figure out why he was getting the brush off other than the sheriff wanted the whole thing to be over.

"Sir, I think Eustice may have killed his wife. I would like to pursue that."

"Where is she then? The boys went all over that island with a fine tooth comb, they didn't find her or any evidence of her. Look for her if you want, Henry, but on your own time. I have enough to deal with right now." And the sheriff walked ahead of him.

The truth was, they all had a lot to do right now. The sheriff had dropped his bid for re-election. Henry had stepped up to run, not wanting the job to go to his opponent. While the sheriff had been vilified while Esustice was on the loose, the town had come back to him once it was all said and done and their daughters and wives were no longer threatened. But the sheriff didn't want the job anymore. He was sixty-eight, and after the last few months, had decided it was time to hang up his badge and leave it to a younger man to take his place. The truth was, Henry wasn't sure he wanted the job either. The town had pushed him to do it being the deputy and also having lost a sister at the hands of Eustice. It felt like sympathy, and Henry wasn't sure that was enough of a reason to run.

"You'll be great at it, Henry. I couldn't think of a better man for the job." The sheriff had told him, slapping his big hand on his back. Henry had never thought about being sheriff until he found himself running for the job. The election was in a month, and it looked like he was going to win it. A whole new world of responsibility was gettin ready to fall onto his shoulders. As much as he hated it, looking for Eustice's wife would have to wait until after the election.

One of several things that Henry had to deal with was what to do with Eustice's body. As it turned out, he had no living family that Henry could find. Seeing no reason to spend the extra money on a casket and burial plot, Eustice had been cremated. It had looked like the children's bodies were headed for the same until Henry talked to the manager at the funeral home. After explaining some of what the children had gone through, she had agreed to donate coffins and two plots in the cemetery. "Sounds like the poor souls deserve some peace."

"That they most certainly do."

"To be honest with you, Henry, I always thought they were a strange family. You never saw them in town all together and when you did see them, they all looked half stunned. Looking back we should have known something wasn't right, but I don't know what we could have done." She had said. Henry nodded. It was the same all over town. They had been that strange family out on the island. No one had really paid any of them much attention. Eustice was an odd guy, only coming over every once in a while and wearing that ridiculous hat. He would sit at the bar, nurse a few drinks and watch TV. Talk to people if they wanted to be talked to, would leave when the bar closed and go home. But everyone knew to stay off the island, or Eustice would come after you and he would have his gun.

"We all should have known. We all could have done more, and we would have done more if we had only known." Henry assured her. He would have, he knew that. He would like to think most of the people in town would have done something to help the family out if they would have known what they were suffering.

After the funerals came fall, and with it, the election. Henry was now sheriff. The leaves turned and fell off the trees, the ocean breeze now had a distinct chill in it. The town slowed back down to its normal rhythm. The days were growing shorter. Henry had taken to going out to the dock and staring at the island in the evenings after he had finished for the day. The island had always had a bit of a mystique about it. The fog had always done weird things on the island, and now it sat abandoned, looking spookier than ever.

Sucking in the ocean air, he would let it clear his head of the day's events and he would concentrate on one thing. Figuring out what he had missed. What clue there had been that not all was right over there. What clue Eustice had left them that told them all the time what he was doing. What clue would have told them that his family was suffering out there. Some clue as to where the wife was. With every day that passed, Henry was more and more convinced that Eustice had killed his wife. So where was she? Henry was fairly confident she wasn't buried on the island. They had searched it extensively. So where was she?

'Why didn't she tell us?' Henry asked himself. All she would have had to do was tell them on one of her trips to town and Henry would have done all he could. *'They had a phone in the house, she could have called while he was out.'* Eustice's wife wasn't his only victim that he thought about. Henry did not allow himself to think about what the victims of Eustice had suffered at his hands. But when the evening had gone quiet, when it was only him and the island standing alone in the dusk, he would wonder about his sister's last moments.

They had not been able to determine if Eustice had killed the women before or after getting to the island. He hadn't buried them alive, according to the coroner, which had been one nightmare of Henry's. The notes left by the son and the daughter all indicated that the women were dead when they arrived. Gerald mentioned them already being neatly wrapped in tarps and tape when he arrived. It was that unknown amount of time between Eustice abducting the women, and Gerald being summoned to bury them that haunted Henry's thoughts. Had she known she was about to die? How had he gotten her? She was a smart girl, raised by a cop with a cop for a brother, so she knew not to trust anyone, but if he had looked like he needed help, she might have stopped. The worst thought of all was, had Eustice picked her because he knew she was the deputy's sister?

"Stop torturing yourself." Meg came up behind him, she pulled her sweater tight around her shoulders. Meg's book shop was right up the road from the dock. He would often stop in there to say hello to her and his brother before heading home for the night. Henry was standing in darkness now, the late afternoon turning to evening without him even noticing.

"Who said I was?"

"It's written all over you, Henry."

"I could have helped her. The wife."

"You didn't know she needed help." Meg said matter of factly.

"Why didn't she tell anyone Meg? You saw her a few times, did she ever say anything to you?"

"For the hundredth time, no. I thought she was just shy. Now that I think about it, the poor thing was scared. I think she was afraid of what would happen if she said anything. So she didn't."

"Where is she though?"

"You don't think she ran away like the sheriff said?"

"Hell no. I don't think she would have left the kids behind."

"No one knew her that well Henry. Maybe she decided she had to leave or he would kill her. Kids or no kids."

"Then where is she? There are no parents for her 'to be staying with'. No family to speak of at all. No driver's license in her name, she hasn't voted, she doesn't own a car. She just vanished."

"You'll find the answer Henry, but stop torturing yourself every night about what you missed. You caught him, you saved the town. As a woman in this town, I am sleeping better at night thanks to your efforts. You should be happy."

"I can't let it go. It's not adding up for me."

"Well, you are going to have to give it up for the night. Your mother called, she went to the doctor today and he didn't like one of her test results. He's admitted her to the hospital so they can run more tests in the morning."

"What tests? She's all right?"

"She sounded fine on the phone. Gave me a list of things she wants you to get for her at the house." Meg handed him a slip of paper.

"Why didn't she call my cell?"

"She says you never answer it when you know it's her."

"Well that is crap." Henry snatched the paper away from her. " Great. I get to go through my mother's underwear drawer."

"You want me to come with you?" Meg offered. Henry was a good man. He was also his mother's youngest boy, and since the death of his sister, the youngest child. Her mother in-law had taken to coming up with new and ever creative reasons for Henry to come by now that he was sheriff. He always went, bless him. "I'll stop by and get this and head on over there. Thanks Meg." Meg turned and walked back to the shop. Henry took one more look at the island and then walked back to his car. The island would keep its secrets for another day.

17

"Leave him alone." His mother yelled, grabbing the arm that was swinging back for another blow.

"And what are you going to do about it?" His father had turned his anger towards his mother, shaking off her grasp and pulling her so close to him she could smell dinner on his breath.

"Leave him alone." She repeated through gritted teeth. Gerald held his ribs and watched for a second as his mother drew the abuse away from him and onto herself. He could tell from looking at his father he wasn't done yet. His mother threw him a look and he ran for his room still trying to get a deep breath from the last punch to his gut.

"I'll do whatever the hell I want with my own son." He heard his father say, and a small cry from his mother as he landed the first blow. Gerald managed to get to his room before the tears started. You couldn't show tears in front of Eustice because they made it worse. Half running into his room, he turned and threw the lock. The beating had started downstairs. He could hear the blows being landed and could have even told you what part of the body he was hitting based on the sound it made. Gerald sat on the bed. His face sore and swelling more with each passing moment. His ribs were bruised, but not broken. His father had landed a punch to the face and three body blows before his mother had gotten there.

Gerald was a coward. He felt a coward anyway. His mother had always stepped in where she could. It depended on what kind of night Eustice was having as to whether he took the bait or not. Gerald had always promised himself that when he was older it would be the other way around. He would take the beatings for his mother. He was bigger than she was, he should be able to take it, but here he was in his room listening to the beating going on downstairs. The tears rolled harder down his cheeks. He couldn't cry too hard, it hurt his ribs. There was a small knocking on the wall next to the head of his bed.

"Ger…" He heard her whisper. "You okay?" Gerald scooted to the head of his bed and leaned his head against the cold wall.

"He's beating her Vic. I should do something?"

"Do what Ger?" Gerald shook his head. The siblings had discovered this method of communication several years ago. On nights like tonight it wasn't safe to leave your locked room, but they could check in with each other this way.

"He should be beating me." Gerald finally answered, his voice small and timid.

"He did beat you Ger, I heard him. No one made Mom get in the way. She did it because she wanted to."

"I know, but I should be protecting her."

"You protect me."

"But I should be protecting her too."

"Don't be stupid Ger, you can't protect everyone. You protect me and Mom protects you."

"But no one protects Mom."

"Which is why we have to get Eustice away from here." Gerald had always dreamed of leaving the island. Victoria had a different approach, get Eustice to leave it. She would often fantasize about him trying to come back to the island after running to the mainland only to find his children carrying his shotguns and not allowing him to dock the boat. This is what they talked about now. Gerald would come up with ways they could leave the island. How they would change their names and go to some far away place so that Eustice would never be able to find them.

"He'd be here all by himself on the island." Victoria said.

"He'll starve. There will be no one to fix his breakfast, lunch and dinner."

"He'll get so upset having no one to beat that he'll have a heart attack."

"He'll die gasping for breath, unable to call for help because he knocked the phone off the wall too many times ." The thought drew a smile from Gerald. The man should suffer. Lost in their musings, they hadn't realized things had gone quiet downstairs.

"I think I heard a door close." The screen door on the back of the house made a particular 'slap' sound when it closed. It was this that brought them back to the present. They sat in silence for a bit, listening for any signs that their father was still in the house. There was nothing.

"Mom, wake up. We need to get you upstairs." Victoria whispered to her mother who was laying on the floor in the living room. Her mother was lying where she had fallen, and they didn't have much time to get her upstairs, which would no doubt take some time with her injuries.

"Leave me here." Her mother insisted.

"Come on, I don't know when he will be back." Victoria ignored her. The bruises were already a dark shade of purple on her face and arms. There were no doubt dark bruises on her stomach from the way she was holding herself. Eustice liked to kick you while you were down.

"Go away Victoria."

"You can't stay down here."

"I'm not moving." Victoria tried to pull her mother up. This resulted in a sharp cry. "Just go." Her mother begged and turned her face to the floor to hide the tears. Victoria left, and for a moment, she thought her daughter had finally left her in peace. Then she heard her soft feet approaching again and a blanket fell over her. Gently, Victoria lifted her head and placed a pillow underneath her.

"You sure you don't want to come up? You can stay in my room tonight." She just wanted to sleep. She was so tired, she just wanted to sleep. It didn't matter where, but moving hurt, so she might as well stay here.

"I'll be fine Vitoria, just go to bed." The girl gave her a kiss on her forehead and then ran up the stairs. She turned her face to the floor again. She shouldn't cry, if he saw her crying, it would make it worse, but she couldn't even bring herself to reach up and wipe away the tears.

Victoria climbed the stairs without their mother. Gerald was keeping watch in one of the upstairs windows. "You need help?" He asked. He didn't think Victoria would be able to get their mother up the stairs by herself, but Vic hadn't wanted him to help.

"She won't come up. I covered her up down there." A movement in the window drew Gerald's glance. Their father was coming out of the woods towards the house.

"What do you mean she won't come up? She's just going to lay on the floor for the rest of the night?" Victoria shrugged her shoulders.

"She said to leave her, Ger. I tried to pull her up and she screamed. He probably broke her ribs; it looked like he was kicking her." Gerald looked out the window again. His father was half way up the yard. There wasn't enough time to get her up here before he entered the house.

"Damn it!" Gerald said, hitting the wall. Even if they both went down there and carried the woman up the stairs, it would take too long with her injuries. He had just wanted to make her comfortable. The back door opened and closed. They froze, listening to Eustice's foot fall walking through the kitchen and then towards the stairs. Their mother lay next to the stairs. There was a small yelp as Eustice kicked her as he walked past.

"Still alive then." And then his footsteps quickly climbed the stairs. They stood frozen in Gerald's room, not making a sound. Eustice should be heading for bed. It was nearly morning, and it had been a busy night, but it was hard to say with Eustice. When he was in a mood, he could keep going all night andhe certainly seemed to be in a mood.

His footsteps did not turn towards Gerald's room. They paused in front of Victoria's. Victoria grabbed Gerald's arm and dug her nails in. The footsteps continued to Eustice's room, and the door shut. Gerald and Victoria let out a breath of relief, and Victoria let go of his arm.

"Should we go and get her now?" Victoria whispered so quietly Gerald could barely hear her.

"No, there is no way we are going to get her up the stairs without making noise and waking him."

"She is just going to sleep on the floor by herself all night?"

"I'll go check on her. She can sleep in your room tomorrow night." Gerald waited what he thought was enough time for Eustice to fall asleep. Opening his door quietly and carefully, he escaped to the landing and looked over the side. His mother was still there curled up in the blanket Victoria had placed over her. Quietly as he could and with a constant eye on Eustice's door, Gerald ventured downstairs where he placed a light hand on his mother.

"You okay?"

"I'll be fine Gerald. Go to bed." She said. Even in the dark he could see the pain in her face. It had been one hell of a beating.

"We have to get out of here Mom." She smiled as much as she could with her split lip.

"I don't think that is going to happen tonight."

"We can't live like this."

"You and Victoria stay together tonight. I'll be better in the morning."

"I'm going to get us out of here."

"You're a good boy Gerald. I know you would get us out of here if you could, but right now go to bed."

18

She stood on the dock, her toes playing with the nails in the wood, her cotton robe wrapped tight around her shoulders. Giving up on sleep, she had come out here to find some peace. Her ribs hurt too much to lay down anyway, not that standing up felt great either. Tears fell silently down her face. There was no reason to wipe them away. He wasn't there to see them. She stopped crying in front of him some time ago, it only made it worse. This was where she cried. Where only the man in the moon could see her. The lights from the mainland were visible in the darkness. How long had it been since she had been over there? Such a short distance, but she wasn't allowed to even go that far anymore. Had anyone noticed she hadn't been seen for a while? Did anyone ever ask Eustice how his wife was doing? What would he say if they did? There was no telling what he had told them about her. What would they say if they saw her walking down the street now? Battered and bruised, barely able to take a deep breath for the broken ribs. Would they help her, or would they pretend they couldn't see her? Maybe she was invisible. The thought had occurred to her that she was already dead and just didn't know it yet. Every day was the same.

Nothing changed for her.

The thought occurred to her to yell. Yell as loud as she could. Maybe someone over there would hear her. Wonder what was happening on the island and come find her. One look at her surely would be enough to tell them something wasn't right. She no longer looked in mirrors because she didn't want to see what he had done to her, but she could feel the swelling under her eyes, and she could taste the blood from her split lip. She didn't need a mirror to tell her that, or that she had a broken rib. The beatings were getting worse. This was the third time he hadn't stopped until she passed out. How much longer before he beat her to death? Gerald had tried to stop him. Eustice had found that funny. Gerald wasn't a boy anymore though. He was nearly a grown man and had the muscles to prove it. Eustice would be surprised when the day finally came where Gerald landed his own punch. Fresh tears fell. What had she done? Raised children with a monster. Raised children who had always lived in fear, and she had done nothing about it. What was there to do? They were trapped here. There was no one to call for help. She hadn't been smart enough to figure out a way to get them off the island. If only she had been smarter. If she had been smarter then none of this would have happened. She would have seen Eustice for what he was.

Looking at the inky water over the edge of the dock, she took a step forward and looked down, letting her toes curl around the last board. If she stepped off the side, there would hardly be a splash. The darkness would surround her and she could escape this place. She could escape him and all the pain. Death couldn't hurt anymore than breathing did right now. Turning around, she looked back at the house. It would all be over with before they even knew she was gone. Just slip below the water. She wouldn't even fight it. She couldn't fight it, she couldn't lift her arms without pain. *'But what about your babies?'* Her inner voice reminded her. Whether they would miss her or not she couldn't say. She thought they would, but who would protect them? Not that she could do much anymore, but she was used to taking the beatings. Just because she was gone wouldn't lessen Eustice's desire to hurt. He would just turn to someone else. That she couldn't do. She couldn't leave her babies alone with him. Taking a step back from the dock, she tried to take a deep breath, the pain bringing her up short. No point in thinking about it then, she took a step back from the edge of the dock.

Her tears all spent, she was so tired she thought she would fall asleep standing up. *'No point in standing here crying about it.'* There would be an end to it all. There had to be. This couldn't be life. This couldn't be all there was for her in life. To be Eustice's punching bag and then die. Something would happen, something that would end it all. Maybe she would get lucky and he would die of cardiac arrest in his sleep or something, but it would end somehow, some way. Taking one more look at the moon, the stars and the lights across the way, she wiped the tears from her face and turned back towards the house.

Walking back up to the house, she caught her reflection in the window. 'I look like a ghost.' She thought to herself. With the moon shining down on her white robe and nightgown, she did look ghost-like. Her bloodshot and bruised eye was the only indication she was alive. *'I'll haunt him all his living days.'* She promised herself, gently touching the swollen area around her eye. That had been the blow that had knocked her out. If he did kill her, at least she would have the privilege of haunting him into an early grave. The thought of his face when she appeared in front of him, his dead wife, untouchable. It was enough to make her smile. Leaving her reflection, she went into the kitchen. It was going to take her longer to make breakfast. Best to get a head start.

19

"There she is." Her father said, his reading glasses perched on his nose and his laptop open in front of him. Twain ambled up to Julia and threw his weight against her legs. Julia tousled his ears and Twain ran back to take up position next Evelyn who was frying bacon.

"Good morning, dear. Breakfast is almost ready. You feeling okay, Honey?" her mother asked.

"Yeah."

"You need to stop staying up late reading. Food will do you good." Her mother never thought she was eating enough. Julia needed time to herself, and with her bedroom no longer the sanctuary it used to be, she thought she would head outside today.

"What's the plan for today?"

"Well, we are going to be on the island most of the day, actually. I promised your father he could fish. I was going to stay here and get some research done. The island has some interesting history, but I haven't found anything about the house yet." Evelyn was not ready to share with Julia what she had found out so far. The child was having enough trouble getting to sleep as it was.

Julia had seen her mother catch the research bug before and knew her mother wouldn't stop until she had gotten all the answers to her questions. There would be a book written and off to the agent before the summer was over. These two months were supposed to be a break from work for all three of them, but Julia had no doubt that her mother would have a binder of notes and would have interviewed most of the town by the time they left.

"Do you think you can find something around the island to entertain yourself with today?" her mother asked.

"I think I'll take my book and walk around the island. See what I can see, maybe read a bit." She doubted it would even take the full day since the island was about the size of two football fields. The idea of being the only person combing the beaches for what the ocean had thrown back was exciting. She already had an art project planned for what she found on the beach.

"You going to take Twain with you?" Julia nodded. "Well, be careful, take your cell phone. I would plan on being back here around four. We are planning on heading into town for dinner."

Julia finished her breakfast and then bounded up the stairs to get dressed. In half an hour she was back downstairs, her backpack loaded with a camera, book, a bottle of water, a sandwich, and her cellphone, of course. She gave her mother a kiss and then headed down the hill to the dock to collect Twain. Coming down the hill, she could see the golden retriever sitting on the dock next to her father, his yellow fluffy tail wagging, eyes steady on the water, just waiting for her father to pull in a fish for him to lick. Her father sat next to him, feet dangling in the water, and his horrible floppy fishing hat on his head.

Letting out a whistle, Twain jumped up and ran to her. Giving a wave to her Dad, the two set off for their own adventure. Hitting the beach, Twain took off after a flock of seagulls then ran back to Julia with his tongue hanging out and looking rather pleased with himself. This was a bit of a vacation for him as well. Certainly better than being in a crate all day while they were all at school and work. Julia found a stick and threw it for him. Twain bounded after it and then brought it back. He grew tired of this quickly, though, and just carried the stick as they walked. She couldn't blame him because the sun was strong, and it was getting warmer.

The waters around the island were shallow, and therefore, did not cause the big waves normally associated with the ocean. Because of this, their walk was a rather quiet one with only the sound of the lapping water and their feet pressing into the sand . It was hard for Julia to imagine a place as quiet as this. Without the sounds of civilization. There weren't even any cars. Humans were so noisy. Instead of putting her headphones on as usual, she listened to the sound of the breeze in the trees, the seagulls overhead, and the water coming onto the beach. It sounded like the sound machine her mother used to get to sleep, only these sounds were real. She didn't hate it so put her headphones back in her backpack.

Julia was unusual in that she neither minded her parents nor her own company, and actually preferred it to many of the people she went to school with. Most of the girls she went to school with would have viewed a two-month vacation with their parents alone on an island as torture, but it hadn't bothered Julia at all. She and her parents all shared a love of books and discussing books. They had some fantastic discussions and always seemed genuinely interested in what she was reading. However, she had spent three solid days with them and had been slightly thrilled at the idea of having a whole day to spend in any way she saw fit. As she walked, the town to her right across the water fell behind her and more open ocean was visible. She could feel her muscles loosening. Twain had settled down into a steady trot next to her, taking off when another flock of seagulls came into view, and looked pleased with himself for having gotten them out of the way.

To her left was an increasingly thick pine forest. They hadn't really seen any wildlife since they had been there, and Julia wondered if the island even had any to speak of. She made a mental note to explore the woods the next time she had a free day. Stopping to take the occasional picture, they were soon rounding the island. Here the water was a little choppier, the wind stronger, nothing but open ocean for as far yas the eye could see. The beach was littered with some fantastic driftwood, and Julia spent a fair amount of time crawling over it and under it, looking for other interesting things that had washed up with the tide. How long did a tree have to tumble around in the ocean before it became the bleached, dried up piece of driftwood in front of her? Picking up some interesting shells and what-nots, it was midday, and she was only half way done with her trip around the island.

He left the safety of the house for only the second time since he had crossed over. Neither he nor Vic left the house for fear of him, but the girl was going out there by herself, and he feared what would happen to her on her own. They were stronger than they had ever been, but that still wasn't very strong. Vic had proven the previous night that it was enough to scare someone, but probably not much more. Gerald knew if they were growing in strength though, so was he. The living seemed to know nothing about him yet. Despite Vic's best efforts, they didn't seem to be aware that they were sharing the house, but he suspected that was all going to change. Gerald left the safety of the house to make sure nothing happened. What he was going to do about it if it did, he didn't know yet.

20

They stopped for a break and some water, which Twain half drank and half slung around, but seemed grateful for all the same. Julia found a large piece of driftwood to climb up on and let the salt air hit her in the face until her cheeks hurt. A smile on her face. There was something very freeing about being alone surrounded by mother nature. She would have to tell her mother that this was probably why there was no other house this side of the island. The winds were fierce compared to their side of the island which was protected from the wind by all the trees surrounding the house. Her stomach told her it was time to eat, and not wanting her sandwich to taste of salt, she and Twain walked on to find a less windy place to eat their lunch. Not finding a break in the wind, Julia climbed up into the trees a little, letting them break the wind for her and sat on a pile of dead pine needles to eat. Twain begged for a little bit but then opted for a midday snooze.

Not wanting to disturb him, and with plenty of time before they had to be back, Julia pulled out her book and read while she ate. Turning her ears to the trees, their needles rustled with every gust of wind. The scene was tranquil, and Julia thought she could stay there forever. Her sandwich finished and three chapters read, her butt started to go numb, and she wasn't sure how much island there was left to walk. As soon as she picked up her backpack to move on, Twain was on his feet again.

They came around another corner of the island, and the wind all but stopped, which was a relief. Looking at her watch, they would be home a little bit before her mother had wanted her, which would work out well. She was playing fetch with Twain again when she felt someone watching her. Not thinking much about it, she turned around to see who it was, only then realizing that there shouldn't be anyone since they were alone on the island. Seeing nothing, she turned and continued walking, but the feeling continued and, if anything, got stronger.

'It's nothing, you are all alone and you know it.' Julia's senses were alive; she was more aware of the breeze moving the upper branches of the trees, the sound of lapping water, and which direction the bird song was coming from. As a result, Twain was more on guard. He was still prancing next to her, but he was no longer looking at her or waiting for her to throw the stick. His ears were up, and he was looking around. They were feeding off of one another. Kneeling down next to him and ruffling his ears, "We are just winding each other up, aren't we, boy?" Twain looked at her with adoring eyes, his tongue hanging out the side of his mouth, and Julia felt herself relax. She was a city girl, not used to being in such a remote place on her own, and after the other night, she had let her imagination get the better of her.

Twain's ears perked up, and the adoring look went out of his eyes. He pulled away from her hands and turned to face the woods. He was standing in his defensive pose and scanning the woods. Julia stood up. She too was looking towards the woods, but she could see nothing. The woods in this area were dense and closer to the beach. If there was someone just behind the trees, she wouldn't be able to see them, and if they came out of the woods, they wouldn't be that far away. Twain barked, and Julia jumped. He kept barking and focused on the woods straight ahead of them. Julia continued to scan the woods looking for any indication of what he might be barking at. She could feel someone looking at her and was sure something or someone was looking at her from just beyond the trees. "Come on Twain." She said and started to walk in the direction of the house. Twain was focused on the trees and was not following her. She kept walking and whistled for him. This got his attention, and he followed her, looking over his shoulder to bark. Julia had convinced herself Twain was barking at wildlife and had turned her back completely on the area when she heard a branch snap behind her.

Feeling his father was close by, Gerald got closer to the girl. He was hoping to not scare her, but he would feel better if she went back to the house. Feeling his father get closer, he yelled with all his power, 'Run!' Something yelled next to her ear. Julia could not tell if she had yelled it to herself, but run she did. "Twain!" The dog was now half running, half stopping to bark at whatever was behind her. Her efforts were made more difficult by the sand, so she was not getting as far as she would like as fast as she would like. Twain was running next to her now, barking as they went.

Run faster! The voice next to her said again, and she doubled her efforts despite the pain in her side. She didn't dare turn around for fear of seeing whoever it was running after. Twain was no longer barking but running to keep up with her. She couldn't hear the footsteps of the person behind her because of the sand, but she imagined them to be right behind her. The curve of the island was right ahead of her. If she could make it there, she wouldn't be too far from the house and could call for her parents. She could feel herself slowing down, her muscles worn out from running in the sand, and she could hardly breath. The stitch in her side hurt like Hell, but she kept running.

Rounding the curve, she could see the end of the dock that her father was sitting on earlier that morning, but he wasn't there now. "HELP!" she yelled, hoping that he wasn't that far away, but it sounded like a whisper to her own ears. *Don't stop, whatever you do, don't stop.* She heard in her head.

She couldn't spare enough breath for a decent yell.   Leaving the beach, she turned left and jumped a small ledge, cutting across a thin slice of woods. It was up hill now, and she felt like she was crawling. Twain was beside her, tongue hanging low. Julia wished he would bark now so her parents would hear it and come out to see what was going on, but it didn't look like he had any breath to spare either.

"HELP!" Again, it sounded like little more than a whisper to her own ears, but maybe they would hear it. Julia heard leaves and twigs breaking behind her and knew now that whoever was chasing her was not far behind. They had just broken through the tree line right behind her.

Not too much farther, RUN. For God's sake RUN! The voice yelled again. It gave Julia the boost she needed.

Knowing this was it, this was all she had left in her, Julia pushed on. With solid ground underneath her, she gained ground, and the distance between her and the house grew shorter. "HELP!" This scream cost her, and she stumbled on the path. She was sure they would get her now. Twain stopped next to her and started to bark again. Julia got herself back to her feet, but she had lost her momentum, and her legs felt like jelly. Nothing will make them move any faster than a walk. She heard the storm door to the house open, but she was not focused on that. She was focused on the footsteps behind her. She could not hear them, and she thought that meant they were right behind her.

He stayed with her even though his father stopped chasing her at the edge of the woods. Not trusting him, he waited for the parents to come and get her. Gerald could feel his excitement. His father had stopped chasing her the closer to the house the girl got, but he had not gone anywhere. He was enjoying her fear too much. The girl was not safe here. In the house maybe, but for how long? He had not been this close to his father since the day he died and it was not a comfortable feeling. Gerald waited until the girl's parents came out of the house and then he escaped inside where he knew his father would not go.

Her mother looked around confused, but then saw Julia and her face turned to fear. Mark was close behind and saw the concern on his wife's face looking at Julia and then to Twain who was again barking at the woods. Evelyn ran to her daughter, wrapping her protectively in her arms. They heard her. They are here. Relief and exhaustion took over as Julia fell to her knees and vomited.

"Honey, what is it?" Her mother's voice was panicked, but Julia was so out of breath she couldn't answer. Mark stopped briefly to make sure his daughter was all right and then walked further down the path. Twain had found new energy and was pacing in front of the woods and barking.

"Get her into the house and call the cops." Her father's voice said over her head, and they both lifted her up.

"Person…. woods." The words came out almost a whisper, but her mother heard them. "She says there was someone in the woods." Julia had never seen her father fight anything. He jogged and fished and taught in a university. He really didn't have a need to prove himself in that way. Hearing there was someone in the woods, she saw him change in an instant. A look came over his face, and he grabbed the axe next to the front door used for cutting firewood and marched off in the direction of the woods. "Get in the house. Lock the door." Evelyn wanted to argue with him but saw there was no point, and did the best she could to quickly get Julia in the house. Evelyn then walked over to the phone hanging on the wall and called the number for the local sheriff, watching out the side window as her husband and Twain walked down to the beach and back.

21

"Hello, Sheriff's office? This is Evelyn over at the island house. Our daughter just got back from walking the island and said someone was following her. I was wondering if you could send someone over?" She stopped while the person on the other end of the line talked. "My husband is out there now, and we are in the house." Another pause. "Did you see anyone, Julia?" Her mother asked, putting a hand on Julia's shoulder.

"No, but I could hear the footsteps behind me."

"Did you hear that? Okay, thank you." And Evelyn hung up. "They are going to send a boat over. She said the sheriff is going to take the boat around the island first and see if they spot anything. You okay?" Julia's breathing was finally starting to return to normal, but she couldn't take her eyes off the door. The footsteps had been so close behind her that surely her father could see who was chasing her. Would he fight the person? Would the person run away? Who could it have been? She didn't know anyone here, what could they have wanted?

Julia almost jumped out of her skin when her father appeared in the window, walking around to the porch and coming in the front door. "I ran both directions until I couldn't see the dock anymore and didn't see anyone. Did you call the police?"

"They are sending a boat over. They are going to circle the island first and then they will come speak to us."

"You okay, Honey?" Mark kneeled down in front of his daughter and put a hand on her shoulder. Julia just shook her head.

"Gerald, I can feel him. He's not far away." Their father was still hanging around the house. Enjoying the chaos he had caused. "He's the one who chased her. I knew he would try something, so I followed her."

"You said we shouldn't talk to them." She reminded him.

"What was I supposed to do?" Gerald had been watching Julia. He knew she was at risk with his father out there. Now his sister knew he had been watching her and it annoyed him.

"Are you sure it was him?"

"It was him. He'd been watching her since she passed the driftwood."

"Do you think he can actually do anything?"

"I don't know, but he wanted to. She is just his type."

"Do you think they will leave now?"

"If they're smart." The mother was calling the sheriff, which made him somewhat happy. Nothing would upset his father more than seeing the sheriff on the island again. Watching the mother cradle the girl made Gerald miss his own mother so bad it hurt. Even now, he longed to feel her hand on his face. He remembered what a comfort having your mother around can be, and he was glad Julia had that comfort now.

"I know it's selfish, but I want them to stay." Victoria said. It was selfish, but he felt the same way. This also annoyed him. "Are we going to warn them?" She asked. It was a question he had been asking

himself since the family got here, and he still didn't know the answer. Hopefully, today was enough of a warning and they would make up their own minds.

He had not gone back to his spot in the woods once the brat's parents had arrived, but rather hung back in the distance. The father running after him had amused him. Chasing a ghost. Like the children in the house, he was still learning what this new energy meant. The girl's fear had fueled him. Allowed him to chase her all the way back to the house. Their combined fear fueled him now. He could feel it pulsing through him the way his blood had pulsed through him when he was alive. His fun had been ruined when the police boat circled the island. The sight of them still angered him. His fun over, he went back to the woods to wait for them to leave. He wanted more of what he had today. More of the girl's fear, more of watching her run, unable to escape him. He had even enjoyed the mother's face when she had seen the fear in her daughter's eyes. It had rejuvenated him. He would be able to feed off their fear for days. All he had to do was stay in the woods and feel himself growing stronger. Next time, he might even be able to catch her.

While they waited for the sheriff to arrive, Julia had calmed down to the point where she was starting to get sleepy. "I hear their boat." Mark said. He had taken guard on the front porch. Evelyn had noticed he hadn't put the axe back by the fire wood, but had laid it in the rocking chair on the porch. Just in case.

"They are pulling up to the dock." Mark was a little disappointed to see the man was barely winded after coming up the hill to the house despite being dressed in full uniform and in summer. He was a tall man with a healthy head of dark brown hair. If she had not seen the star on his chest, Evelyn would have still known this was a man used to being in charge from the way he stood in the room. Feet wide apart, shoulders squared, and eyes looking directly at her. He nodded to all of them in the room and then focused on Julia who was sitting on the couch, Twain draped across her lap. He too was worn out from the morning.

"Good afternoon, I understand we had some excitement. Are you up to telling me about it?" He asked Julia. She nodded that she was. The sheriff turned to the deputy behind him who pulled out a notepad and flipped it open.

"So, you went out for a walk?" The sheriff prompted her.

"Yeah, around the island. I thought it would be neat to see what the rest of it looked like since it's so small."

"When did the person start to follow you?"

"I was almost home, more than halfway around the island when I felt like someone was watching me. It was right before I turned and could see the house again. The woods are closer to the beach there and it felt like someone was standing just beyond the trees, watching me. Twain turned and got defensive. He usually loves everyone, but he was barking, really barking at whoever it was. I went to continue walking. I had almost convinced myself that it was just me being weird about being on my own, but then I heard a branch snap. I took off running after that."

"Did you get any glimpse of the person behind you out of the corner of your eye?"

"No. I felt them, but I was too afraid to look. When I got closer to the house, I turned and ran through the woods that lead to the path next to the house. I could hear them behind me then. They were close."

"Did they say anything to you?" Julia stopped for a second to think about this. Did they say anything? Someone had told her to run. But that had been the voice in her head surely, it had just seemed like it was someone yelling in her ear.

"I don't think so."

"Did you see a boat, or anything pulled up on the sand while you were walking?"

"No. I saw rather large pieces of driftwood, but not boats."

"We did a pass around the island on our way over here but didn't see any craft. I've got a deputy out there right now doing a slower pass to see if he can see any marks in the sand to show where someone would have pulled a boat onto land. I'll let you all know if we see anything. How far did they chase you?"

"All the way up to where the woods end at the footpath up to the house." Julia answered.

"I saw her running up the house looking absolutely petrified, and we ran out to see what was going on. When she told me someone was following her, I took off for the woods, but I didn't see anyone." Mark offered.

"I'll go through there with my deputies and see if I can find any sign of them. They should have at least left foot prints. I can't promise that we will find out who did this, but I will send a patrol boat out this evening to make sure they know we are around. I'm sorry this has disrupted your vacation folks. I'll let you know if we find anything."

"Thank you, Sheriff." And the sheriff and his deputy went out to search the woods. The sheriff had a bad feeling in his stomach. This was only the second time he had been back to the island since the day Eustice had died. The first time had been after they found the bodies of the missing women. "What do you think?" His deputy asked him. "Think she's just wanting attention from the parents?"

"She seemed genuinely terrified. Probably local kids wanting to scare off the tourists. Make sure if there is someone on the island, they know we are here." The deputy took off for another part of the island. The sheriff walked the small patch of woods Julia had run through between the beach and the house. He found Julia's foot prints with little effort, the toe dug in where she had been running. He followed them back to the beach where there were similar prints. The dog's paw prints close by. Looking at the sand, there were only the two sets of prints. It looked like a girl running with her dog. Going back to the woods, the sheriff saw something he didn't like. Julia looked like she was about five foot four. Whoever had caused the twigs of the branches to bend on the path leading to the house had been taller than that. Despite this, he could find no other sets of prints on the ground except Julia's and the dog's. What would break branches six feet up but leave no footprints? An idea had occurred to the sheriff, but he discounted it. He wasn't even convinced it was possible and certainly would not look good in a police report. Leaving his deputies to their jobs, the sheriff went back to the boat. When he got back to the office, he pulled the Eustice file. The well-worn, brown folder was never far away. He opened the file to the picture of the victims. All young girls in their early twenties. Julia looked like she was still in high school. He looked at their familiar faces and closed the file again. "And he's dead." He explained to himself, burying his head in his hands.

"Now I'm wondering if I did hear anything." Julia said in almost a whisper over her dinner that night. They had planned to eat on the mainland anyway, but after the events of the afternoon, it seemed even more appropriate.

"Don't doubt yourself, Honey. Something made you feel unsafe out there, and you said yourself that Twain was barking at something." Her mother assured her.

"It could have been a squirrel."

"He only barks at people, Jules, you know that." Her father said sitting across the table from her. "If it had been a squirrel, we would all be in the woods searching for Twain because he would have run after it. I'm glad he was there with you. If he hadn't been, I wonder if this person would have tried harder." And he ruffled the hair on top of Twain's head. They couldn't have left him home after he had been so brave that day. They had even ordered him an ice cream for dessert.

It was true. Twain never barked at animals. At the park, he pulled on his leash until she thought her arm would break. He only barked when people were around. A shiver ran down Julia's back. What if she hadn't taken Twain? What would have happened then? Evelyn's phone rang.

"Yes?"

"Good evening. This is the sheriff. I still have my deputies searching, but right now, we aren't finding much. Now, I don't know your daughter, and she seems like a level-headed young lady to me, but I wanted to ask someone who knew her better."

"Are you asking if I think she made this up?" Evelyn sat up straighter, prepared to defend her daughter.

"I don't know your daughter, but I do know sometimes teenagers do things to get attention or to make a point. I was just wondering if you thought there was a possibility that this might be the case here."

"My daughter is not like most teenagers. If she says there was someone chasing her on that beach, then she had reason to think that there was someone chasing her on that beach." Evelyn was preparing her speech on 'this is why more women don't report attacks'. Mark had stopped eating his dinner and was also looking defensive.

"That's enough for me." The sheriff answered in his low steady voice. Evelyn relaxed a little. He hesitated before speaking again, but it was clear there was something else he wanted to say. "I understand you were at the bookstore the other day buying books on the history of the island."

"How in the…"

"My sister-in-law runs the store and told me you might be stopping by to ask me some questions."

"I was beginning to wonder if we had picked a police state to vacation in. Yes, Julia and I stopped the other day. We are both suckers for a used book store. I had actually intended to call you today to see if you would be willing to talk to me."

"I would be happy to speak with you about the town. How would lunchtime tomorrow work?" Evelyn was a little thrown by his willingness to speak but decided she should take him up on it before some crime was committed and he no longer had time.

"That would be great. You decide where we should eat, and it will be my treat." He agreed and gave her the name of a diner and directions.

"I will see you then. There will be a patrol boat out around the island about ten tonight to cruise the island and make sure there isn't any trouble. If there is anything else, or if the young lady remembers anything, please give me a call."

"Are we in danger here? I mean, we are kind of sitting ducks out there. I'm wondering if we should maybe move into town."

"There were some townspeople who weren't thrilled about this place being turned into a rental house. Thought it should stay in the hands of a local, not out of town investors. I'm thinking it was either someone making a point or some grumpy fisherman going out of his way to defend his fishing hole. I'm not sure your daughter was in any real danger, but I do regret that she felt like she was, and we will do our best to make it clear such behavior will not be tolerated." And he hung up.

"What was all that about?" Mark asked.

"The sheriff didn't find any sign that anyone else had been on the island, but he thinks it was likely some local who doesn't want tourists around. He is going to have a patrol boat come around tonight. Make their presence known so whoever it was won't come back." She looked pointedly at Julia while she said this.

"What was all that about lunch?"

"Turns out he's the brother in-law of the book store owner. She mentioned I may want to talk to him about local history, and he offered to do it over lunch."

"I thought you were taking the summer off?" Mark asked, not seeming surprised at all that her promise hadn't lasted a week.

"This is a hobby, not work." She could tell from the looks on their faces that neither Mark nor Julia bought this. Hell, Twain didn't even buy it.

22

Evelyn showed up at the restaurant ten minutes early the next day. Mark and Julia had come over with her because Julia had found a paddle boarding school that had a class. Mark had probably never considered paddle boarding in his life, but after yesterday, he was not going to deny his daughter anything. The restaurant was actually more of a diner and very much off the beaten path. To her surprise, the sheriff was already there, sitting in a corner booth. Evelyn's eyes were immediately drawn to a manila envelope sitting next to him on the bench.

"Hello again." He said standing up to greet her.

"Yes, hello. Thank you again for meeting me like this. I know you have other things to do with your time."

"Always willing to speak to authors who have agreed to read their latest book in my favorite sister-in-law's bookstore." Now Evelyn understood. Oh well, she was going to do the reading anyway, so she might as well get something out of it.

"I understand you know all there is to know about the island." The sheriff leaned back in his seat, his hands splayed out in front of him.

"I know the parts you want to know about."

"How do you mean?" She didn't want to lead him.

"I understand you bought several books on the history of the island. How far have you gotten?"

"Not very, the house hasn't been built yet."

"Hmmm, that won't happen until the 1940's."

"So, when does the part I want to know about happen?"

"Early 2000's. I was a deputy back then." Evelyn pulled the notepad and pen out of her bag. The sheriff sipped his coffee until she was ready.

"That's rather recent."

"Mmm. Does it matter that isn't in the distant past?" Evelyn could feel the sheriff starting to pull away.

"No, I don't suppose so. Sounds like I would have been reading for a while though before I found anything of interest."

"Oh, the island has a history. Mostly centered around fishing. There have been fishermen in this town since it was founded. Sometime in the 40's the town decided it wanted to be respectable, so they built a house out there on the island and made all the bachelor fishermen stay out there. You can imagine what it must have been like. It is still believed amongst residents that decent people don't go there. You know people of a higher moral standard." Evelyn gave him a surprised look. "You are given a pass. Not being from around here, you wouldn't know such a thing." He smiled over his coffee cup. "Back when I was in high school, it was where people went to go make out. You had to be careful you didn't get caught by Eustice though. People around here wondered what would happen when they heard the island and house had been bought. Considering its history. I have a feeling your daughter found out yesterday." Now this was sounding scary.

"What do you mean?" The sheriff looked around

uncomfortably and placed a hand on the envelope next to him.

"I don't go in for all that spirit stuff, but Meg, my sister-in-law does. That being said, if there was ever a place that should be haunted, it's that island, and that house." The sheriff rubbed his chin and brought up the envelope and started to open it. "When I came on as a deputy, it was because they needed more experienced law officers. I had been a police officer in the town since I was twenty-one. I was thirty-one when women went missing in the town. There had not been a missing person in this town for ten years. In that case, the girl had run off with her teenage boyfriend and both were found safely. These girls were going missing without a trace.

"It started in June of that year. We would no sooner get a lead on one girl before another one would go missing. At first, the sheriff thought it was just young girls running away from home. At the time, this was a town where everyone left their doors unlocked and no one thought twice about walking home alone in the dark. We weren't finding bodies, just a string of missing girls in their twenties most having finished a shift at a bar or restaurant late at night or even the early hours of the morning." The sheriff put a page filled with pictures of young girls' faces in front of Evelyn. They were the ones she had seen in her own search, but she looked at them again. Tried to burn their faces into her memory.

"When did you think it was something else?"

"There were just too many of them going missing without a word. The sheriff thought maybe it was someone from outside the town. Like I said, we hadn't had any trouble before, nothing like this. But if it was someone from the outside, he was sticking around because it kept on happening."

"Did you eventually get a break?"

"We found one of them. Marcy Grey. She was the third to go missing and was found behind the dumpster of the place she worked. Coroner found evidence that she had been sexually assaulted and then strangled to death with the killer's hands. It had rained that night, so we didn't find much evidence around the body, but by a stroke of luck, a volunteer found makeshift handcuffs made out of duct tape. We were able to lift prints off the duct tape. They even ran it through the state database for us and came up with a name. The lab was also able to lift DNA, though we wouldn't get the results until later."

"So, you had a lead?"

"We did. Eustice was a local man born and raised, and we had his print on file from an old arrest. About twelve years ago we had booked him for assault, a bar fight. His prints were still on record. He had a wife and kids out on the island. He was known to be a grumpy bastard and a bit peculiar, but no one had him down as a killer. We obviously wanted to ask him some questions. It was fairly early in the morning when we left the harbor. Another girl had been reported missing that night and we had all been out searching for her.

" The sheriff was under a lot of pressure from the town. They were accusing him of not caring and being in over his head. We got the print results back, and we didn't waste any time following them up. We knew Eustice wouldn't let us on the island without a warrant, so we had one in hand when we pulled up." Evelyn could tell that the sheriff was looking back through time, his gaze staring past her shoulder to that morning on the island.

"I take it he wasn't happy to see you?"

"No, he wasn't. Eustice must have seen us coming and panicked. As you know, from the house, you have a pretty good view of the water heading towards town. The sheriff and I had no sooner pulled up to the dock then Eustice came running down the hill with his shotgun ready. Shots were fired, but Eustice was using a shotgun, and when he stopped to reload, I took him down. We started to make our way out of the boat when this kid came running down the hill with a shotgun in his hand and yelling at us. I was on land and yelled for him to stop. He kept coming, still yelling. I couldn't tell what he was saying. Henry fired from the dock and shot him." The sheriff threw his arms up in the air and sadness in his eyes. He pulled out another piece of paper with the young man's picture on it. The picture had been taken at the post mortem. Under his picture was the pathologist's notes.

"Gerald Thompson, seventeen years old. He knew what his father had done, and seeing us coming, he had taken it as an opportunity to make sure his father was held accountable. He was running down the hill to help us when we shot him." The sheriff fell silent for a moment, and Evelyn let him have it. The boy in the picture looked so young. Child like, even though he had the lean, muscular look of a teenager. She didn't know if she would have acted any differently had she been on the beach that day.

"Says here he had three broken ribs healed, but not set, and evidence of a broken nose. Sounds like a prize fighter, not a kid."

"Turns out Eustice was a real jackass. He bought the island and the house so that he would have complete control over his wife and kids. They weren't allowed to leave the island without him. It had been years since his wife had been seen in town. Eustice told everyone she was afraid to leave the house. The only reason we found any of this out was because Gerald

Thompson told us as he lay dying that he had papers hidden in his room. The kid had been keeping a secret diary for months, which he kept well hidden in his room. I think he had only meant it to tell us where his father had buried the bodies, but it then went on to describe what life was like for them. It was hidden in the pages of a book. If he hadn't told us they were there, I'm not sure we would have found them."

"So, Eustice was the killer?" The sheriff nodded his head.

"Eustice made his son dig the graves for a few of them." There was a sharp intake of air from Evelyn. "Apparently, he didn't like digging graves in bad weather. The kid was able to tie the dates his father came to the island with the dates the girls went missing and told us where to look for their remains."

"The poor boy."

"Cadaver dogs found a burial ground right where the son said it would be. Some distance from the house. Almost in the center of the island. Eustice had put some work into hiding his crime. It wouldn't have been easy to carry a body from the dock in front of the house to where he buried them." Evelyn remembered how hard it was getting the luggage up that hill. Eustice must have been rather fit.

"So Eustice is leaving the island to kill young women in town, and getting his son to bury them. What an absolute nightmare." Evelyn said, looking at the pictures laying before her. "And you all found everything out because the son was taking notes?"

"Mmmm. At one point he explains he didn't want to do it, his father made him. That if there is a punishment for what he has done he understands. It was very clear from reading his letter that he wanted it made clear, he had wanted no part in any of it."

"What a nightmare." Evelyn repeated.

23

The sheriff ordered nothing but a cup of coffee and a danish despite the fact that it was lunch time. Evelyn had been planning on lunch, but ordered the same anyway. She was getting a lot of good information, she could eat later.

"What about the women in the family? You mentioned a wife and kids, plural."

"The daughter we found in the house deceased.   The post mortem revealed she had died of sepsis. Eustice hadn't allowed the son to go and get medical help." Evelyn found her picture in the stack. Victoria Thompson, it said at the bottom of the page. Again, the picture had been taken post mortem. She still looked so young. Her hair framing her pale face. Pathologist's report said she was fifteen. "She was pregnant." Evelyn announced reading through the pathologist notes.

The sheriff nodded his head. He still had reservations about this woman, but she was sharp and had no trouble reading between the lines, which was helpful.

"Pathologist said she wasn't far along. He didn't think it was what caused the sepsis, but it obviously didn't help any. Without medical help, there was no chance." Evelyn looked at the report again. The girl was the same age as her daughter, and she could not imagine Julia pregnant. She was still so much a child.

"You said Eustice never let them leave the island."

"I hadn't seen Victoria since she was about six years old. The sheriff at the time said he saw her maybe around the age of ten. She came over with Eustice, but he couldn't really be sure."

"That means one of the men on that island was the father." And she thought she knew which one. Jesus. Henry reached across the table and took the file back before anyone who cared saw that she had it.

"Where the hell was the mother while all this was going on?" Evelyn asked.

"We don't know. We haven't found her yet." Henry was rather pleased with himself. She had gone right where he had wanted her to go. "Gerald's diary mentions he had discussed with his mother various ways they could get off the island and away from Eustice. Shortly after this conversation, she goes missing. Just wasn't there one morning. When Gerald asked Eustice where she was, he was informed that she had left and wouldn't be back. The next day Eustice seemed so sure that she wasn't coming back, that he was burning her clothes in a fire out in the backyard. Gerald hoped that his mother was able to escape and would send for him and his sister soon, but he was disturbed by how calm Eustice seemed and suspected that something else may have happened to their mother."

"You think Eustice killed her?"

"We could never find any trace of her." Evelyn feels like he is leaving something out.

"What do you think happened to her?" Henry leaned back in his seat and uttered the words he had not allowed himself to say out loud.

"I think he killed her. He had already killed and gotten away with it. For all he knew, no one suspected him, so why not kill again? No one saw his wife anyway, so she wouldn't be missed, and his kids never got off the island and were firmly under his control."

"Then why didn't you find the body with the others?"

"That I don't know. Cadaver dogs went all over that island and didn't find her. Ground penetrating radar found a location where the soil had been disturbed, but there were no human remains found there."

"Like a grave had been dug and then filled back in?" The sheriff nodded. "There's a possibility he threw her into the ocean, but he hadn't done that with any of the others. He had made a small cemetery with all of his victims carefully laid out in a circle. Hers wasn't there." The sheriff stopped talking while Evelyn made hasty notes.

"What do you know about the mother?"

"Not a lot. She wasn't from around here. We saw her from time to time when they came to shop or go out to dinner. When they had kids, we didn't see her as much, and then we didn't see her at all. By the time all this happened, no one had seen her in years. I think we all hoped she had gotten off the island."

"But you think Eustice killed her?"

"Yep." Evelyn waited for him to offer more, but when he didn't she prompted. "What makes you think she didn't just leave?"

"I don't think she would have left the kids behind. I think if she was still alive, she would have reached out when she learned the kids were gone. We haven't heard a thing." Evelyn couldn't argue with his logic, but Eustice was what was fascinating her. A man lives his entire life in one area and then one day, just starts killing.

"Was Marcy Grey his first victim?" Evelyn asked.

"No, she was the third." Well, there went that theory. "Why?"

"Two things really. Eustice has lived here his entire life. All right, he's an oddball who abuses his wife and kids, but then he starts killing. How did it start? Why didn't it start with his family? According to your timeline, he had been successful at covering his tracks and then Marcy Grey is found behind a dumpster. If Eustice took that much time with his victims, why was Marcy Grey left behind a dumpster?"

"We think he got interrupted. We aren't sure what happened, but that's the theory. He liked time with the victims. He would assault them and then kill them. It seemed that part of it was done fairly quickly, but after that he would carefully wrap them in tarps. It was done with great care. I think he got interrupted. Behind the dumpster wasn't a great hiding spot. It was at the back of the parking lot where Marcy worked. We'll never really know, but I think something spooked him. Either he had already cut the handcuffs off or he had the presence of mind to take the evidence with him. They were found on the dock, some distance from the body." Evelyn looked out the window of the diner and thought about what the sheriff had told her.

"And all this went on during the course of one summer?"

"One summer."

"Any idea as to why he started doing this when he did?"

"I passed the case to a criminal psychologist after we found out it was Eustice. We had hoped to find out from Eustice himself why he had done what he did, but that wasn't going to happen, so we had the psychologist do a profile."

"And…"

"She thought the first time he killed may have been by accident. He liked to hurt people, that was clear. The type of abuse inflicted on the children shows he liked to hurt, liked the control he had over them. She thought it had been an assault that went too far, but instead of being terrified by what he had done, Eustice had discovered he liked it. He could control whether the person in front of him lived or died."

"Jesus."

"The fact that he took their bodies back to the island was not just to conceal evidence, but by placing them close by, he could visit them. Revisit the killing and maintain that control over them as well. They were sort of a collection for him." Evelyn was beginning to be sorry she asked. As a woman and a mother of a young woman, she would rather be left ignorant of the existence of people like Eustice in the world. She would sleep better anyway. Henry leaned across the table at her and stared at her with those purposeful brown eyes.

"Your daughter would have been just his type." Henry said. Evelyn locked eyes with him for a second. She couldn't get why he had said such a thing. Henry leaned back seeing the fear in her eyes. "Eustice never liked stranger's on his island. Obviously, he had secrets he wanted to keep. I can't help but wonder what he would have done though seeing her walking the island by herself yesterday." Evelyn wasn't sure what kind of conversation she was having anymore.

"But Eustice is dead. You said the sheriff shot him."

"Yes he did. Very dead." A thought had occurred to her.

"Do you think the island is haunted? That my daughter was chased by Eustice's ghost?" The sheriff took a deep sigh and looked down at his coffee. There was both relief and dread in his face. He ran his hand through his hair and took a deep breath. Spreading his hands out in front of him, he searched for the words to explain as logically as he could.

"After all that happened, no one would go near that island except my sister-in-law Meg who seemed determined to put to rest any unsettled spirits." The sheriff had mentioned before that Meg was into spirits.

"Meg thinks she can speak to dead people?" Henry nodded. Evelyn couldn't make this match with the well put together woman she had met in the book store. "I drove her out there on the boat. I don't go in for all that, but bad things had happened there." Henry didn't bother mentioning that the real reason he had been willing to take Meg out there was so she could tell him if his sister was okay.

" Meg wasn't there fifteen minutes before she came running back to the boat. Said Eustice's spirit was there as well as those of the children, and he wouldn't let them go. She was white as a sheet. Now I don't doubt Meg saw something, but I'm not sure I believe it was Eustice. What I do know is that chasing a young girl while she walks alone on a beach is exactly what Eustice would do. Now I'm still looking for a flesh and blood person who might have been out there yesterday. Lord knows there are some fisherman around here who would defend their fishing hole, but I thought you should know about the place you are staying."

Evelyn didn't know what she felt. Her pen lay limp in her hand. Like the sheriff, she did not consider herself a spiritual person, but she did not relish the idea of staying in a house previously occupied by a serial killer either. Especially now that the thought of it being haunted by said serial killer had now been planted in her head.

"Are you telling me this because you think my family is in danger?" The sheriff shifted in his seat.

"To be honest, I don't know. Like I said, I don't buy into the spiritual stuff. I'm not sure I believe in ghosts. But I saw Meg's face when she stepped into the boat that night. Whatever she saw seemed real enough to her. I'm sure the rental agency didn't mention any of this when you made your arrangements. I'm sure all of this sounds incredibly insane, but Eustice was a vile human being, and if there is a chance that some part of him is still on that island, you and your family need to be careful."

24

Evelyn walked toward the boat dock in a daze. Everything the sheriff had said was spinning around her head like a tape on repeat. Evelyn had never thought of ghosts as being something real. When you died, you left. End of story. That being said, she did think that buildings absorbed some of the life that lived in them. It's why she couldn't understand someone living in a converted church and thought old prisons incredibly creepy. Walking down the hill, she could see the dock where she had tied up the boat, to her left was the bookstore. Without thinking about it, she turned and walked into the bookstore. When the bell chimed over her head, it seemed to bring her out of the fog she had been walking in. She looked around for Meg and began to wonder what she was doing there. What was she going to say to Meg? *Hello, your brother-in-law tells me you like to speak to dead people in your spare time. Would you mind coming over the house and asking the spirit of the serial killer who used to live there if he could kindly leave my daughter alone?* Meg appeared out of the stacks, a customer- ready smile on her face, which turned serious when she saw Evelyn.

"You look like you need a drink." Maybe Meg did have

some extra abilities after all.

Meg waved Evelyn to follow her to the back of the store. There was a small kitchen at the back that seemed to have been converted from a closet. There was a small counter just big enough to hold a coffee pot and a few mugs. From the cabinet beneath, Meg pulled out a bottle of Jack Daniels and poured a healthy amount into one of the coffee mugs and handed one to Evelyn.

Evelyn took a sip and coughed. "Henry said he was having lunch with you." Meg offered while Evelyn recovered.

"That was perhaps the strangest lunch I have ever had." Evelyn answered honestly.

"Mmm. He still wrestles with what happened on the island that day. Jeb, the sheriff at the time, didn't run for re-election afterwards. He would have won. Despite people making noise when it was happening, they credited him with catching the killer, but he couldn't stomach the job. Lord knows what those guys found on that island. Henry still won't talk about it."

"Do you really think it's haunted?" Evelyn had finally found her voice and had used it to get right to the point. Meg didn't answer right away. She took a sip of her drink and then a deep breath, taking the time to look Evelyn over. Measuring her answer.

"Yes." She finally said. "I wanted Henry to talk to you as soon as I found out where you were staying, but he told me to wait and see what happened. It was years ago, after all. But they get their energy from the living, you see. There were murmurings when the builders were out there doing work on the house. Enough for me to be concerned when I learned you would be staying out there for two months solid. I feared once there were living people on the island that Eustice would come back."

"So, it was the ghost of Eustice that was chasing my daughter along the beach yesterday?" Meg shrugged.

"No idea, Love, but I think it's possible. Could have been the kids. I think I felt them when I was out there. I definitely sensed Eustice. His evil vibrates off the place."

"What the hell am I supposed to do about that?" Evelyn asked honestly.

" Do me a favor, and if the house doesn't feel safe anymore, get out of there."

"And go where? We have the house for the summer?"

"Come to my house if you need to, but don't wait around to find out what Eustice is capable of. That man tore this town apart once, and I have no doubt that he would do it again if given the chance."

"He does seem to have a thing for young girls. The sheriff showed me pictures of the victims."

"Did he tell you one of them was his youngest sister?" Evelyn almost dropped her glass. "I didn't think he would." Meg continued. "Neither one of them talked about it, Henry or my husband. It killed their mother. Not right away, of course, but she was never the same after Gertie went missing. No one is entirely sure how he picked his victims or why. Mind you, it wouldn't have been hard. Back then women in town thought nothing of walking home alone at all hours. Eustice would wait for them, tape their hands behind them, tape their mouths shut, and then rape them. When he was done, he would strangle them. Gertie would have put up a fight though. Henry has always worried that Eustice chose her because he was a cop. Their father was a cop too." Evelyn had a strong urge to go back to the house and hug her daughter. "I can't imagine what went through those girls' minds before they died." Meg said into her cup.

"The sheriff says you are a medium? Couldn't you....?" Meg smiled slightly and nodded her head.

"Henry took me back to the island to see if his sister was still there and to show her to the other side if need be. Poor man, he isn't sure how he feels about my abilities, I know, but he wanted to make sure his little sister was okay in the only way he knew how. I did it as much for him as I did for her. He wasn't sleeping, and with Jeb not running for re-election, the town wanted him to run for sheriff. The man was a mess."

"He said you weren't there that long."

"Eustice buried those girls so that he could visit them whenever he wanted. He didn't want to let them go. He still guards their graves." Meg took another sip of her whiskey. "Your mother wants you to know she is doing well. She's no longer in pain, and actually, she looks very young. She is surrounded by lavender." Meg said without warning.

Evelyn took in such a sharp breath it hurt her chest. Tears immediately appeared. Her mother had died a month ago. She had not mentioned her since arriving here, hoping that by doing so, she would be able to let go of some of the emotions that had held her so tightly in their grip.

"Lavender was her favorite scent." She finally sputtered. "She bathed with lavender scented soap."

"She says to please give JuJu a kiss from MawMaw." The glass of Jack Daniels hit the floor, brown liquid spilling all over.

25

It had taken Evelyn a full half an hour to collect herself. "Don't worry about it dear. A slight smell of whiskey mixes well with the old paper smell. You have simply added ambiance to the place." Evelyn had sat helplessly on the floor while Meg had cleaned up the broken coffee cup and whiskey. She was having the most peculiar afternoon, and her mind kept trying to find a way for her to understand what it was impossible for her to understand.

After twenty minutes, Evelyn's breathing had returned to normal, and she managed to get to her feet. "You okay? Do you want me to call your husband?" Meg had offered.

"I have so many questions." Was all Evelyn could say.

"Most people do, dear, but you have had a hell of an afternoon. Like you said. Why don't you go home and come back Thursday night? Meet me at Gill's Seafood Bar. We'll eat some oysters, and you can ask me all the questions you want."

"Deal."

By the time Evelyn pulled the boat up to the dock in front of the house, she was calmer but no less amazed by the afternoon she had experienced. She didn't want to say anything about it in front of Julia, but she couldn't wait to talk to Mark. It looked like they had a good time paddle boarding because there were two paddle boards pulled up onto the beach. *How are we supposed to get those things home?* It was just like Mark to try something once, fall in love with it, and then buy everything having to do with it. When she got out of the boat, there were wet footprints on the dock. They had been out paddle boarding recently then. Somewhat lifted by the fact that her family had apparently had a good day, Evelyn climbed the hill to the house. Clouds were rolling in and there would be rain by dinner time. A soft yellow light came from the side window, lighting the pathway for her. She could hear Twain start to bark. Despite what she had been told about the place today, the house seemed warm and inviting.

"Hello," This was towards Twain who had run up and greeted her, his tail wagging. Julia was sitting on the couch with an open book in her hand, but she was firmly engrossed in the TV. Mark was in the kitchen, which Evelyn knew was a mixed blessing. He was cooking, bless him, and he was a damned good cook, but the kitchen would take two hours to clean afterwards. "Has no one fed you?" Julia was Twain's true love, but if he wanted a walk, he went to Mark. If he wanted to be fed, he came to Evelyn.

"That was a long lunch. I was beginning to worry." Mark said from the kitchen, the broad smile on his face indicating that he had not been too tortured.

"I see you two found your way home."

"Don't worry. They are rentals." Mark quickly read the tone in his wife's voice. "But we did have a good time, didn't we, Honey?" Julia said nothing. Evelyn came around the kitchen to get some idea of the mess she would be dealing with. "Hope you don't mind, I thought I would get dinner started." Mark leaned over to give her a kiss. "I'm making Chicken Piccata." There was a pot for the pasta and a frying pan for the bacon, another frying pan for the chicken, and the containers that had held all the ingredients were strewn all over the counter. Evelyn mindlessly started picking up the wrappers and putting them in the trash. "You must have been out paddle boarding most of the day. There were still wet footprints on the dock when I pulled in."

"No, the class finished about one. We liked it so much, we rented the boards you saw out there and then boarded all the way home. A little ambitious for our first time probably. My arms and legs were on fire by the time we got here. I barely had enough in me to walk up to the house. She's been vegged out there the rest of the afternoon. I took a shower, answered some emails, and then started dinner." Mark seemed to have glanced over the wet foot prints, but if they hadn't left them, then who had? Evelyn casually went over to the window that overlooked the path to the dock. The footprints had almost dried now, but she could still see them. Whoever left them must have done so right before she pulled in, but the dock had been visible long before she reached it, and there had been no one. She remembered thinking they looked like Julia's foot size when she had seen them. Looking back at Julia, she was dry and had obviously been sitting there for some time, just like Mark had said. The happy warm feeling that she had felt coming home was now gone.

She looked again at Julia on the couch and decided not to mention it right now. The prowler in the woods was still fresh in her mind. Should she call the sheriff? And say what? That there were footprints? They weren't men's foot prints, Evelyn was sure of that, which meant it wasn't Eustice. This was small comfort in that it raised the questions of who else it might be.

"You okay?" Mark asked.

"Fine. Just tired." Evelyn answered too quickly. "I need to stop reading those books halfway through the night and actually sleep." As she said this, she realized there would probably be very little sleep tonight. The sheriff's words were still spinning around in her head to the point the real world seemed like background noise. And then there was what Meg had said. So much for a relaxing summer vacation.

"Why don't we have wine with dinner tonight?" She suggested, going back to the kitchen to find one of the two bottles they had brought with them.

"We are on vacation after all." Mark said, and found two glasses in the cabinets and held them out for Evelyn to fill. He tried not to read too much into it when she drained hers right away.

"Was your meeting productive?" Mark asked, looking a little concerned. Evelyn almost jumped when he mentioned it.

"Extremely."

"Get a lot of good information?" Evelyn locked eyes with him.

"More than I know what to do with." Evelyn answered, refilling her glass.

26

Even with the wine, Evelyn could not let go of what she had learned that day. Stone circles in the woods, crying mothers, and wet footprints stirred in her mind until she felt sick. The fact that the house she had chosen to rent for the summer was the home of a serial killer and the fact that her new best friend could speak to dead people were constantly vying for attention in her thoughts.   In the end, she hadn't said anything to Mark about the footprints. They had such a lovely dinner together, and Mark had been in such a good mood, she hadn't been able to bring herself to tell him what she had seen, and when he asked about her visit with the sheriff, she had quickly turned the conversation to something else. Thanks to the three glasses of wine he had with dinner, Mark hadn't put up an argument. "You said something about murders though. You wanted to talk to him about a murder that had happened out here."

"Yes, and we did." Evelyn didn't want to go into detail tonight. Not while she was still stirring things around in her head. Looking at Mark leaning back in the bed, the book in his hand not being read and his eyes growing heavy. She also didn't think he would be able to stay awake for the whole story anyway. Now Evelyn was lying awake in bed listening to the house breathe, ears waiting for any sign that a ghostly figure was making the rounds. Julia had been sure it was a man following her through the woods, but Evelyn had felt the footprints were feminine. Could footprints 'feel' feminine? When she first saw them, she had been sure they were Julia's, why was that? Their size? Was it one of Eustice's victims? God, she hoped it wasn't Eustice. Did it even matter that there were ghosts in the house? I mean, they couldn't really do anything to the living. Could they? Exhaustion and the wine finally took hold, and Evelyn fell asleep as soon as her eyelids touched, but she did not rest soundly.

It was night time. She could smell the dew on the grass. Her chest hurt because she was being chased, not along a beach, but through the woods. Evelyn's heart was racing, and she kept looking over her shoulder to see if he was gaining on her. It was him. She knew immediately who it was. She didn't know his name, but he seemed familiar to her, and Evelyn knew what he would do if he caught her, and that was why she was running so hard. Then she wasn't running. She was looking up at the sky. The ground was wet under her back. Evelyn knew she should run, that she shouldn't stop now, but she couldn't make herself move. It took a moment to realize that she was moving along the ground, but she was not doing anything to facilitate this. It was with a start that she realized he must be moving her. She could feel his grip on her ankles. Evelyn tried to move her arms, grab the trees and the bushes that were passing her. Pull her legs out of his grasp, anything, but she couldn't make her body obey. She was still in the woods, the earthy scent was strong, like freshly turned soil. Evelyn knew what he was going to do and also didn't know at the same time. She knew if she couldn't get herself loose that she would die. But she couldn't die. She had to get back and warn Julia. Julia must get as far away from here as possible. She tried again to move, but she couldn't, and tears started to form at the corners of her eyes, not only because she knew she would die, but because she knew she couldn't do anything about it.

When the first shovel of dirt hit her face, Evelyn woke up with a start. Her heart was racing, and the t-shirt she wore to bed was clinging to her. She had never had a nightmare that left her out of breath. But that was what woke her up. She could still taste the dirt in her mouth.

She woke Mark. Seeing what a state she was in, he sat up concerned. "You ok?"

"I don't know." Evelyn was trying to take deep breaths, but her body was still half convinced that she was choking on dirt. She focused on the dresser in front of her and the items there, convincing herself she was in her room and not being murdered out in the woods. All her effort went into taking deeper breaths.

"What the hell were you dreaming about?" Evelyn shook him off. She couldn't think about it right now because she was dizzy, and her heart was beating so fast. Mark was not used to seeing his wife like this, though, and after threatening to take her to the hospital under suspicion of a heart attack, Evelyn finally told him about her dream. Then she told him what the sheriff had told her at lunch the previous day. By the time she finished, dawn was peaking over the horizon. Evelyn still didn't mention the foot prints, though. She wasn't entirely sure why except she was tired of talking.

Both she and Mark assumed that the bad dream was nothing more than the result of a rather unsettling afternoon spent learning that the house they were sleeping in was once owned by a serial killer. For the next three nights, Evelyn had the same dream. Every night there was a little more to the dream. She knew she was running from Eustice. In the dream, she was not only worried about her daughter, but her son. On the third night, she knew that she was not only running away from the person chasing her, she was running towards the house. This house. The one she was sleeping in. She recognized the back of it, focusing on the screen door that led from the back of the house to the woods.

Waking suddenly again when the dirt hit her face, Evelyn didn't wake Mark. Instead, she got out of bed and went to the window. Looking out, she could see the backyard and the woods beyond. That was where it happened. She was still not sure who she was in the dream, although she was clearly one of Eustice's victims, but right down there in the backyard was where that poor woman ran for her life. Where her last thoughts had been of her children. Thinking of what would happen to them if she didn't make it. She couldn't figure out why the woman thought the house would make her safe from the man chasing her, but it was clear in the dream that getting to the house was the woman's goal. The tears dripped off Evelyn's cheek before she knew they were there. Evelyn's fear was overtaken by curiosity. *What the hell happened on this island?*

27

After three nights of the same nightmare and waking up out of breath, the thought entered Evelyn's mind that maybe they shouldn't be here. For reasons she couldn't even explain to herself, she said nothing to Mark. If they left with no reason, Evelyn rationalized to herself, they would lose all the money they had paid in advance. She had already checked the lease. And really, what for? Because the house has a history? She was the only one who seemed to be having a problem after all. Julia, while not completely recovered from her experience on the beach, seemed to be enjoying herself. Mark called the paddle board rental company, and they now had the paddle boards for another three days. Julia had been going out every day. Mark had started lying in a hammock, and though he had not caught a lot of fish, he seemed to enjoy trying. They were having such a good time during the day. It seemed a pity to end it all because she was having a run of bad nights.

More and more, Evelyn could be found on the porch reading up on the history of the island and making notes while watching Mark fish off the dock and Julia paddle boarding. Twain had been splitting his time between waiting for Mark to pull up a fish for him to lick, and running up and down the beach chasing Julia. Twain apparently decided that Julia needed to be rescued and swam out. The problem was that Twain only liked to swim when his feet touched the bottom, so his bravery soon failed him, and he had to turn back.

"I wish we had a dog." Victoria said. She was doing what she normally did these days,watching the young girl ride a surfboard over the flat water. She knew Gerald would make fun of her for spending so much time around them, but she had also noticed him joining her more often than not . She couldn't blame him. They didn't really see a lot of people when they were living, much less after they had died. A happy family that enjoyed each other's company was what she liked the most. Victoria had often wondered what such a family would be like. They could stay forever if it was up to her.   Gerald was worried again, she could feel it vibrating off of him. The mother had been having nightmares, and he was worried Eustice was causing them. He was, of course, but what could they do about it?

"Mom said you were allergic." Answering her about a dog.

"Eustice would have killed it anyway, but it would have been nice. Look how he runs after her." They watched as the dog ran into the water, turning back when he got too deep. The mother on land laughing, the daughter out on the board in the water slapping the water and encouraging the dog to come out further.

"I can feel him. He's getting stronger."

"I know." Was Victoria's simple answer. "It stands to reason that if we are getting stronger, he is too." She really didn't want to talk about him. She wanted to enjoy the day with the family.

"Vic, the only way to keep things calm is for the living to leave." She looked at him with her big eyes.

"I don't want them to, Ger. They are what we could have been if we

had a normal family." Gerald looked back at the family on the beach. He could hear them all laughing. The daughter on the surfing board was almost doubled over in laughter as the dog swam through the water at her just to turn around and swim back to shore. The mother met him there. Once out of the water, the dog shook himself, flinging water everywhere. The mother put up her hands to avoid the spray. Gerald could not remember the last time he had heard laughter on this island. It was being selfish to let them stay. He knew they should be coming up with ways to scare them out of the house before Eustice got so strong. He would scare them on his own, but the laughter sounded so nice. They seemed so nice. A nice family that loved each other. Maybe they could wait just one more day.

Mark had been watching the women in his life play and laugh. Without a reason, he looked up at the house. Specifically the back room, the one they weren't using. There was a face there. It had been a teenage boy, but Mark could see the wall through the boy's head. Mark blinked, and the face was gone, but the curtain was still moving . He looked at the girls to see if either one of them had seen it, but they were still playing with Twain. Mark looked again at the window. The curtain was still, and Mark tried to convince himself that he hadn't seen anything.

"Anyone want something to drink?" Mark said, getting up from the dock. The girls waved him off. Julia was paddling back to shore, still smiling. Evelyn was trying to catch Twain and dry him off with a towel. Mark walked up to the house, grabbing the axe left for wood chopping before he went in. He would get some water, but he was going to check the rooms first. Coming back out of the house, glass of water in one hand, he flung the axe back into the log where it rested. Convinced he had seen nothing, and absolutely no reason to upset everyone's fun by mentioning it.

28

Evelyn left that evening to have dinner with Meg. When she left the house, Mark and Julia were sitting together on the couch under a blanket watching something on TV. Twain was snoring at their feet. "Don't be too late." Mark had said when she leaned down to give him a kiss. The sun was just starting to make it's descent in the evening sky as she started the boat and headed to the mainland. Having parked the boat in the dock (something she was pleased to be getting rather good at) she followed Meg's instructions to the restaurant. One thing she did like about this town was that everything was within rather easy walking distance.

Stopping herself before entering, Evelyn was nervous walking into the restaurant to meet Meg. To her knowledge, she had never had dinner with a medium before, and she was a little worried about more messages from her mother coming through. Well, if she was honest with herself, she was worried Meg would be a crackpot who had imagined the whole thing and had actually not given her a message from her mother. Taking a deep breath, she opened the door and walked in.

Meg was sitting in a booth at the back of the restaurant and met her with a warm smile. White wine was already sitting on the table. "What are Mark and Julia doing tonight without you?"

"Binge watching something on TV. They had a pretty active day actually. I wouldn't be surprised if I find both of them asleep there when I get home." Evelyn said, sliding into the booth, her hand going automatically for the glass of wine. Nerves forgotten, the women slipped into easy conversation.

"Who's running the store while you are out tonight?"

"Privilege of being the owner. I closed early. The crab cakes are delightful if you don't mind me suggesting something." Meg said, looking at her menu. Evelyn was still looking at hers, but crab cakes sounded good. "I've been worried about you since the other day. I feel like we gave you more information than you could handle." Meg was looking over the rim of her reading glasses.

"It was a lot. Not least of which is your ability to communicate with the dead. My head was still turning over Eustice and all that he did, and then you blind sided me with that."

"It's okay if you don't believe me. It's not going to hurt my feelings." Evelyn believed that it wouldn't hurt her feelings if she didn't believe her. Meg had the special talent of being who she was despite what other people thought about her. A confidence not many people possessed.

"Well, I would love to not believe you, but I also can't figure out how you knew what my mother called my daughter and vice versa. Between the house possibly being haunted and you being able to speak to dead people, I'm not sure what I believe anymore." Evelyn took a gulp of her wine. Meg smiled at her.

"You are taking it rather well though, I have to say."

"I'm on vacation." They ordered their food. Evelyn got the

crab cakes and Meg ordered the salmon.

"It must have been hard on the sheriff and your husband to lose a sister that way." Evelyn finally said. She had been intrigued that the sheriff hadn't mentioned that his own sister was one of Eustice's victims. "Especially since he was one of the first people on the scene when the bodies were discovered." Meg took a sip of her wine. "It was horrible. It was a horrible time for the whole town, but when Gertie went missing. My husband was the oldest. We were already married and our son was in school. Henry had just been promoted to deputy by Jeb, the sheriff at the time. It hit Henry particularly hard. I think he thought he should have done something to stop it. She was the second one to go missing. People had started to be more careful, but you have to keep in mind, no bodies were found. Until Marcy Grey that is. It was thought that maybe the girls were running away." Meg had mentioned a husband a few times, and she was wearing a wedding ring, but Evelyn noticed every mention of him was past tense. "Henry came to the house to tell my husband that they had found Marcy's body. He knew then that the sister was dead. Henry was as white as a sheet."

"I guess it's hindsight, but Eustice seemed like a good place to start, especially with the island as a place to hide the bodies."

"Yeah, I mean if you look at Eustice now, knowing what we know, of course it was him. But this is a small town, and we have our share of characters. He had lived here his whole life. It just seemed impossible that it was a local."

"Did you know him?"

"Yes and no. He was a few years ahead of me in school. A rough kind of guy, but nothing that would make you think he would do what he did. Shocked the hell out of everyone when he bought that island, though. He certainly didn't come from money."

"Perfect place to put your family if you want to isolate them from the world." Evelyn thought about pouring herself another glass of wine but thought better of it. Driving a boat was still driving, and she would now have to find the dock in the dark.

"Apparently. I still feel bad about not knowing what was happening out there. They were good kids, what I remember of them."

"I asked the sheriff what happened to Esutice's wife, but he didn't really answer me."

"They don't know, really. Jeb should have tracked her down, but he was so overwhelmed with everything else that the poor woman just kind of got forgotten."

"Henry said ground penetrating radar found a grave that had been dug up and apparently filled back in, but there were no human remains in it."

"It was assumed that either Eustice was planning on killing again and had prepared the ground, or was planning on burying the daughter in the grave. She was dead when Henry and Jeb got there." They sat in silence for a bit, Evelyn thinking about Eustice's wife.

"Surely the woman would have come back if she had fled after finding out that her children were dead."

"That question was raised at the time, but like I told Henry, she didn't come back because she is dead."

"You sound sure about that."

"I felt her presence when I went to the island to see if Gertie was at peace. She's very faint, but she is there. I got the feeling she wanted to tell me something, but Eustice surprised me with how threatening he was. I just wanted to get off the island. I've been meaning to ask you, how is Julia doing? Henry told me she had a scare while walking the beach."

"She's all right, actually. She's discovered paddle boarding and is spending a lot of time out on the water."

"She's a great kid. I love it when kids are into reading. It gives me hope for the future." They talked through the rest of the meal. Not circling back to Eustice or ghosts, but instead Evelyn's reading and book signing at Meg's store. Meg was very happy to hear that the publisher had agreed to ship a box of Evelyn's new book out to the shop.

The women were laughing when they parted, Meg walking Evelyn to her boat, and then walking the short distance back to her bookstore. Evelyn was smiling as she crossed the short distance back to the house. She had texted Mark to let him know she was coming home, but assumed he was asleep. Evelyn was quite proud of herself steering the boat to the dock in the dark and managing to 'park' it by herself. It had been a good day. Her family had the type of day they hoped for when they planned this vacation, and she had made a new friend in Meg. Evelyn was feeling good about things when she read the word 'RUN' written in water on the dock. Evelyn looked around her for any sign of the person who had left it, but the woods were dark. She ran to the house, taking as long a stride as she could manage up the hill to the house. Once inside the house, she closed the door behind her and locked it.

Mark and Julia were asleep on the couch, Twain still at their feet snoring. The show they had been watching had long gone to another program. Evelyn caught her breath and then hurried to her room to change into her pajamas. Coming back down stairs, she stole what part of the blanket was still available and went to sleep on the couch with Mark. There was no way she was going to sleep alone in her room after that.

29

When they woke the next morning, the fact that Evelyn had joined them in the living room instead of enjoying a comfy night alone in her bed was the source of amusement. For a moment, Evelyn forgot why it was she had chosen to sleep in the living room with them. Then Mark asked her how the dinner went. With a flash, Evelyn remembered coming home from the dinner and the letters written on the dock. For most of that day she tried to convince herself she hadn't actually seen the word 'RUN'. That somehow the sunset tint played on the wet dock and it just looked like it spelled out the word, but she couldn't sell it. Not even to herself. Evelyn knew with every fiber of her being that she had seen exactly what she thought she had. Still, she hesitated in saying anything to Mark. It wasn't until the evening when Evelyn and Mark were sitting up in bed reading that Evelyn asked, "Do you believe in ghosts?"

"Why would you ask that?" Mark asked back, thinking about the mysterious boy in the window. He laid down his book and looked at her with his glasses resting low on his nose.

"Well, there is no denying that some strange things have been happening here since we arrived. Like the sheriff said, if there was any place that deserved to be haunted, this is that place."

"Do you believe in them?" He asked. They had talked about this before, but it had been several years, and with her mother recently dying, Evelyn may have changed her mind on the matter. She didn't answer immediately, picking at the blanket to the point where Mark was sure she was going to say she did now believe in ghosts.

"I don't think I would be surprised if they existed, but I can't say beyond a shadow of a doubt that I believe in them." Evelyn somewhat surprised herself with this statement. Despite the strange things happening at the house, she couldn't say that she thought ghosts were the ones doing them.

Mark closed his book. Took his glasses off his nose and folded them as well. "I think I'm with you on that. I don't think I would be surprised." Evelyn looked at him. Mark was such a logical person. She had really been counting on him to form a logical, irrefutable argument against there being ghosts. "I saw someone in the window the other day." He clarified "A boy. He wasn't really there. I knew that even when I was looking at him, that he was not a real person in the house. He was transparent for one thing. It didn't stop me from coming inside the house and making sure. But I saw him, there is no denying it, and for the life of me, I can't think of another thing that would look like a teenage boy looking out a window...to the point where the curtains moved. Unless there was something there. I can also not think of a logical situation where I would be able to see the picture on the wall through their body. " Evelyn sat up on her elbows.

"Why didn't you say something?"

"We were having a great time on the beach, and it was over

in an instant. I wasn't even sure of what I had seen."

"It was a young boy?"

"Well, a teenager. Maybe seventeen, eighteen years old."

"Shit, maybe the place is haunted by Eustice and his family."

"What makes you think this kid is connected with Eustice?" Mark thought it was just as likely it was a fisherman from way back. Why did all the ghosts in the house have to be connected to this Eustice guy?

"Eustice had a son who was killed the same day as him. The police saw him running down the hill to the dock carrying a gun and screaming, they assumed he was avenging his father, so they shot him. He was seventeen and was, in fact, trying to force his father at gun point towards the police. Eustice had been keeping them hostage on the island for years. Meg says us being here is making their spirits stronger."

"Well, that's a horrifying thought."

" I thought about us leaving, but we would lose all the money for the rental and then what? We just go home?" Mark bit his lower lip and nodded his head.

"I'm still getting over the fact that we are now people who believe in ghosts." Mark leaned his head back on the head board. "I mean, it couldn't be some kindly old woman who fills the house with the smell of cookies causing us to constantly crave chocolate chip cookies and leaving the island twenty pounds heavier than when we arrived? No, our first haunting is a serial killer and his strange family. What does Meg say about this? She seems to be the local expert."

"She told me to be careful."

"That isn't incredibly helpful, is it?"

"There's something else I haven't told you. When I came home last night, something was written on the dock. The word

'RUN'."

"Jesus. Why didn't you wake me?"

"I don't know. You both looked so comfortable, and you and Julia had such a lovely day. I didn't want to wake you and cause a panic."

"That's why you were on the couch with us in the morning?"

"It wasn't the first time I've seen something on the docks either. When you and Julia went paddleboarding, I came back from the mainland, and there were wet footprints going from the water to the house. They were fresh. I thought it was Julia having just gotten out of the water, but you said you guys had been in for hours."

"What the hell is going on here? Did you tell Meg about this? And your dreams, you've been having those nightmares." Mark pushed himself up in bed, sleep the farthest thing from his mind now.

"No, I didn't. I don't want to sound crazy."

"Wouldn't that be something, went on vacation to save our sanity after a hellish year only to find out we're too late."

"I'll call her tomorrow and see if she has any other recommendations."

"We may have to leave, Evy. I mean, it's not going to be a relaxing summer being chased by ghosts, is it? We can live without the money, but I don't ever want to see that look on Julia's face again." He was right, of course. At a certain point, it would be stupid to stay even with the lost money.

"Something I've never understood about ghosts, can they actually do anything to the living? I mean it's scary having someone dead standing in front of you, but other than that, can they do anything?" Evelyn thought out loud. Something had chased Julia and scared the life out of her. But could it actually catch her?

"I have no idea. I've been haunted for just about as long as you have." Mark shrugged his shoulders.

"I have to go to the book shop tomorrow to check on something for the book reading with Meg. I'll ask her." Mark nodded and picked up his book, a murder mystery which seemed a bit sarcastic under the circumstances. Evelyn picked up her book but re-read the same page five times before giving up and going to sleep.

Evelyn dreamed that night, but she was not being chased through the woods by the faceless man. She was calm and looking down from the tree tops. It was very dark, and it took a moment for her to see what she was looking down on. There was a man bent over the ground. She could hear him grunting and smell the sweat coming off of him. The white sheet lying next to him now shone bright white in the moonlight. Though she wasn't scared this time, she was confused, she didn't know what she was looking at or how she got in the treetops. What the man was doing became clear when he stopped working and stabbed a shovel into the mound of earth next to him. Leaning back to stretch his back, he looked around and then grabbed the white sheet and dragged it into the hole he was digging. The sheet made a heavy 'thud' as it hit the bottom of the hole, and the man started piling dirt back into the hole again. But Evelyn was no longer watching the man. She was looking at the woman lying on her back at the edge of the woods. Her pale face shone. Her eyes fixed, staring at the sky. The woman was dead. Evelyn was almost sure of this. Her heart stopped. The woman looked familiar, but Evelyn wasn't sure until the man pulled on the dead woman's legs to get her close to the hole in the ground. The woman's face turned and stared directly at Evelyn. She was looking at her own dead form being buried. Evelyn watched in silent horror as the man pushed her body into a hole and started shoveling dirt back into it. Evelyn felt the dirt hit her face. She opened her mouth to scream, but dirt filled her mouth, choking her. It was the choking that woke her, once again.

"Are you okay?" Was the greeting she got from Meg when she entered the book shop later that morning.

"Do I look that bad?"

"Are you sick?"

"No, I just haven't had a decent night's sleep in about a week. I keep having these strangely realistic nightmares thanks to that brother in-law of yours."

"You've been having nightmares ever since your meeting?"

"Yeah. Why are you looking at me like that?" Meg set a cup of coffee in front of her, brows coming together in concern.

"Tell me what these dreams are about." Meg's interest is a little alarming, but Evelyn took the offer of coffee gratefully. Evelyn had a cup before she left the house, but this one was having the same soul refreshing affect. She told Meg about the dreams, how each one was different, especially the last one. Evelyn watched Meg's face go from one of deep interest to one of deep concern.

"What?" Evelyn said.

"It may be nothing. It may be exactly what you said it was, a product of your imagination and your meeting with Henry."

"But..."

"The dead are limited in how they are able to communicate

with us. Dreams are one of the ways."

"It's Eustice. The man in my dream. I can't see his face, but it's him. I know I'm one of the victims. I think I might be his wife. I saw the back of the house in one of the dreams, and I was determined to get back to it."

"They never found his wife. According to the son's diary, he thought Eustice had killed her as well. He went to bed one night, and the next day his mother wasn't there."

"But they never found her body either. If he didn't bury her with the others, where did he put her?" Evelyn asked. Meg shrugged. A very casual gesture considering the conversation they were having. Evelyn buried her face in her hands.

"Tell me what it means Meg. I'm too tired to try and figure it out. Should we leave? Are they trying to scare us off? I mean, I don't want to, but I also don't want to be stupid about this either."

"If this is the wife, I think she is sending you a message, woman to woman. But other than confirming that she is dead and Eustice is the one that did it, I'm not sure what else she might be trying to tell you."

"All the houses in Washington state, and we had to rent this one."

"Maybe you were meant to find it." Evelyn looked up to see if Meg looked as crazy as she sounded, but Meg was smiling at her.

"I'm glad you can find humor in this."

"I'm serious. That house has been empty this many years and here you come. I think maybe you were meant to find this house for some reason."

"Like what?"

"Who the hell knows? You could also just be unlucky. What

are you guys doing tonight?"

"Nothing, why?"

"Why don't I come out to the house and put a ring of protection around the foundation?"

"What would that do?"

"Make the dreams go away for one thing. The spirits can't cross the ring of protection or influence you once you are inside the ring. If I put it around the house, then once you are in the house, they can't bother you."

"That sounds worth a try." Why not? If this ring of protection worked, maybe they could live on the island along with the ghosts and still have a relaxing summer. That was if it worked.

"Great, I'll come over tonight. Henry can bring me after he gets off work."

"I'll cook dinner, what kind of wine do you like?"

"Any kind."

"Fantastic. Ghost busting and a dinner party." Evelyn felt a little better already (though it also could have been the two cups of coffee). "I almost forgot, the whole reason I came in here today was to discuss the book reading. Have you had anyone RSVP?"

"I sent out invitations, and so far, not only has everyone confirmed, but I have had requests for more invitations. We are going to be a packed house. I have ordered extra books, and if you don't mind signing some of them afterwards...."

"Of course not."

"Excellent. Fifty percent of the proceeds are going to go to the Fund for Fallen Heroes. It's a local charity for fallen rescue workers."

"Meg, that's fantastic. I can't wait." Evelyn felt lighter leaving the bookstore.

30

"Here she comes." Evelyn saw the police boat coming across to the island. They had informed Julia of what was going to happen, obviously. To Evelyn's surprise, Julia had not been freaked out but rather thought it was 'cool' and asked if she could video it. "If anything happens, my Insta account is going to blow up."

"Well, you'll have to ask Meg." Evelyn said, trying to figure out if that was a normal teenager response, or if she should be concerned.

"Hello!!" Meg yelled from the front of the police boat. She waved her hands over her head, a bottle of wine in her right hand. Evelyn wasn't sure what she had expected the vibe for the evening to be, but it seemed that Meg was coming for a dinner party where they might speak to ghosts, with an emphasis on the party. Henry looked the same serious person he always did.

"Hey there, Sheriff. It's good to see you again." Evelyn said as he got out of the boat. He almost looked like he was there against his will, and Evelyn almost felt sorry for him.

"Thanks for inviting me." Evelyn introduced Meg and

Mark, and they all walked up to the house together, chatting away. Meg walked into the house and stepped forward, looking around the empty room purposefully. The bottle of wine still in her hand.

"What?" Evelyn asked. They had all stopped in the doorway to give Meg's physic abilities room to work. Julia had her phone out in a flash and was recording.

"Is that lasagna I smell?" The group exhaled at once. Julia rolled her eyes and put her phone away.

"Jesus, Meg, we thought you had found a ghost already." The sheriff said.

"Relax Henry, you'll know when I am talking to the spirits because I will call on my spirit guide to protect me." Meg said, hitting her brother-in-law lovingly on the arm.

"Yes, it is lasagna and garlic bread." Evelyn answered.

"Good. I interpret the spirits better on a full stomach. Carbs are a good conduit."

"What does the wine do?" Henry asked.

"Opens the mind." Meg answered matter of factly.

"Is that that one that shot you?" Victoria asked. The children watched from the roof as the boat arrived. The woman could hear them. There was a light that surrounded her that drew them to her. They stayed out of the house. Not sure they wanted to be found by her.

"No, but he was there." Gerald remembered the man kneeling over his father. Looking up in surprise as he ran down the hill at him.

"I don't like him." Vic said sternly.

"You don't even know him."

"They killed you, Ger."

"I was running down a hill with a shotgun in my hand, Vic. What was he supposed to do?" Gerlad had replayed the day he died several times in his head. It had been stupid to run out there with the

shotgun. "I just wanted so badly for Eustice to not get away with it. I was sure he would turn on the charm and they would buy it and go back to the mainland. You were already upstairs, and I couldn't face living here with just him."

"If it weren't for them, you would still be alive."

"And what would that get me? Mom was gone. You were gone, and Eustice was gone. It would have been just me."

"Are you saying you would rather be dead then alive?"

"I would have liked to have known what life off the island was like, but then who would I share it with?"

After enjoying a truly delightful dinner, Meg said, "I guess we better get down to what we came for. Everyone hold hands." They did as they were told. Meg then closed her eyes. Evelyn wanted to ask what she was doing, but Meg seemed to be doing something spiritual, so she didn't. "I am asking my spirit guide to protect us from any that should wish us harm." Meg explained. "Then I will open myself up to the spirits."

"What does a spirit guide do?" Julia asked. Evelyn shot her a look. She wasn't sure it was polite to interrupt someone when they were talking with their spirit guide.

"The spirit guide is on the other side. They know whether the spirit you are communicating with wishes you harm. If they do, you can close yourself off to them. It is like an interpreter for the spirit world." Meg answered. Evelyn thought she saw Henry roll his eyes.

"They are pulling me outside." Meg stood up and, without being shown where to go, went to the back door and out into the yard. The group followed behind her. Julia once again had her phone out. The dewy night air filled their nostrils as they stepped out onto the grass. It was full darkness now, which had a whole different meaning out on the island where there was not the glow of city lights. A million stars shone over their heads, but without the light of a flashlight, a person would quickly disappear into the blackness.

"There are two spirits here, a boy and a girl." Meg was standing in the yard with her eyes closed, hands spread out in front of her as if she was grasping for the spirits that were around her. "They are younger. Highschool age. They stay with the house. They are waiting for someone to come and get them. They don't leave the house, they are very clear about that. I think they are afraid to leave the house."

"Why?" Henry asked.

"Their father. He's in the woods. They say he doesn't come to the house, and they don't go to the woods." Henry looped his thumbs through his belt loop. The answer he got didn't seem to make him happy.

Since they could apparently ask Meg questions, Evelyn asked, "Are they dangerous?"

"No, they are harmless. They like having you here. They have never seen a happy family before. They are sorry if they have frightened anyone, but they aren't sure of their abilities."

"It's no problem." Evelyn said out loud before realizing the people she was saying it to were not in the room and were, in fact, dead. Julia was circling the group, her phone held out in front of her.

"Are they here now?" Victoria asked.

"They are dear, but I doubt you will catch them on that. They aren't solid enough to be seen right now." Meg closed her eyes again and with her hands held out in front of her, she said, "I'm being pulled out to the woods." Meg stopped and seemed to be leaning back towards the house. " The children are telling me not to go out there."

"Then maybe you shouldn't." Henry said, but Meg was walking slowly in that direction. Evelyn wasn't sure she wanted to follow her. It seemed the woods held all the bad things. She didn't know who these children were, or if she even believed in them, yet she found herself thinking that maybe they should take their advice.

"What does your spirit guide say?" Evelyn asked. If the spirit guide said they shouldn't go into the woods, she definitely wasn't doing it.

"She is telling me to be careful."

"Her spirit guide is a woman." Evelyn said out loud.

"What does that mean?" Mark asked, walking next to her.

"I don't know if it means anything. Just never thought of a spirit as having a gender."

"It would have the same gender it would in life wouldn't it?" Evelyn shrugged.

"Are spirits and ghosts the same thing? I thought ghosts were people who had once been living, but spirits had always kind of existed in the...spirit world?" Mark shook his head.

"I have no idea. I didn't even believe in this shit until a few days ago."

"Maybe we should go back and put the protection on the house. We don't have to speak to whoever is in the woods tonight." Evelyn suggested. With the exception of Julia, they all knew who was in the woods. Evelyn didn't really want to draw Eustice's attention to them if she could avoid it.

"I need to know what we are dealing with so I know what kind of protection is needed." Meg answered. Evelyn looked at Mark who shrugged his shoulders at her. Julia seemed transfixed by the whole process, staring open mouthed through the screen of her phone.

They walked across the grassy lawn and headed towards the tree line. Evelyn felt a sense of déjà vu. This was the path she had used to run away from the faceless man in her dreams. She instinctively looked down at the grounds as if she was going to see the drag marks from where she was dragged to the grave. It was a creepy feeling, and she wrapped her arms around herself.

"Something wrong?" Evelyn almost jumped out of her skin. Henry was looking at her with his cop eyes.

"It's nothing really, just these dreams I've been having. This all seems a bit real."

"The ones where you are Eustice's wife and he is dragging you to a grave?" Evelyn whipped her head around in surprise. "Meg told me." He said answering her unspoken question. Of course she had.

"Charmingly, in the last one, I was the victim and watched as my own body was placed in the grave. Does Meg tell you everything about our conversations?" A grin broke his usual serious face.

"Yes. Everything. Whether I want to hear it or not. Tell me about this woman and maybe we can figure out who you are in the dreams."

"I'm running away from him and scared out of my mind that I won't see my two kids again and what will happen to them." The sheriff shook his head.

"None of the victims had children. Most were women in their early twenties. Marcy Grey was pregnant, but we don't think she even knew about it. Her mother didn't."

"His wife had two children, though." Evelyn thought. Two children who were still in the house waiting for someone to come and get them.

"We never found her body. Or any proof really that she was dead. Anything else?" Evelyn shook her head. "Jeb, the previous sheriff, always thought the wife had run away. I never did. I also don't think Eustice would have let her go. I think he killed her. We just haven't found her."

"You think I'm the wife in the dreams?"

"I think it's a good possibility. Keep me posted if you dream anything else." Evelyn couldn't believe what she was hearing. Mark interrupted their conversion, walking up between them.

"I have to admit, this is spooky. I half expect something to jump out at us." Mark said, coming up next to her. The sheriff gave her a purposeful look and went to go join Meg who was once again feeling the air around her with her outstretched hands.

"Julia would be thrilled if something happened and she had something to post on Instagram." Meg stopped walking when she reached the tree line. A strong gust of cold wind came at them from the tree. Strong enough to make the trees rustle and groan.

"He doesn't want us here." Meg said.

"Then why the hell did he call you over here?" The sheriff asked.

"He didn't." A cold chill ran down Evelyn's spine when Meg said this. She had been so convinced it was going to be Eustice. " A woman guided me here. She wanted me to see what he's doing." There was a pause.

"Well? What is he doing?" Henry asked.

"He's guarding them." The sheriff shifted his weight, looking more at attention.

"Guarding who?" He asked calmly.

"The souls of the dead. There are at least twenty of them."

The sheriff ran his hand through his hair. It was fairly clear that considering the history of the island that the 'him' in question was Eustice, who as far as they knew, had killed only five women. The four women from town and most likely his wife. Was it possible that this had merely been the end of his killing career and he had been taking lives longer than anyone knew?

"They are all crying for help, to be released." Meg said.

"Where did they come from?" The sheriff asked with some urgency.

"They were here before him. Souls who passed before Eustice did, but he has trapped them here. He has become a soul collector." A chill ran down Evelyn's back and she leaned in closer to Mark. She noticed Julia was standing closer as well.

"He says you took the bodies, but their souls stay with me." Meg was looking straight at the sheriff when she said this. Meg stepped away from the tree line, and her body posture became more relaxed.

"My spirit guide says we should leave." Meg said, starting to walk back towards the house.

"Perfectly fine by me." Mark said, "The sooner we are back in the house the better." The group had no desire to see what was hidden within the trees. Meg didn't walk back into the house, though. She got to the middle of the yard and started walking in all different directions.

"Meg?" Henry asked.

"I'm looking for her."

"Who?"

"The woman who was leading me. She's here. I can feel her, but she doesn't seem to be anywhere. Her energy doesn't get stronger no matter where I go." The sheriff couldn't help with this. Meg tried calling her forward, asked the spirit to guide her, and got nothing. Meg eventually shrugged her shoulders. "I guess she was done talking to me. Strange though, she was the one pulling me in the direction I needed to go, but then she just disappeared." Meg stood still in the grassy backyard and looked around her, walking in one direction and then another looking for the communication to get stronger in one direction or another. With a shrug of her shoulders Meg turned back to the house.

"Follow me." Meg said, she took off towards the house with determination. Finding her purse on the chair, she dug around for a moment and then pulled some bottles out. "I think you are going to need something stronger. Eustice is a baddy, but that doesn't worry me nearly as much as how strong he is." Evelyn buried her face in her hands. How could this possibly be the reality they were living in?

"Now, who do you want to allow in, and who do you want to keep out?" Meg asked.

"Well, I don't think we want any of them in the house, do we?" Evelyn asked Mark who nodded his head. "I think we could live without any ghosts in the house."

"But what about the teenagers, the ones who are afraid of the man in the woods? You can't throw them out." Julia piped up. Her mother gave her a confused look.

"You want to allow two ghosts to stay in the house? Won't that be a little frightening?" Mark asked.

"Not now that I know who they are. I mean, it's a little creepy when you can feel someone staring at you, but you can't see them, but if I know it's one of them…" Evelyn couldn't argue with this logic and so conceded to allow the teenagers to stay. Meg pulled out a bottle of black salt and headed to the outside of the house. "Black salt will create a barrier around the house. Anything inside the house will not be able to leave and anything outside the house will not be able to get in, including Mr. Eustice." Leading the group back out to the yard, she sprinkled a thin line around the house while praying to St. Michael to protect the house and all who lived in it against the darkness of evil. With a dramatic toss of the last granules, she turned to her awaiting audience and said, "I declare this house…clear."

"I think you are enjoying this just a little too much." Evelyn smiled. To her amazement, she did feel a little relieved that it had been done, which meant she put more stock in such things than she thought .

"We should be getting back. It's getting late." The sheriff reminded them. Evelyn looked at her watch. It was almost midnight.

"Good lord, you're right. We are on vacation, but you two have work tomorrow." And they moved back inside the house to gather their things.

"You have work tomorrow too, don't forget." Meg reminded.

"Oh yes, the reading and book signing. Eve's publisher was thrilled she was willing to push the new book while on vacation." Mark said.

"It's the least I could do after all this."

"And the free books." Julia reminded her. The mood walking down the hill to the dock and the boat was light-hearted. Julia and Mark were walking with Meg who was telling them about the author that made her swear she would never do book signings in her store again.

"This was before I moved here and opened the store. I was still living in California at the time…."

"She certainly has enjoyed herself this evening. I didn't know talking to the dead could be so uplifting." Evelyn said. Somehow she was walking with the sheriff again.

"Meg always gets like that after a reading." The sheriff said. Evelyn found him a quiet and calm presence and thought these were exactly the traits you would want in a sheriff. Someone who thought about the situation before jumping right in.

"When did her abilities first appear? I would think that would be an interesting thing to find out about yourself." Evelyn asked, half joking. The sheriff looked up at the back of his sister-in-law.

"Meg was a bit of a late bloomer. She didn't start talking to the departed until after my brother and nephew died." It was not only what he said, but the look on his face when he said it that stopped Evelyn walking down the path. The sheriff continued on, seemingly not noticing the effect his words had on her. Meg seemed so light hearted, Evelyn was surprised she had suffered such a loss. "I had no idea." The sheriff shrugged his shoulders and walked to the boat. Evelyn felt numb as she said good night to Meg and the sheriff. She waved to them, along with Mark and Julia, as the boat backed away from the dock and headed back to the mainland.

"Well, what a strangely but not unpleasant way to spend an evening. I bet none of your other friends will attend a dinner party turned seance." Mark said to Julia.

"I can't wait to go back over the footage tomorrow and see if anything appeared." Julia said.

Arms wrapped around herself, Evelyn had to agree. What an extremely strange evening it had been.

31

"You okay?" Mark asked, getting in on his side of the bed.
Evelyn was sitting on her side rubbing lotion into her hands and
staring at the wall with a confused look on her face. Her look
had been so intent, Mark had looked to see what the source of
confusion was. The wall had been blank though.

"Yeah, why?" Evelyn snapped out of it and looked at him.

"You've been quiet ever since Meg and the sheriff left. Did
something get to you?"

"Just something the sheriff said as we were walking down to
the boat afterwards."

"What did he say?"

"That Meg didn't start communing with the dead until after
her husband and SON died."

"She lost both of them? Did he say how it happened?"

"Some accident I would think . It's just that looking at her,
you wouldn't think anything that horrible had happened to
her."

"Well, if she can talk to them still, I would imagine that takes
some of the grief away."

"But still…"

"You are wondering if she really does have abilities or if this is some elaborate way for her to deal with the death of her son and husband?"

"Yeah. I've been replaying the events of the evening in my head. The sheriff never seemed to doubt what she was saying was true, but he was also the one asking the most questions. I mean, what did we really see out there this evening? Not a whole lot."

"You think Meg was playing on our emotions to make it seem like she was speaking with someone?" Evelyn knew Meg better than he did, and he also knew that Evelyn would not have entertained an evening like this if she had thought Meg was a fake.

"I don't know. Meg doesn't seem like the type of person who would do something like that. It's not like she asked for money either, and having dinner was my idea."

"So maybe she believes she can communicate with the dead."

"Yeah, but can she?"

"I guess we'll find out." Mark gave her a kiss. "Don't stay up too late worrying about it, Hon. If what she did worked, then things should calm down around here. If it didn't work, then I would imagine we will be hearing from Eustice in the near future." Evelyn looked down on her husband.

"Well, that's a comforting thought to go to sleep with, thank you dear." Evelyn did stay up too late thinking about it. Rolling the entire evening over in her head and finally falling asleep when she was too tired to keep herself awake.

The cold water surrounded her, and she felt it lift her arms and hair as she floated down. She looked up and could see the moonlight on the surface of the water growing dimmer. The rope binding her feet to the weight rubbed at her skin. She struggled to free herself, but her bindings wouldn't move. *'They will never find me here.'* Fear gripped her at the thought that no one would ever know where she was if she sank to the bottom. Looking up, Evelyn could see the moon shining through the water. The light grew dimmer as she sank. She kicked her legs harder to free herself from the rope, the fibers scraping her skin, but the weight was too heavy. Evelyn opened her mouth to scream, to let someone know where she was. It was the choking on water that woke her.

When her eyes opened, she was sitting up in bed trying to get a deep breath. Her hand went to her chest, and she was surprised to find her pajamas dry. They had clung to her as she tried to free herself from the weight pulling her deeper into the water. It took these facts, the dry bed and dry pajamas, to convince herself she wasn't drowning. Evelyn reached for Mark, but he was already out of bed. Morning light filled the room, and the smell of coffee was coming from below. Evelyn had no question as to what the dream had been about. She knew without a doubt that she was Eustice's wife. Jumping out of bed and feeling for her phone, she called Meg.

"Hey Meg, it's Evelyn. I know where he put the wife's body."

<h1 style="text-align:center">32</h1>

"….and at last Margret had the answer she was looking for." Evelyn looked up from the last page of her novel and searched for Mark in the crowd. They locked eyes, and Mark smiled at her and gave a little wave. This is his purpose at these events, and he tried to stand in her line of sight. It calms Evelyn before she is forced to look out on the crowd and allows for a dramatic pause before she gives her closing remarks. "Thank you again for coming out and listening. You were a delightful audience." Meg came up and stood next to her, clapping and smiling from ear to ear.

"Wasn't that fantastic? That was from her new book as well. Evelyn has kindly agreed to autograph her books for anyone who would like one. We have a limited number of her new book as well as a number of her earlier books." Meg added, waving her hand in the direction of a table covered with hard back books. The crowd got up and started moving around the room, leaving a path for Mark to make his way to his wife.

"You should be happy with that. They seemed to love it." Evelyn had no problem promoting her books until it was time to stand in front of a crowd and read. Having Mark there to lock eyes with over the sea of strangers was the only way she could get through these readings.

"Are you and Julia going to go back now?" Evalyn asks him.

"You forget, we only have one boat. We are going to have to leave together unless you want to paddle board back in the dark." Evelyn found Julia in the crowd, looking incredibly grown up for a freshman in high school. None of them had brought really nice clothes, but somehow Julia managed to look elegant in a long button up shirt dress, simple platform heels, a long thin necklace, and way too much eye makeup for a girl her age (if for no other reason than it made her look twenty-one). "I'm not extremely comfortable with how mature our daughter looks." She said to Mark.

"Tell me about it. The only comfort I have is she is completely oblivious to the male attention in the room."

"The bored look on her face isn't helping. What male attention?"

"I caught a few eyes looking. She is a little mad actually. I wouldn't let her read her book while you were talking. I think I'm going to have to get her out of here before she does actually die of boredom."

"Why don't you go get something to eat or something while I finish up here." Mark gave her a kiss on the cheek.

"Don't be too long." He walked over to Julia who was picking her nails and leaning against the wall. Throwing his arm around her neck and directing her in the direction of the door, he said, "Come on kid, let's go get a beer."

"Really!"

"No."

"Evelyn?" It was Meg. Looking away from Mark and Julia,

Evelyn looked around at the meandering crowd, most of whom were lined up and waiting for their book to be signed.

"Yes, sorry." Putting her public smile into place, Evelyn took her place behind the table and spent the next two hours signing books. Mark had been texting for over an hour to ask when she would be done. Signing the last book, the bell over the door dinged shut, and Evelyn slouched back in the chair and felt herself relax. Meg was making her way around the room, clearing away used cups and napkins from the bookcases and tables, a genuine smile across her face.

"That was the best book reading we have ever had."

"Was it really?"

"It was only our third, but by far, our best." The door dinged, and they both placed smiles on their face as they turned to politely tell the person the store was closed.

"Henry." The sheriff was taking off his hat as he entered the shop. Evelyn wondered if he was ever out of uniform. It seemed no matter what time of day or night she saw him, he was in uniform. "To what do we owe the honor?" Meg asked, going up and placing a kiss on her brother-in-law's cheek. "I was going to make a cup of tea, anyone else want one?" Meg asked.

"Yes please." Evelyn said, Henry nodded his head.

"Well, I come bearing news actually." He was looking at Evelyn. The tiredness left her and she sat up straight.

"You found her?" Henry nodded.

"We found her."

"You found the wife? That was fast." Meg said from the kitchen. The sheriff sat down in a chair across from Evelyn and gladly took the cup of tea Meg handed him.

"Well, acting on a tip," He gave Evelyn a look, "I was able to get the dive boys out. It took the better part of the day, but we found her. We won't know it is her for sure until they get her back to the lab, but who else would it be?"

"You found her in the water?" Evelyn felt numb. She wasn't used to communicating messages for the dead and would rather it had just been a bad dream. The thrill that the body had been found was replaced by the dread that she had accurately translated a message from a dead woman.

"There isn't much left of her at this point, I'm afraid. She was tied to a large rock and tossed on the far side of the island where the currents are stronger. I'm sure Eustice was hoping she would be dragged away a bit before she settled. He should have chosen a smaller rock."

They sat in silence for a moment, sipping their tea.

"So, what now?" Evelyn asked.

"We'll have to go back tomorrow and get her out of the water and then the lab will take a look at her and see if they can determine the cause of death."

"I don't suppose there is any way at this point to tell if she was still alive when she went into the water?" Evelyn asked, though she wasn't sure why. The dream was still vivid in her mind, and she had been extremely aware of what was happening to her, which she probably wouldn't have been if she was dead. Eveyln couldn't imagine the fear she would have if she knew she was drowning. She hoped the woman's last moments had not been filled with fear.

"Not for sure, but if they can determine how she died, they may be able to determine if she died instantly." Small comfort. "I can arrange it so that you can be there when we pull her out of the water if you want." To her surprise, Evelyn found the sheriff was looking at her.

"Me?" He nodded.

"Since you helped us find her."

"I would like to be there. Thank you." Evelyn answered to her surprise.

"You look beat, and I'm sure your husband and daughter are waiting for you. Go on home." Meg said. Evelyn looked at her watch. It was almost midnight.

"Good lord." Evelyn grabbed her purse and made a B-line for the door. "I'll talk to you tomorrow. Thanks for letting me do a reading. I'll see you tomorrow morning sheriff."

Evelyn texted Mark on her way out the door and started for the dock. She would wait for them in the boat. They appeared a few minutes later, and she regretted making them wait so long. Mark wasn't drunk, but he looked the part. His tie undone, eyes heavy, and walking somewhat slouched. Poor Julia looked like she had just woken up. Having abandoned her platform shoes, she was walking barefoot, and her long brown hair was now pulled back into a messy bun. Evelyn had to smile a little though. She looked less like a bored model in her twenties and more like a tired child wearing her father's dress shirt. Evelyn started the engine. Out of the three of them, she thought she was in the best shape to drive back to the island.

"What time of night do you call this?" Mark said, half stumbling into the boat.

"Sorry, I didn't realize what time it was." He kissed her cheek and said, "Price I pay for being married to a successful writer, I guess."   Julia just rolled her eyes at her mother and plopped into the boat, and using her father's jacket as a pillow, closed her eyes again.

The house felt blissfully empty when Evelyn opened the front door. Mark was half walking and half carrying Julia up the path. For some reason, she had half expected to walk in and find their new ghost friends watching TV.

"Can you get yourself up the stairs?" Mark asked Julia.

"Mmmm." Was her answer and she went to go up the stairs.

"Goodnight dear. Thanks for being a good sport." Evelyn caught her shoulder and placed a kiss on her head. They stood there for a moment listening to her progress up the stairs.

"Well, I thought it was a good night. Decent crowd." Mark said, sitting heavily on the couch.

"It was a good night. Best crowd yet. Maybe I should only do small book shops in small towns from now on. From the look on Meg's face, she thought it was a good night as well."

"Well, if you managed to sell that large stack of books on the end of the table, then I think she did all right. Tea?"

"Oh, yes please. Starting to get a bit of a headache." At the offer of tea, Evelyn plopped herself onto the couch and watched Mark make his way around the kitchen. "The sheriff came in right as the last person was leaving."

"Yeah."

"He'd been out on the water all day."

"Because of that dream you had?"

"Yeah, they found her. They found the wife's body." She was looking at his back trying to gauge his reaction. When Mark turned to look at her, his eyes were no longer heavy.

"Where did they find her?"

"Far side of the island. The sheriff thinks he threw her there so that the current would carry her farther away. I'm going to go out with them tomorrow when they bring her up." Mark brought the tea over and sat on the coffee table right in front of her. Normally, this annoyed her, but it was one in the morning and they were talking about bringing dead people out of the water. The normal rules of polite society could be relaxed.

"Are you sure you want to do that?" Mark looked fully alert now.

"To be honest with you, no, but I told him 'yes' without even a thought when he asked me. I know it sounds strange, but I kind of want to meet her, or at least see her. I mean, I know she's dead and all, but she's been in my head almost since we got here. The sheriff indicated that there really wasn't much left of her, but it's the closest I'm going to get. It doesn't make sense, I know."

"If you need to do it, then do it."

"You seem very calm about all of this. Your wife has a dream she is drowning, and the next thing you know, the woman who used to live here is discovered in the water behind us . This doesn't freak you out just a little?"

"Well, I certainly don't understand it. I don't understand any of what has happened on this island since we got here. We are apparently not only people who believe in ghosts all of a sudden, but people who are in some way communicating with them. It's never happened before coming here, which makes me hope that it won't happen once we leave."

"I asked the sheriff if they would be able to tell if she was still alive when she went into the water."

"What makes you think she was?"

"I was choking on the water. I was aware I was drowning. I knew if I sank to the bottom no one would find me." Mark sat next to her on the couch and pulled her towards him.

"You sure you want to go do this tomorrow?"

"I think I need to."

"Do you want me to come with you?"

"No, that's okay." She leaned her head on his shoulder. "Thank you
    though." Evelyn took a sip of her tea.

33

Julia tried very hard to climb the three flights of stairs to her room without waking herself up. She had been fantasizing about her bed for the better part of three hours now. The room felt cold, but that didn't seem strange to her. For a moment, she thought about crawling into bed in her clothes, but decided against it. She took her necklace off and hung it on the side of the mirror with her other necklaces. Her clothes were unceremoniously thrown into the corner with the rest of her dirty laundry. Putting on the large t-shirt that passed for a night gown, she climbed into bed. She picked up a book and looked at it, but decided she was too tired to read tonight and put it back on the nightstand. Turning off the light, she rolled over onto her right side and closed her eyes. Sleep was just starting to pull her under when she heard a noise in her room. It was not the noise that opened her eyes, more the feeling that someone was watching her. Turning her light back on, she half expected to see someone standing at the end of her bed.

There was no one there, and Julia convinced herself it was a dream when she saw the necklaces on her mirror move like they would if someone had run their hands across it. A white mist formed next to the mirror, growing in density and shape while she watched. The shape of a girl formed in front of Julia, a girl's body which had no defined shape, but Julia could make out her face and her long hair. Frozen to the spot, Julia wanted to scream, but she couldn't make the sound come out of her mouth. The girl turned to look at Julia and smiled. Julia tried to convince herself it was fine. It was the teenager. They were the only ones allowed in the house, but seeing them was more than a tad scary.

"Please leave." Julia said with as much authority as she could muster. To her amazement, the figure faded away.

"You gotta stop touching stuff, Vic."

"She has pretty things, doesn't she?"

"She saw you." Gerald pointed out.

"They said we could stay."

"I don't think that meant they wanted to invite us for dinner."

"Maybe they can help us. That woman came with them, the one who can hear us."

"I keep telling you, no one can help us. No one can beat him, just give up." Risking further temper, "That sheriff stopped him pretty good." Victoria added calmly. The vibrations coming from him were almost like a high-pitched hum now. Gerald stormed away.

"Did you hear something?" Evelyn asked. She had a chill run up her arm.

"Who would Julia be talking to this time of night?" So, he did hear it. It sounded like someone was having a hushed conversation upstairs. Mark got up and went to the bottom of the stairs to listen better.

"I don't think she's talking to anyone, she didn't have her cell in her hand." Evelyn could see it half out of her purse where Julia had thrown her bag in the chair.

"She wouldn't be reading...." Every door in the house slammed shut. Evelyn and Mark froze and then locked eyes. There was nothing that could make that happen. Mark went racing up the stairs to Julia's room. Julia met her parents at the top of the stairs. Twain was barking so loudly there was no chance of hearing anything else.

"What the hell was that?" Julia asked, running down the stairs and almost crashing into Mark's arms, and then it was over. The noise that had filled the house was gone and silence surrounded them. The house was so silent, that for a moment, they wondered if it had really happened. Twain was standing behind Julia, ears up and alert. They stood there, motionless on the stairs, looking around them for any indication that what had happened was going to happen again.

"Well, that went completely unnoticed." Victoria said as Gerald stormed out of the house. She could tell he was no longer there. She could no longer feel his energy. She stayed to see what happened. Gerald hadn't meant to slam all the doors in the house. He seemed very concerned with frightening the living, but they were both having to adjust to the fact that they could affect the world around them again. It was one of the reasons she wanted the family to stay. How long had it been since she touched something, and it moved?   And she loved having another teenage girl around. She couldn't admit this in front of Gerald because it upset him. Using the energy of the living to make themselves stronger did seem a bit mean, but she wasn't the one who made the rules. She didn't choose to die, didn't choose to stay here, didn't choose any of it. She watched as the family ran to each other in fear and collided on the stairs. 'I'm sorry, don't be scared.' She tried to whisper, but they showed no sign that they heard her, and she didn't

want to shout. Gerald was right, no matter what they did, they were bound to scare the living, so she just watched.

That night they all slept in the living room with the lights on. Mark and Evelyn stayed awake until Julia was asleep, just like they had when she was a baby. Twain was lying on her legs, his soft snores a comforting sound.

"I'm not sure we can stay here too much longer. Things are getting a little strange." Mark said, calmly watching Julia sleep.

"I know, but home is the only place we can afford to go."

"It might still be less stressful than here." They agreed Mark would call the rental company in the morning and plead their case to see if they could get any sort of a refund. He was more level headed when it came to these things. Evelyn was more likely to end up yelling and threatening to sue. The sky was starting to turn light and Evelyn had completely given up on sleep that evening. Closing her eyes, she was surprised to hear the alarm go off a few hours later. What little sleep she had gotten had thankfully been dream free.

34

Mark and Julia were still asleep when she stepped out onto the porch and made her way down to the dock where the sheriff was going to pick her up. What she saw in front of her stopped her cold. She could see no farther than the woods right off the back of the porch. A thick fog had rolled over the island and lingered in the trees. Evelyn's mind went to the trapped souls Meg said Eustice was keeping and a shiver went up her spine. Looking to the side of the house, Evelyn could see that the fog seemed to be confined to the trees, the path to the dock was clear. No longer needing coffee, Evelyn ran down the path to the dock. The fog thinned but still hung low over the water . She was trying to figure out where the water ended and the fog began when the sound of a boat motor drew her attention. The police boat glided through the water more slowly than Evelyn had remembered, but with just as much accuracy. The sheriff brought the boat up alongside the dock.

"Beautiful morning we have, isn't it?" The sheriff said with the closest thing to humor Evelyn had heard out of the man. She forced a smile on her face.

"Excellent weather to go find a body." He helped her into

the boat. They said little on the way to the site. The sheriff was concentrating on navigating the fog and Evelyn was happy to let him do it. The farther they got out to sea, the thinner the fog got.

"You told me the island got the title Ghost Island because of the fog. I have to admit, I didn't believe you." Evelyn said, looking back at the island that still looked completely emerged in the fog.

"It's also haunted." Evelyn turned to look at him just in time to see the smirk disappear from his face.

"Are they going to be able to get her out of the water today with all this fog?" Evelyn asked. The sheriff had slowed the motor and so she assumed they were getting close.

"As long as there isn't fog under the water, they'll be fine."

"Is there such a thing as fog under the water?" He smiled at her.

"No."

The sheriff had been right. To her surprise, there was a lot of activity already at the site. Despite the early hour and the fog, she and the sheriff were the last ones to arrive. There was another police boat with the divers on board already dressed in their dive suits and checking their gear. There was another fishing boat with one lone, round man on board. "The coroner." The sheriff said. "He has his own boat, so he drove himself. Not a fan of early mornings."

"You have a coroner?" Somewhat surprising considering the size of the town.

"He's retired. Came down here for the fishing. I agreed to pay his fishing license every year if he would act as coroner when we need it. Considering how often we needed it, he got the better end of the deal."

Evelyn wrapped her jacket more firmly around her. "So,

what happens now?" Evelyn asked.

"They'll dive down to the location that we marked last night, bring the body up, and then search the scene for anything that might be evidence." Evelyn readied herself for what she might see when the body came out of the water. The divers were lining up along the side of the boat, even a diving novice like herself knew that meant they were about to go into the water. "They will bring the body up in a bag." The sheriff added. Evelyn let go of her breath, the ball of tension in her stomach unwound. "Really?" He nodded.

"Like I said, there isn't a lot left of her." Feeling much better about the situation, Evelyn watched with still calmness as the divers fell backwards into the water. One, two, three. The bubbles they created soon disappeared and the water was calm again. "And now we wait." The sheriff said, sitting back in the captain's chair. "Coffee?" He produced a thermos from under the seat.

"That would be wonderful, thank you." Evelyn held the mug in both hands, the heat taking the cold out of her. It was hot and delicious. Evelyn felt more capable of handling the day now.

"I'm glad she'll finally be put to rest." She said, almost to herself.

"Yeah, living with Eustice was no picnic. If there is anyone out there that deserves a peaceful rest..." The sheriff watched the water and sipped his coffee. He looked very relaxed with his foot resting on the steering wheel.

"There is one thing bugging me though." Evelyn said. The sheriff looked at her with those piercing eyes that made her uneasy.

"What's that?"

"The dream in the water, that wasn't the first dream I had where I thought I was his wife. In the previous ones, I woke up choking on dirt. I assumed he buried her with the others, but we found her in the water." The sheriff shrugged his shoulders.

"He obviously killed her on land. Maybe he buried her temporarily until he had a chance to bring her out here."

"Seems like a lot of trouble to go through just to get rid of a body." Evelyn had never had the trouble of figuring out what to do with the person she had just killed. Digging a grave just to dig it back up again seemed like a lot of extra work.

"Hmmm. More personal though, more emotion. The girls he wanted to keep close, wanted to possess them, didn't want to let them go. By burying the wife farther away, he may not have wanted her around his other kills. Maybe he wanted her erased completely. I mean, look how long it's taken us to find her. The girls were buried and at least had markers." Evelyn took a sip of her coffee and thought about that. It was going to bother her that they would never know for sure . They sat in silence for a bit, until Evelyn couldn't handle it anymore. "Can I ask you something about Meg?" They both kept an eye on the water while they spoke.

"Sure."

"Do you believe she can speak to the dead? It's just the other night, I got the impression that maybe you didn't." The sheriff looked at her over his coffee cup in a way that made her want to confess to the blunt she smoked in college. For a horrible moment, she thought she had offended him.

"Do you believe she can speak to the dead?" He asked her. Evelyn knew this trick from interviewing people herself. Answer a question with a question.

"I don't know what I believe anymore. That's what this

place has done to me. Mark and I were talking only last night that before we came out here, we didn't consider ourselves believers in ghosts, and now we not only believe in them, but are entertaining the thought that we are living in a haunted house and that Meg can communicate with them. And me for that matter. Through those dreams. That was right before we were interrupted by the hushed conversation the ghosts in our house were apparently having soon followed by all the doors in the house slamming shut." The sheriff looked out over the water without answering. Evelyn was getting ready to ask the questions again when he said, "I think Meg believes she can speak to the dead, and that's enough for me. Did she tell you how my brother and nephew died?"

"No, she told me your sister was a victim of Eustice's, but she didn't mention her husband or son at all." Evelyn thought she saw him flinch at the mention of his sister, but it was barely noticeable.

"Single car accident." He said, bluntly. "His vehicle left the road and collided with a tree. They were killed on impact. It was a clear night, and my brother was driving roads he had been driving his whole life." The sheriff locked eyes with her. "It didn't make sense. I was called out to it. I had just been elected Sheriff. They said the driver was dead, and the passenger had been sent to hospital with severe injuries. They didn't say who the driver was. Hell, they may not have known. I knew it was his car as soon as I got to the scene. He and Meg were high school sweethearts. My deputy offered to tell Meg for me, but I couldn't do that. On the way to her house, I found out my nephew had died at the hospital. I couldn't let a stranger tell her that the two most important people in her life were gone. Telling her the news is still to this day the hardest thing I have ever had to do in this job." Evelyn wiped a tear away before he could see it.

"How old was her son?"

"Seventeen. Meg completely shut down. To the point where she was going to lose the shop, and if she didn't open it back up again, she was going to lose the house. I did what I could, but it wasn't enough. She was dead. She just hadn't died yet. Then one morning she called me, and she sounded like old Meg. Told me Dave and Tim came to see her in a dream and they talked. Said Dave told her that he swerved to miss a deer and hit the tree. Dave apparently told her they were fine, they were happy, and that she saw Tim smiling behind Dave. From that day to this, she has been the old Meg." He shrugged his shoulders, "Except now she talks to dead people."

"But do you really think she does though? That communication with people beyond the grave is possible?" The sheriff shifted in his seat.

"Did she speak to Eustice that night at your place? I don't know. But you had a dream, and now we are out here pulling a body out of the water. So, who's to say?" There was noise from the other boat, and they both turned to look. Bubbles touched the surface, so the divers were coming up. A balloon came up first, and the other police boat moved closer to it. A diver broke the surface and then a second one. Evelyn could see the white bag just below the surface of the water. The diver swam to the boat pulling the bag behind them aided by the balloon. The officer on the boat grabbed one end and pulled the bag up. The whole process was captured by the coroner who was taking pictures from his boat. The bag lifted completely out of the water easily, but it took both divers to lift the rock out of the water, the rope still attached. Evelyn reached for her ankle, feeling the burn of the rope on her skin.

It was at times like this that Evelyn wished she was a religious woman. She wished she knew a prayer to send up for his wife (she didn't even know her name). *Hopefully you are at peace.* Was all she could think of. She couldn't imagine being down there all this time, no one knowing where she was, and not really looking for her. A tear escaped and she wiped it away.

"What was her name?" Evleyn was pretty sure he could hear her voice crack when she spoke.

"Helen. Helen Sinclair, forty-two. Married Eustice when she was eighteen." Helen. Finally, a name for the woman whose last moments she had been reliving in her dreams. "Thank you for letting me come out here today. If it wouldn't be too much to ask, do you mind letting me know when they find out the cause of death?"

"Sure, let's go see if Bertie has any ideas right now." The sheriff turned over the engine of the boat and pulled up on the other side of the police boat that would carry Helen's remains to land. The rotund coroner had managed to get from his boat onto the police boat and was bent over the white bag taking pictures.

"Whatcha got, Bertie?"

"Morning to you too Sheriff. It's a female. That's about all I can tell you right now. We are going to have to pull medical records to positively ID her."

"Any idea what killed her?"

"You mean other than the rock tied to her ankles?"

"We have reason to think she was dead or at least injured when she went in the water." The coroner shrugged his shoulders and looked back into the bag.

"At first glance, I would say blunt force trauma. Most likely she was dead when she hit the water. If she was alive, she certainly would have been unconscious. Let me get her back to the lab and I'll be able to tell you for sure."

"Weapon?"

"Something flat. Doesn't look like she was hit with a round object."

"Like a shovel?" Evelyn asked. She could feel the sheriff's eyes on her. The coroner looked at her as if noticing her for the first time. "Possibly. Do you always bring your dates to such romantic locations, Henry?"

"She's just a friend, Bertie, and mind your own business. How soon do you think you'll have something for me?"

"Tonight." They nodded to one another, and the sheriff threw the boat into reverse. They moved away from the activity and turned the corner of the island, heading back towards the house. The fog had almost disappeared now, though some of it was still clinging to the trees. The sheriff slowed the engine on the boat and said, "How did you know what she had been hit with?" Evelyn shrugged.

"It was in the dream."

"Maybe you should tell me about these dreams. All of them. All the way through."

"It wasn't just one dream. I've been having them since we got here. She follows him to the woods. I can't see what he is doing, but then I'm running, and I know if whatever is behind me catches me, I'm dead. Then there is a flash of silver metal, and I can't move. I'm thinking about my kids, that I need to get back to them. Who is going to look after them if I'm not there? He drags me further away from the house. The house we are staying in. It's the back of the house as you see it when you are coming out of the woods. I'm aware of what's going on, but I can't make myself move. I thought he had buried her. In the first dream, I can smell the dirt and feel it hit my face when he starts to fill in the grave. It wasn't until this last one that I was in water. I woke up choking on water. When I woke up, I knew without a doubt that she was in the water."

"Have you ever had dreams like this before?" The sheriff asked. Evelyn half laughed.

"No, thank god."

The sheriff rubbed his face with one hand and suddenly looked very tired.

"It's ridiculous, isn't it?" Evelyn offered.

"Yeah, but here we are. I just can't figure out how I'm going to phrase this in my report." Evelyn got out of the boat and watched as the sheriff backed the boat up and turned towards the mainland. She wrote fiction, and even she wasn't sure she could write a situation as strange as this.

35

When Evelyn got back to the house, it was only ten in the morning, and Julia was sitting up at the kitchen table looking like she had been through the wars. Julia had dragged herself from the couch to the kitchen table and was leaning heavily over her phone, thumbs going a mile a minute. "Texting the girls about last night." Mark informed her.

"Morning dear." Evelyn said to the top of Julia's head.

"Mmmmn." Was the reply she got. Mark made her a cup of tea and put it in front of her. "Did you find her?" Julia asked as if realizing her mother was in the room. Evelyn was a little surprised by this because she had not talked to Julia about Eustice or her dreams for fear of adding to an already strange situation. Julia was a smart child, though, and had always paid more attention to things than she let on. Evelyn's first instinct was to sugar coat it, make it less than what it was, but Julia was a big girl now. Almost an adult, and if she had figured out this much on her own, she deserved to know the rest.

"Yeah, we did. Her name was Helen Sinclair, and now she can be laid to rest properly." Julia nodded.

"Good, I'm sure that will make her kids happy."

"Her kids?"

"The ones who haunt this place."

"Are you for sure that's who they are?"

"Meg said they were teenagers, and I kind of get that feeling when they are around. One of them was playing with my necklaces last night, before all that stuff with the doors happened."

"Wonder what got them going last night?" Mark asked, placing a cup of coffee in front of his wife.

"What do you think about us going home early?" Evelyn asked Julia.

"And do what?"

"Not living in a haunted house for one thing." Mark offered. Julia shrugged in that way universal to teenagers.

"I've got so many hits on my Insta account from the other night. I kind of wish I had been recording last night."

"So, you want to stay?" Evelyn was a little surprised considering last night. She wondered if Julia would answer the same way if she asked the question again around bedtime. Julia shrugged again.

"I know it's scary, but I don't think they mean any harm. Do you?" Julia asked. Evelyn didn't know what she thought, but they couldn't go through many more nights like last night.

Though exhausted, no one wanted to sleep, and so the rest of the day was spent doing the things they liked. Julia got back on the paddle board. She was so good by now she could take a book out with her. She paddled out into the water and then lay on the board reading. Mark worked a crossword in the hammock while Twain napped in the shade underneath. Evelyn got out her laptop. The events of the past few days were swirling around in her head so fast it was making her dizzy. She typed up the events of the last twenty-four hours in hopes of getting some perspective on the situation. At the very least, they would be notes she could reference back to if she decided to write a book about it. Helen was weighing on her mind. When she was done, she wasn't sure how much perspective she had gotten, but she felt better. *'Who knows? There may be a book in it.'* She told herself. *You would have to label it fiction. No one would believe it.* She answered. The world would be a better place if people like Eustice only existed as fiction.

It was surprising how quickly the day went although they did nothing, and how quiet the house felt. It was hard to think of it being the same house that had terrified them the evening before. The heat of the day finally ushered them all back into the air conditioning. Julia was looking very sun kissed and was pleased that she had finished her book. She stomped up stairs to find the next one. "I'm going to have a few to hand back to Meg soon." She proclaimed as she went up the stairs.

"I have a copy of my new one if you want to read it." Evelyn floated out there. Julia had never read one of her books, which was a bit of a joke between them. Julia rolled her eyes. "Mystery isn't my thing, Mom." And she continued up the stairs. Mark came in looking sleepy . He had finished half the crossword puzzle before falling asleep. Twain's barking as Julia paddled her way back to shore had woken him.

"What are we going to do for dinner? It's amazing how doing nothing has given me an appetite."

"How about meatloaf and mashed potatoes?"

"Sounds fattening and delicious." Evelyn nodded and started pulling what was required out from the fridge. Mark looked up the stairs to see as Julia was coming down and then added. "How are you doing?" Evelyn turned around.

"Fine, why?"

"You saw a woman's dead body pulled out of the ocean this morning. A body that you told the police to look for after a dream you had. Just thought you might have some feelings about that."

"I do have feelings about it, but I don't know what they are." She placed the pot of water onto the stove.

"Was it gruesome?"

"No, I was dreading that, to be honest. That moment when they pulled her out of the water and seeing what so many years in the ocean can do to you, but they already had her in a body bag."

"Imagine being the diver that found her…"

"I know, that had to be a sight. No, I don't know what is really bothering me, but now I know her name." Evelyn wasn't looking at him. She had turned around to chop the potatoes. "Before, I just knew how scared she was, not only to get away from him, but to make it back to the house for her kids. She was afraid of what he would do to them. I've never known fear like it. It was easier when it was just a dream, but now I know her name was Helen Sinclair and she felt a fear that no living being should ever feel. It makes me want to dig Eustice up and kill him all over again."

"Does Helen have any family?"

"I don't think so."

"I assume she will be buried once they have investigated everything they need to?" Evelyn looked at him.

"I would assume so, why?"

Mark shrugged. "I say we give her the burial she deserves."

"You want to give her a funeral?"

"Not that far, but I think we could attend and say a few words while she is laid to rest and spring for a head stone. You can make sure her name is never forgotten again."

"That would be really nice. I'll talk to the sheriff about it, see where the kids were buried. Maybe we can reunite them after all this time." Evelyn was holding back tears for all she was worth. She was once again surprised by the warmth of the man she married. Evelyn leaned across the counter and kissed him. "Thank you, that is a fantastic idea. Expensive, but fantastic. The sheriff said he would call me when they know what killed her, so I'll mention it then." Evelyn did feel better, lighter. They enjoyed a quiet evening. Having worked up an appetite paddle boarding, Julia even had seconds. Enjoying the effects of a blissful food coma, they settled down for the evening. Mark found a game on TV which interested absolutely no one else, so Julia placed her head phones in her ears and started on her new book. Evelyn followed her daughter's example and picked up a book. She felt like she had enough of local history for the day, so picked up the mystery she had been reading before they came out.

Not surprisingly, Julia called it an early night, yawning that she would let them know if she saw anything weird when she got up there. Mark had fallen asleep on the couch. Evelyn, too, was beginning to feel the pull towards bed, but it was only ten o'clock, and she was about to find out who the killer was in her book. Turning on all the lights as she went, Evelyn crossed the living room into the kitchen where she pulled down a glass and filled it up in the sink. Without thinking, she looked out the window. There was a man standing by the woods, which was surprising enough, but he was not a solid form. She could see the trees behind him, but he was solid enough that she could tell it was a man. The same fear gripped her that had gripped her in her dreams, and without a doubt, she knew she was looking at Eustice. The blood in her veins went cold, and the glass of water fell out of her hand. She couldn't look away. Completely frozen, she could not make herself turn her head or even blink. The black orbs of Eustice's eyes looked straight at her, and she knew he saw her. He knew she was there just as much as she knew he was there. He stayed on the edge of the woods, staring at her. He was sending her a message. Eustice turned away and went back into the trees, turning so that Evelyn could see what he was carrying at his side. A shovel.

"What are you looking at?" Mark said at her side. Evelyn jumped and smacked Mark at the same time. "What the hell?" Mark asked, covering his cheek and backing away a step. The look in her eyes concerned him, wide open but not seeing. For a moment, he thought she may have been sleep walking though she had never done it before. Then the light came back into her eyes.

"Never do that again." She yelled as tears welled in her eyes.

"Honey, what happened?"

"He was there! He was right there looking at me."

"Who?"

"Eustice. I think he's pissed I found his wife." Mark held her. She was shaking so hard it was clear she had seen something. All he saw was the dark night and the trees.

36

There had been little to no sleep for Evelyn that night. Mark had managed to calm her down and get her to bed, but every time she closed her eyes, the image of Eustice at the edge of the woods came back. Teenage ghosts who slammed doors were bad enough, but she had felt the fear Eustice caused, and she understood the fear was what he liked about killing. The fear they felt when they knew they were about to die. He liked having that kind of power over someone. She tried to finish her mystery, take her mind off of it. What was the point when you were living your own murder mystery? As soon as she saw the sun rising, she got out of bed and headed down to the docks, leaving a quick note for Julia and Mark.

The early morning air felt good, and for the first time since she had seen Eustice, she felt like she was able to take a deep breath. It felt good to be doing something. Fear was part of the human experience, but it was not an emotion that Evelyn was comfortable with. She did not go to scary movies, and she did not like roller coasters. If she was afraid of something, she would take action to stop being afraid of it, but what could you do against a ghost? Backing the boat out of the dock, she turned it around and headed full steam towards the mainland. It was still very early when Evelyn walked up the main road to the book shop. There was no one around other than the fisherman who gave her a nod as she passed.

The sign on the book store said CLOSED obviously, and Evelyn realized she didn't actually know where Meg lived. She had always seen her at the bookstore. Feeling silly for just standing there, she knocked as hard on the door as she could and then looked inside the window for any sign of activity. Seeing none, she knocked again.

"What?" Evelyn looked up to see a disheveled, robed Meg looking down at her from her bedroom window. "Evelyn? What the hell do you want at this hour of the morning?"

"Help."

"Stay there." Meg disappeared back inside the window. When she appeared again, it was behind the bookstore door. She had run a hair brush through her hair on the way down the stairs.

"What happened?" Meg greeted Evelyn and then turned around making her way to the coffee maker.

"Eustice." This netted the appropriate response. Meg stopped and turned.

"Where?"

"On the edge of the woods, but he was looking at the house. With a shovel in his hand."

"And he was solid enough you could tell it was Eustice?" Evelyn had to think about this for a moment. How did she know it was Eustice?

"He was solid enough for me to tell it was a man. I sensed it was Eustice. I got the same feeling I did in the dreams." Meg didn't say anything for a moment, looking at Evelyn as if she was trying to figure out if this was a bad joke.

"What else?" She asked.

"I think he's upset I found his wife."

"I would think so. He went to a fair amount of trouble to make sure she was never found."

"How strong is that ring of protection, Meg? I don't want him near us." It was clear to see the fear in her friend's eyes, and though they hadn't known each other long, Evelyn seemed more like a fighter than a runner. If Eustice had caused this much fear in her, there must be a reason.

"It's as strong as I know how to make it."

"What does that mean?"

"I've done rings of protection before, Eve, but none of the dead were Eustice. Before this, the dead I've dealt with have been grumpy old people who refused to admit they were dead, so refused to leave the house they lived in. Eustice is a different ghost altogether because he was a different sort of person. If he was solid enough for you to see him, then he is gaining in strength, and that can't be a good thing."

"Is there a way to keep him from gaining energy?"

"Not really, just your being there is enough to do it. The energy that surrounds you, the power you are using in the house, all of it is energy he can feed off of. Thunderstorms can do it even." Evelyn hid her face in her hands. "What are we going to do Meg? We don't want to go home despite living in a haunted house right now. We would lose all the money we paid for the summer, but then there's Eustice now. Can he actually do anything?" Meg put up her hand to give her a minute. She finished making the coffee for both of them and then sat down in one of the arm chairs, inviting Evelyn to do the same.

"The short answer to your questions is 'I don't know'. Most of the injuries and such that have come from hauntings have been because the person was so scared, they had a heart attic or ran into something. Along those lines. Then there is possession. Some people think that only a demon can take over your body. Others think it can be any one in the spirit world. I have never come across someone who is able to say from personal experience." Evelyn took a sip of her coffee and felt the warm liquid take hold.

"What would you do, Meg?" Meg looked into her coffee cup for a moment.

"I have never had a spirit cross that line of protection, but none of them were in league with this. You have a right to be nervous."

"The kids are bad enough. The other night all the doors in the house slammed shut. That was after Julia saw one of them playing with her jewelry apparently, and now we have Eustice and his shovel in the backyard. This is not the vacation we envisioned."

"I would say give it a little longer. I'll send you with some more black salt to lay around the house and try not to worry. Worrying may actually bring Eustice around more. Like a moth to a flame. He was by the woods, which is where he tends to be. Could be he's been there all the time looking at the house, and you just didn't know it because you couldn't see him.

"Thank you. I feel better just talking about it really."

"I bet he is a little upset you found his wife though."

"Poor thing deserves to rest in peace. I can't imagine what living with him must have been like."

"We always wondered how he got her to marry him. He wasn't a bad looking guy, and apparently, he had some money stashed away somewhere. More than one mouth dropped when he bought that island."

"Did you know her?"

"His wife? A little, I knew of her. She seemed like a nice girl. Came in here a few times looking for books for herself or the kids. Eventually, she faded away. We didn't see her a lot and then we didn't see her at all. Like you said, can't imagine what living with him was like. We all thought she must have married him for his money, not that he had a whole lot after buying the island. But there he was, only a few years out of high school, buying an island. Turns out his father had left the money to him when he died. It was supposed to last Eustice a lifetime, but he blew it all in one go."

"Did she have any family?" Meg thought for a minute.

"I don't think so. Not around here anyway. If I remember correctly, her parents moved here when she was younger. They died not too long after she married Eustice. Her father had cancer, I remember because we had a fundraiser for him when I was in high school to raise money for his treatments.

"Mark and I are going to give her a proper burial. I feel like I need to." Meg nodded her head, but she looked concerned. It wasn't the response Evelyn had been expecting.

"That's very nice of you."

"She deserves to rest in peace."

"She certainly does. Evelyn, don't get too tied up in all this, okay?"

"I'm not Meg, but I saw the woman pulled out of the water. I feel like I need to see her laid to rest."

"I know, but if you get too attached it can be dangerous. Henry was very impressed with you, by the way."

"Oh yeah, in what way?"

"Well, for one thing, you didn't vomit when they brought

the body up. For another, he can not explain logically how you have a dream about Helen and are then able to lead them to her body. Not that I think they looked all that hard to begin with. Henry doesn't like it when I say that, but the truth of the matter was, they had six bodies to deal with if you include Eustice and his son. There was no sign that the mother had been killed, just a note in the kid's diary saying his mother was there one day and then gone the next."

"Well, I'm glad Henry was impressed, but to be honest, I will be a lot more comfortable when I am no longer having dreams that lead me to bodies."

"I think he is going to be a little weirded out if the murder weapon does end up being a shovel."

"He told you about that? Well, I'm sure that's what it's going to end up being. Especially after last night." Meg smiled at her and took a sip of coffee.

"What makes you so sure?"

"In one of the first dreams I had where I was Helen, I saw a flash of silver before I went down on the ground. While he was dragging me away, I could hear something. I never paid much attention to it because I couldn't figure out what it was, but last night, when I saw Eustice's shovel, I figured out what the sound was."

"And?"

"It was the sound of a shovel being dragged along the ground."

37

Evelyn pulled back into the dock feeling better than she had when she left. After strong coffee and a good conversation with a medium, Evelyn felt like she was in control again. She immediately poured the black salt around the house, whispering a prayer to St. Michael for protection. When she finished, she was standing at the back of the house, her back to the woods where she had seen Eustice. Infused with courage, she walked towards the spot where she had seen him. Eustice was scary because of what he had done in life, but Evelyn would be damned if she was going to let him get to her. He was dead for Christ's sake. He would get no pleasure from seeing the fear in her eyes. That being said, Evelyn could not bring herself to step into the woods by herself. She knew that down a path towards the center of the woods was where Eustice had placed his grave yard where his victims were buried so that he could visit them when he liked and remember their fear at his hands.

Evelyn looked back at the house. She was standing where Eustice would have been standing the night before. It had seemed closer last night. She was sure he had known she was standing there, but it actually would have been difficult to see if anyone was standing in the window. But then the spirit world didn't really rely on 20/20 vision. Evelyn was about to walk back to the house when something caught her eye in the ground. A cut in the ground as if something sharp and heavy had been dragged from where it rested into the woods. Something like the point of a shovel.

Refusing to run, Evelyn walked very quickly back to the house.

"Where have you been?" Mark was in the kitchen as she came in the back door. He was still disheveled from sleep and looking at the clock on the microwave. Evelyn realized it was only eight O'clock.

"I went to see Meg."

"At this hour of the morning? She must have been thrilled. Everything okay?"

"I just had some questions for her."

"About last night?"

"Yeah, she gave me some extra salt stuff to place around the house."

"He really freaked you out, didn't he?" Mark put his hand on her arm.

"It was a bit of a shock to look up and see him there, yeah, but I'm fine now." Evelyn didn't mention what she had just seen in the ground where Eustice would have been standing. To admit it to herself would have erased all the strength she had gained that morning after talking to Meg.

"You look exhausted, Hon. Why don't you try and get some rest?"

"I will in a little bit. You hungry?"

Evelyn tried making breakfast but was too tired to eat. She finally gave in to Mark's suggestion and went upstairs to take a shower. The hot water washed away the previous evening. Her muscles started to relax, and sleep could no longer be delayed. Evelyn fell asleep on the bed with the towel still wrapped around her. She was awakened some hours later by her phone vibrating next to her head. By the time she had realized what was happening and gotten her eyes to focus, it had gone to voicemail. With horror, she realized she was lying naked on the bed, having rolled out of her towel. The number was from her mother's lawyer. She decided to get dressed before calling back. It somehow seemed wrong to have a professional conversation with a lawyer while wearing nothing but a towel. Putting on a pair of jeans and a sweatshirt, she whipped her hair up into a messy bun and made her way downstairs, dialing the number as she went.

"Yes, this is Evelyn Thompson." Evelyn looked serious when she came down the stairs, and Mark gave her a concerned look which she waved off. "No, I'm afraid we are rather remote at the moment. I don't have a scanner or a printer, but I might be able to make arrangements in town." She listened for a while to the other end. "How much longer will you be at the office? I could call you back in about ten minutes. Okay, thank you." And she hung up.

"Everything okay?"

"Stuff with Mom's estate. They found a buyer for the house, they need me to look over the buyer's proposal and either accept it or deny it . Apparently, they have been trying to get a hold of me for a few days. They are worried if there is a delay, they may lose the buyer."

"What are you going to do?"

"Call Meg and see if she knows where there is a scanner/ printer. Where is Julia?"

"Upstairs reading." Evelyn looked at the clock, 5:00 in the afternoon.

"Why did you let me sleep so long?" Mark shrugged.

"You needed the rest, Eve."

"I was asleep on our bed naked."

"I know. I came up to make sure you were all right and there you were. I covered you up."

"Apparently not enough. There were no covers to be seen just now." Mark shrugged again and handed her a tea.

Evelyn took her tea out onto the porch to call Meg. "Thanks Meg." She hung up and stood there in silence for a while 'feeling' the area around her. The air felt light and breezy. No threat of anyone lurking in the woods. Who knew a little salt could work such magic? She turned back into the house. "Meg says the only scanner/printer she knows of is at the sheriff's office. The library doesn't even have one."

"So, you are going to have to go into town?"

"Looks like it. I shouldn't be long. Are you two going to be okay here?" Evelyn looked at her watch. It would be almost 6:00 by the time she got to the office, so she would have to hurry if she was going to make it back before dark.

Mark shrugged in answer to her question. "We'll just continue on as we are. I was going to make tacos for dinner."

"Sounds good. I'll see you in a little bit then." Evelyn grabbed her purse and jacket and went down to the boat, calling the lawyer back on her way to tell them where to send the forms.

Evelyn looked out across the sky as she steered the boat away from the dock. There were some dark clouds off in the distance, and for a second, she worried about leaving. But this offer had to be dealt with. The lawyer had been clear on that. *I won't be that long. Back in an hour.' She said to herself.*

"Gerald ."

"Yeah."

"He's here, I can feel him."

"I know."

"She shouldn't leave. They are going to need her."

"We can't stop her."

"What are we going to do?" Her voice sounded like she was a child. Knowing Vic needed him had always given Gerald courage. He couldn't even remember what he had feared in his father when he was living. Physical pain? Death? None of that applied now, and somehow, yet he still felt fear. It wouldn't hold him back though. Not anymore. He wouldn't stand by and watch Eustice tear apart another family.

"We will do what we can together." And he looked at her. She seemed to have come to the same realization. Their father had already done his worst, so all that was left was fear, and from the look in her eyes, there wasn't much of that anymore.

"Dad? Where's Mom?" Julia came down the stairs looking like she, too, had fallen asleep.

"Had to run into town to sign something for Grandma's estate. They found a buyer for the house."

"When will she be back?" Something in his daughter's voice made him look up.

"Not long. Why? What's the matter?"

"The house feels weird again." Mark didn't feel any different, but he knew better than to dismiss her. "Stay down here and help me cook dinner. Mom will be back in about an hour."

The sun was setting, and within the hour, the house would be surrounded by the darkness of night. Mark secretly hoped that his wife would be back in an hour. Realistically, he didn't see what her presence could do against the darkness, but it seemed like a better idea for them to be all together than apart. She also had the boat, their only means off the island.

Washing the tomatoes in the sink, Mark knew it would not be a normal evening. He had never seen Eustice. Evelyn had, of course, but she hadn't gone into detail about it. He assumed that's who he was looking at, standing on the edge of the woods with a shovel in his hand. He knew Eustice saw him, standing there in the window making dinner. Eustice turned and faded away into the woods again, but it felt like a warning. Mark wasn't sure Eustice cared about a ring of black salt. Cold ran down Mark's back, and he stood frozen until Eustice had completely disappeared into the trees.

"Hurry back dear." He thought to himself. Lightning lit the sky off in the distance. *"Oh good, a storm is coming. Just what the evening needed."*

38

"Hello, I understand you need to use our printer/scanner." The sheriff said, holding the door open for her.

"Yes, thank you. Sorry, to make you stay. The lawyer has apparently been trying to get a hold of me for a few days, so I didn't want to make them wait any longer. It's my mother's house. I didn't think it would sell this fast." Evelyn had seen lightning off in the distance as she crossed over from the island. She wanted to get this done and get back home before the weather hit. With familiarity she would not have normally used, she sat down at the sheriff's desk and opened her email. The sheriff was forced to lean against the file cabinet.

"Things okay at the house?" He asked. Evelyn didn't look at him but shrugged her shoulders in response to his question.

"About the same."

"Meg has really enjoyed having an ally in the ghost debate. She's done everything but say, 'I told you so'." Evelyn found the email from the attorney and after reading the brief instructions, she printed it off.

"She does seem to be enjoying herself more than anyone else. Mark and I still don't know what we think about all of it.

We have a new perspective on it, that is for sure."

"I bet. I was going to call you tomorrow, actually because I got the official report back from the coroner. Helen was killed with something similar to a shovel. She was struck in the back of the head. Looks like the bastard got her while she was running away. There was something else interesting in the report. They found dirt in her mouth." The sheriff could not see the blood fall from Evelyn's face.

"What?" The sheriff pulled a paper out of the folder sitting on his desk and handed it to her. "They found dirt in her mouth and in the upper airway. Pathologist thinks she was alive when he buried her, and he definitely buried her before putting her in the water. It was still there after all this time."

"Jesus Christ." Evelyn said, covering her mouth with her hand while she read what the pathologist had written. "Could he tell if she was conscious when he buried her?"

"No. Not for sure. He suspects she wasn't conscious since there was no dirt under her fingernails, but she has been underwater for a while. It could have washed out. I was hoping you could help me with that part."

"How could I help?"

"What happened in the dream?" The sheriff leaned over his desk and looked her straight in the eye when he asked this. It was effective, but she wished he'd stop doing that. "Um, aah. I was running away from him. In the clearing. I was scared to death because I knew if he caught me, he would kill me and then who would look after the children? I turned to see where he was and something silver hit me in the head. I knew I should move, try and get away, but I couldn't." Her mind was spinning so fast she could hardly find the words. "I don't think she was conscious, but I always wake up in the dream choking on the dirt in my mouth. I don't know if that was what happened to her or not."

"Hmmm." He tossed the paper back onto the file and leaned against the file cabinet again. "The way I see that night playing out is, Helen thinks she knows what Eustice is doing. If she was going to risk her life getting to the mainland or even getting word to us that she thought he was the killer, she wanted proof. So, she stays up late waiting for him. No doubt he came back that night with a new victim. We are almost one hundred percent sure he killed them here and then took them back to the island since we found Marcy Gray dead on the mainland. Instead of calling us, she followed him out to the woods. Saw him burying the body and tried to run back to the house, but he caught up to her. He hit her over the head with the shovel he already had in his hand, dragged her back to the graveyard, and buried her, not really caring if she was really alive or dead. This would explain the grave we found that looked like it had been dug and then filled in again. What I can't figure out is why he then dug her up again and went through the trouble of burying her at sea?" Evelyn put the papers down and leaned across the desk. "I think I can help you there. When I was writing my first book, I spoke with a Criminal Psychologist as part of my research. I reached out to her after our little adventure yesterday."

"What did she say?"

"Eustice didn't want her around the others. He wanted to keep the others there, to visit them when he wanted. Helen dirtied that for him. Maybe it was because she was his wife, maybe it was because he had killed her because she was about to rat him out. You know, he hadn't chosen her to be a victim. I guess we will really never know." A flash of lightning followed closely by a clap of thunder brought Evelyn back to the task at hand.

"Shit. I told him I'd have these back to him twenty minutes ago."

"I'll leave you to it." The sheriff walked into the kitchen with his coffee cup in hand. Evelyn signed the papers where she needed to sign, scanned them, and sent them back. She could hear the rain start just as she got confirmation they had been received.

"Thanks again, Sheriff. Sorry to keep you. And thank you for letting me know about the pathologist's report. Does that mean they are going to release her body soon?"

"Probably."

"Mark and I have been talking, and we were going to see if she could be buried next to her kids. Do you think that's possible?" Another flash of lightning and clap of thunder interrupted her.

"That came up quick, didn't it? Not sure you're going to be going back to the island tonight." The sheriff said. The night had gone pitch black, nothing was visible unless illuminated by lightning.

"Really? You don't think I could make it?"

"The police boat is bigger than that thing you brought over. I could try to get you back if you really need to." Evelyn sighed. She had already kept the man from going home. She didn't want to make him drive through a thunderstorm as well. "No, let me call Mark and let him know I'll at least be late getting back. I told him I would only be an hour." Evelyn dug into her purse and pulled out her phone. Dialing Mark's number, it went straight to voicemail. She hung up and dialed Julia's number.

Julia had run up to her room to get her book. With the storm rolling in, she was planning on staying downstairs at least until her mother got back. She could hear her father downstairs digging out the knives and forks. Lightning flashed outside her window, and a clap of thunder rattled the windows. She looked up to the dark sky moving in quickly over the house. Her vibrating phone made her jump. "Mom, where are you?"

"I'm still at the sheriff's. He isn't sure I'm going to be able to get back tonight with the storm." Another flash of light, and the lights went out in the house.

"Julia?" Evelyn said, a little worried.

"The power just went out." Julia answered, the nervousness clear in her voice. Looking back at the mirror in front of her, it was not her own face that was looking back at her, but the face of a man. A pale, translucent man whose face curled into an evil smile. Julia screamed and instinctively looked behind her. Eustice was there, standing behind her, so close she could smell him. He smelled like wet earth. Julia screamed again. With his smile in place, Eustice grabbed for Julia. Dropping her phone, Julia ran from the room.

"Julia…" Evelyn could hear Julia screaming in the background. Hearing his daughter scream upstairs, Mark dropped the knives and forks and ran up the stairs. Twain left the unattended food and ran after Mark. Julia ran into him on the landing, but she didn't stop. It wasn't comfort she wanted. She wanted to get past him, past him and away from her room. Looking past Julia, Mark saw Eustice appear at the top of the stairs, shovel as always, by his side. Mark wasn't sure what ghosts could do to the living, but he wasn't going to stick around and find out.

"Run…" Evelyn heard Mark's voice in the background.

"MARK!" Evelyn yelled into the phone. She heard Twain bark before the phone cut off. The tone in Mark's voice had told her all she needed to know.

"What's going on?" The sheriff asked, standing with his hand on his belt. He was speaking to Evelyn's back. Evelyn ran out of the sheriff's office, headed back to the boat. She had not bothered with an umbrella or even bothered to zip up her jacket. Grabbing his slicker, the sheriff took off after her.

With blind fear, Evelyn ran down the hill to the boat dock. The rain was hitting her in the face and making the street slippery. Thunder clapped, and the occasional flash of lightning illuminated the street and the path ahead of her. Hitting a puddle, her feet went out from underneath her in front of Meg's book shop. Meg had seen Evelyn running down the road, and thinking she might be heading there for shelter from the storm, was waiting by the door to let her in. Seeing Evelyn fall, Meg opened her door, "You okay?" But Evelyn was up and running again without acknowledging she had even heard Meg. The look on Evelyn's face told Meg she was running against time. Seeing her brother-in-law running down the hill after her in his yellow slicker and sheriff face, Meg grabbed her rain jacket off the hook just inside the door and took off behind them. It was clear something had happened back at the island.

The sheriff's longer stride caught up to Evelyn and over took her. He did not go to her small boat, but instead jumped onto the police boat which was a lot more worthy of being in the water on a night like this. The rain came down so hard now, the sound of it hitting the water was a constant drum. For a moment, Evelyn thought the sheriff had disappeared, his bright yellow jacket gone. A flash of lightning revealed him on a bigger boat to her right. Abandoning her own boat, Evelyn almost fell again trying to slow herself down enough to hop aboard the police boat the sheriff was currently preparing to back out of the dock. Evelyn followed him, pulling the ropes off the dock as she boarded. Meg was right behind her and jumped on as the boat started to back out of the dock. The sheriff looked from one woman to the other until Evelyn yelled, "Go!" Throwing the boat into reverse, they backed out of the dock and started toward the island.

They took shelter under the small canopy over the wheel and captain's chair, yet rain and spray still hit them from all sides. The sheriff was careful backing out, but as soon as he had cleared the dock, he pushed the gear up and sped towards the island with little regard for the weather around them. The blue and red flashing lights revealed a solid wall of rain in front of them, and Evelyn couldn't see anything beyond the front of the boat. For a moment, she worried they couldn't see where they were going, but the sheriff knew these waters better than she did, and even she knew the island was ahead of them.

"What happened?" He yelled once they were on their way.

"I don't know, but something." He nodded his head. That was enough. Turning to Meg she added, "Julia said the lights went out and then she screamed." Meg didn't say what she was thinking, but she didn't think the storm was what caused the lights to go out. If she had to guess, Eustice was using the storm to get what he wanted.

39

"Here he comes." Victoria said. The house felt just like it did when they were living. How did he do that? She felt herself trying not to make a noise, trying to fade into the walls just like she had done all her life. The lights went out. They could feel the energy being sucked out of the house. He was gathering. The girl screamed.

"And there he is." Gerald answered. He knew they should move, go and see what was happening, what they could do to protect the living from their father. But they stayed where they were.

Julia had run past her father and was heading for the door. Mark stood his ground for a moment, watching Eustice walk closer. He could smell the man, the smell of dirt, and could hear the metal of the shovel as it scraped the wood floor. He seemed so solid, yet Mark could see the light switch on the wall through Eustice's chest. Twain was barking at the bottom of the stairs, not sure if he should stay with Mark or follow Julia. At the thought of Julia, Mark ran. There was no doubt in his mind that Eustice wanted her. He took off down the stairs after her, Twain on his heels. Eustice did not run.

The rain hit them in the face like a wall . A flash of lightning showed them the path down to the dock. Julia had wanted to run as far away from the house as possible, but there was no way Mark was going to run into the woods. Grabbing his daughter's arm, they ran to the end of the dock. Mark had half expected to see Evelyn pulling up in the boat, but one look at the water let him know that would not be happening. Wave peaks were hitting the bottom of the dock. The little boat they used to get back and forth would be impossible to handle.

"Dad." Julia was holding his arm tight and trying not to cry. Her hair was soaking, and her clothes hung heavily

"We are going to get out of here, Honey. We are going to get out of here." *But how?* He thought to himself. They could swim it if the water wasn't so choppy. Julia screamed again. Turning, Mark saw that Eustice had made his way out of the house and was now standing on the porch, scanning the woods for a sign of them. A disconcerting smile crept over his face as he saw them trapped at the end of the dock. Twain stood between Eustice and his family, barking and growling. The three of them watched Eustice calmly walk down to the dock.

Mark looked around in desperation for anything to defend them with. There was nothing but an oar from the paddle boards resting on the dock. Not sure what good it would be against a ghost, Mark picked it up and took a defensive stance. Julia followed and picked up the second oar. They weren't going down without a fight.

"Julia, stay behind me." Mark yelled. The water was streaming down his face now, and it was hard to see anything without the occasional flash of lightning. Eustice was now at the top of the hill, the path clear between him and Mark. The creepy grin disappeared from Eustice's face, and his eyes slowly turned to the water behind Mark. Turning to see what had taken his attention away, Mark could barely see the blue and red flashing lights. With the next flash of lightning, he could just make out the front of the boat.

'Hot damn. Evelyn's coming and she brought back up.' Mark thought to himself. It was his turn to sport the grin as he turned back to a seemingly unhappy Eustice.

"It's Mom." Julia yelled.

"You bet your ass it is." Mark felt fingers around his throat, cold fingers that pressed down cutting off his air. He looked at the figure in front of him as Eustice winked at him. Mark grabbed at his neck, pulling away at the invisible hand that was squeezing the air out of him. He opened his mouth wide to try and take in air. The harder he tried, the tighter the grip around his neck. Mark did not take his eyes off Eustice.

"Dad!" Julia came up behind him. "Dad." Mark had gone down on his knees. There was a firm pounding in his head, and a voice in his head told him this was going to be the end. Julia saw the whites of his eyes turn red "Help! No, please." She tried to yell to the boat, but it came out more as sobs. 'Please no, please no, you can't leave me.' Julia tried to say, but she was crying too hard now.

'Where are you going?' She asked.

'I can't watch him kill them, I'm going.' He said. He did not ask her to come along. That would have been asking a lot. She looked at the girl, the fear and heartache clear on her face, and then looked at their father. The smirky grin that was so familiar to them. That smirky grin that had been the background to every beating, every bit of pain. Victoria followed her brother.

Mark was leaning forward now, he could feel the black curtain falling. He tried to fight against it, but it was heavy, and there wasn't much he could do about it. Julia leaned over him screaming . She did not see the white forms materialize in front of them. She did not look up until Mark had taken a deep breath. Mark's eyes opened wide as he inhaled sharply. He coughed and took another breath. Julia looked up to see what had changed and found her view of Eustice blocked by two pale forms. They seemed no more substantial than a whisper, but she could clearly see they were holding hands. Mark continued to cough with lungs that hurt, but he could breathe. The pounding in his head was almost blinding, and he could not make himself stand yet. Grabbing Julia's hand, they backed away to the very end of the dock. Twain moved with them. He had stopped barking and started whimpering instead, dancing from one side of the dock to the other.

'Get out of the way.' Eustice growled at them.

'No.' They could feel the fury in him, but they stayed where they were.

'I'm not going to tell you again.'

'And do what?' Gerald hissed. He had wanted to do this all his life and most of his death. 'What else could you possibly do to me?'

'Stay there and find out.' But Gerald had seen it. It had only been there for half a second, but it was enough for him to see the doubt on Eustice's face. His father didn't know what he was going to do to them, what he could do to them. Grabbing Vic's hand, they would not leave until the living were safe.

"There!" Evelyn yelled into the sheriff's ear. She could see Mark, Julia and Twain on the end of the dock. The sheriff turned on the spotlight and pointed it at the figures on the dock. Why was Mark sitting? Julia turned and waved. "What the hell are they doing out there?" The sheriff asked. Evelyn didn't care

what they were doing out there. She just wanted to get them
and get back to land.   Mark didn't not turn to look at them, but
kept his eyes in the direction of the house. Following the path
from the dock to the house, Evelyn saw Eustice standing at the
top of the hill. Panic struck her. She did not see the pale figures
between him and her family. The boat slowed to an almost stop.

"What the hell are you doing?" Evelyn turned to the sheriff.

"Figuring out what's going on." The sheriff's eyes were on
the dock. Evelyn looked to Meg for help. Meg looked up. She
had spent the entire trip mumbling a prayer to St. Michael to
protect them.

"He's strong. He's very strong."

"What the hell does that mean?" Evelyn yelled. She looked
at the dock and could see the fear in her daughter's eyes. The
sheriff was watching what was happening on land as they
neared the end of the dock.

"Get them out of there!" Evelyn had never yelled at the
police before. The sheriff looked down at her. It was clear he
had reservations about getting any closer, but he put the boat in
a low gear, and they slowly headed towards the dock. Hearing
the engine of the police boat getting closer, Julia grabbed her
father under the shoulder and tried to drag him as close to the
end of the dock as she could. Mark's head was still pounding,
and his throat felt swollen and raw, making each breath painful.
He didn't dare take his eyes off of Eustice, but Eustice seemed to
have noticed they weren't alone anymore.

*Their father was no longer looking through them. His attention
seemed to be drawn out over the water. Gerald was afraid to look for
fear that his father would try something if not watched at all times, but
he felt the heat of anger rising in his father and turned to see what had
irritated him. The sheriff.*

The sheriff kept a steady eye on Eustice as they pulled up. Even dead, it was clear that Eustice was the one to watch though he was not sure how he was going to react if Eustice did something. They pulled up alongside the dock, and Evelyn almost leapt the remaining inches to the dock. It was clear something had happened to her husband since Julia had to drag him to the boat. Meg had joined Evelyn in getting Mark into the boat. The dog was the last one in, still willing to fight Eustice until his family was safe. The storm had not weakened, lightning flashing every few seconds. Henry did not look away from Eustice who was standing almost exactly where he had been that summer day all those years ago. The shovel at Eustice's side was a shotgun that could be raised at any moment. Instinctively, his hand went for his gun,and he moved towards the front of the boat to get a clear shot. He locked eyes with Eustice over the water and felt the cold run from his chest down his arms. Henry grabbed his chest, looking down to see where the injury was to find nothing there. He looked back at Eustice, a wicked smile crawling across his face. Henry felt a tightening of his chest with pain so bad, he dropped to his knees.

"Jesus Christ." He said, groaning, leaning over. It felt like hot pain running down his shoulder.

"Henry!" Meg yelled. Leaving Mark and Evelyn to sort themselves out, she knelt down next to her brother in-law. "What's happening?" Meg asked him. Henry could not speak, every ounce of energy being spent on staying conscious and breathing, but he was still looking at Eustice. Meg followed his line of sight. "No!" Meg eased him down onto the bottom of the boat, hoping that if he was no longer looking at Eustice, the connection would be broken.

"Is he having a heart attack?" Evelyn asked. Meg was white faced as she looked up.

"It's Eustice." Closing her eyes, she added. "He recognizes Henry. We've gotta get out of here.   Eustice's energy is just too strong." Evelyn wanted to help, but the only person who could drive the boat was the one having the heart attack. "He needs medical help!" The panic in Meg's face reminded Evelyn that Henry was the only family Meg had left, and he was dying in front of her. Eustice and the white figures on land forgotten, Evelyn's mind raced. She saw the radio and picked it up. She pushed the button and said, "This is the Police boat. We need medics. The sheriff is hurt." Taking her finger off the button, she realized she didn't know who was on the other end, and with the thunder and rain, she couldn't hear if they had been any reply. Hopefully, help would come. She looked at the wheel and controls on the boat. There were a lot more than she was used to, but the basics seemed to be the same. She pushed the boat forward slowly and turned it around, which was not made any easier by the water pushing the boat against the dock. Julia let out a scream behind her, and Evelyn turned to look. Julia was being pulled out of the boat by Eustice's white hands. Evelyn lunged to the back of the boat, grabbing Julia's leg and pulled her back into the boat. She smelled his earthy scent, but this time she was not afraid of him. Eustice snarled and growled at her. "Defend us in battle, protect us against evil…" Meg chanted while looking Eustice in the face. She had come up beside Eveyln, and was pulling Julia's other leg back into the boat.

"Let go of my daughter, you sonofabitch!" With this there was an extremely loud clap of thunder and a white cloud formed on the beach. *"I can take care of him."* Evelyn heard the words in her head. The voice was familiar. She had heard it in her dreams.

Eustice seemed surprised when Julia slipped from his grip. The smirk gone from his face, Evelyn pulled Julia back into the boat and pushed her towards the captain's chair. Evelyn's eye was caught by something on the beach. The white cloud had formed into a woman with her hair and dress blowing in the wind. *"Helen."*

Helen was focused on her husband who was now aware of her presence. Having let go of Julia, he turned his attention to the beach, and seeing his wife, Eustice let out a primal roar. Helen didn't move. She calmly closed her eyes and lifted both of her arms. To Eustice's surprise, he was lifted off the ground. Taking their mother's lead, the children turned towards their father and likewise closed their eyes and lifted their hands. Eustice rose off the dock, his hands being held at his side by invisible powers. His face contorted with the effort of trying to regain control. Helen opened her eyes and watched as he lifted into the air. It was her turn to give a knowing smile. As one, she and her children moved their hands, and Eustice moved over the water, and everyone smiled at the fear in his face. With no ceremony and no hesitation, they moved their arms wide. Clearly not happy to be over the water, Eustice struggled harder against his invisible bindings, kicking wildly. With a drop of their arms, Helen and her children consigned Eustice to the briny deep. He didn't even make a splash.

The passengers of the police boat watched in stunned silence. With the appearance of Helen, Henry had felt the tension in his chest ease. His arm still hurt, but he was slowly regaining his breath. He was not the only person on the boat who wondered what they had witnessed. Evelyn stared at the surface of the water where Eustice had disappeared and half expected him to resurface and take his revenge. There was nothing. Just the rain hitting the water.

The sheriff groaned from the bottom of the boat and brought Evelyn back to pressing matters. She looked at Mark as well who was lying with his eyes closed, every effort given to breathing. "Mark!" He gave no sign of hearing her. Evelyn leaned down next to his ear and said, "Mark, Honey, if you can hear me, stay with us, please. Don't go yet. I love you." Kissing his cheek, she went back to the captain's chair and threw the boat into reverse.

"Let's get the hell out of here." She said.

"Hold on." Meg said, looking behind them towards the island.

Helen had moved closer to her children. Her white dress billowed around her. She reached out a hand to each of them.

"Time to go now." She said to them. They all turned away from the house and went towards the light that had opened to the left of the house. There was a mighty roar from the water, and Eustice shot out, yelling with anger, and flew toward them, his shovel raised. The children cowered, their mother standing protectively over them. "Nnnnooooo!" Evelyn and Meg yelled, lunging to the front of the boat. With an anger that had been kept suppressed for decades, Helen lunged towards her husband. Her face was no longer one of calm reserve. Her features turned into a growling beast, teeth sharp and mouth wide. The wind gathered behind her, and from behind Meg and Evelyn. Coming together around Eustice, it twisted into a cyclone and spun him back into the water. His strength was gone. Helen knew he would not be able to come back. She knew

how hard it was to escape deep water. Helen looked at him no more. Calmly taking her children's hands again, they continued towards the light. With a gentle nod, she watched them walk through one by one. Before she went through herself, she looked out at the boat bobbing in the water. The falling rain was once again the only sound.

"*Thank you, mothers.*" Giving a little wave, Helen stepped through the light herself, and darkness returned to the beach.

"Can we leave now?" The sheriff moaned from the bottom of the boat. Evelyn, with new confidence, turned the police boat around and headed towards the mainland. She could see a faint glow of the town's lights and used it to guide her. Julia clung to Mark. Twain sat protectively next to him. Meg was crumpled on the floor on the boat with Henry who she was lovingly holding against her, pulling her raincoat up over his head in a vain attempt to protect him from the rain.

As they got closer to the mainland, it was clear that someone had heard the call Evelyn put out. The rest of the department, as well as an ambulance, was waiting for them at the docks. Their flashing lights directed Evelyn where she needed to go.

40

Once they got back to town, everything happened so quickly it
would take days before Evelyn was able to make sense of it all.
The police boat was no sooner pulled up beside the dock than
the deputies were there pulling everyone out of the boat. Julia
was carried out in the arms of one of the bigger deputies. Mark
and the sheriff were loaded onto back boards and carried away.
The EMTs took one look at the soaked and battered group, and
decided that everyone should be transported to the hospital.

"What happened out there, boss?" One of the deputies
asked before the sheriff and Meg were taken to the hospital.
"Attacked." Was all he was able to say. The deputies ran back
to the police boat and took off for the island. Meg started to tell
them there was no point, but realized it would take too long to
explain and let them go. Mark started to regain consciousness.
Although he wasn't able to speak, Evelyn knew he would be
okay. Battered, but okay. Julia had just managed to stop crying,
and she was leaning on Evelyn's shoulder in the ambulance.
She objected when Evelyn told the EMT Julia needed to be
checked out. Julia argued they only needed to pay attention to
her father. "They have multiple doctors, Honey. Someone needs

to look at you."

"Twain?" Julia says. The dog had jumped into the ambulance with them.

"That dog can't come with us." The EMT informed them. Evelyn couldn't leave him. He was soaking wet, and he was as exhausted as the rest of them and didn't want to leave their side.

"I can take him, ma'am." Said a young deputy who had been left behind to man the office. "I'll take him to the station, get him dried and fed up. I think there's some turkey in the fridge I can give him." Tearful, Julia jumped out of the ambulance and knelt down before Twain, cupping his head in her hands. "Who's a good boy? We'll be okay. You go with the nice man, get dried off, and get something to eat. I'll see you tomorrow." The dog licked her face and his tail wagged.

"Ma'am, we have to go." The EMT sayid to Evelyn.

"You are a good boy, and I love you." Julia kissed him on the head and jumped back into the ambulance. Twain barked, but his tail wasn't wagging. Evelyn held Mark's hand all the way to the hospital. He squeezed her hand and he squeezed back.

When they got to the hospital, Mark was hurried back, and a nurse came to get Julia and take her back for examination. Evelyn was left standing in the harsh artificial lights, soaking wet and alone, not knowing where to go. She could feel what little energy she had left seeping out of her. Finally, a kind nurse wrapped a heated blanket around her and guided her to a waiting area. Without asking, the nurse brought her a hot cup of coffee. "It will help with the shock and the cold." Evelyn was so grateful, she could not find the words and so smiled and nodded. The warmth of the coffee warmed her, which made her even more tired, and she slipped into a trance, replaying the

events of the evening in her mind. They didn't make any sense.
How could such a thing happen? But here she was, sitting in
the hospital as a result of it, so it must have happened. She
hoped she never had to see that look on her daughter's face
again. Her heart gave a lurch as she remembered the crumpled
form of Mark on the dock. The look on Eustice's face when he
grabbed Julia made her shiver, so she took another sip of coffee
to chase it away. She didn't realize Meg had sat down next to
her until she spoke.

"You okay? You look like you've seen a ghost." Meg said.
Evelyn turned her head slowly to look at her and was greeted by
a smiling face. Evelyn smiled, and soon the two were laughing
hysterically. Evelyn knew this wasn't right or proper, but the
harder she tried to stop laughing, the more she laughed. Finally,
they managed to get a grip, wiped away the tears, and Meg said,
"One of the doctors just asked me what kind of attack it was.
The deputies radioed back, and they said it looked like an
interrupted robbery." The smile on Meg's face disappeared.
"Apparently, Eustice made a bit of a mess when he chased Julia
through the house. Muddy footprints everywhere. They are
searching the island now for any signs of the attackers." Evelyn
didn't want to think about what happened at the house before
she got there. She could only remember the fear in her
daughter's voice when she had called. She took another sip of
coffee.

"I feel bad for those fellas searching the island in this
weather, but they wouldn't believe me if I told them so…" and
Meg shrugged her shoulders.

"How is Henry? How did you get to go back with him?
They won't let me back with Mark."

Meg shrugged, "They know Henry is all I have left. He's

going to be fine. Thankfully. They are treating it as a heart attack . I'm not sure modern medicine has a treatment for what really happened. Any word on Mark? Julia?"

"No, but they will be okay. Julia was just really shaken up as you can imagine. Mark was okay. I'm not sure he can speak, but he will be okay." Evelyn took Meg's hand. "Thank you. For everything. You and Henry. You were both having quiet lives until we showed up and stirred up the ghosts of the past. I'm so sorry." And tears welled up in her eyes. Meg squeezed her hand and shook it. "Don't you start that. You can't run from the past forever, Evelyn, and if it hadn't happened now, it would have happened eventually. Besides, if you hadn't come along, Helen would still be on the ocean floor wondering if she would ever be found. The world now knows that woman did not run off and leave her poor children to deal with that horrible man. You did that."

"Ma'am." A doctor appeared at the door and gestured for Evelyn to follow him. "I understand you've had a bit of an evening?"

"You could say that. How are they?"

"Your daughter is fine, just shaken up. I've prescribed some sleeping pills. What she needs more than anything right now is rest. There is some bruising on her arm and her lower legs, but no other physical trauma. Your husband sustained severe trauma to his throat. It looks like someone tried to choke him. There are deep bruises forming, and the trauma has caused swelling. Obviously, the throat is not where you want swelling to occur, so we have given an injectable NSAID, and we are going to keep him overnight to monitor the situation. Whoever they were, they tried hard to get rid of him. The bruising goes into the muscle layer of the throat. We took an x-ray of his neck to make sure the trachea and esophagus weren't damaged, and they do not appear to be. His blood oxygen is normal, but he isn't able to answer our questions, and that is normal considering the level of trauma. His vocal chords aren't able to function like they normally would right now. He does seem to be comprehending what we are saying. What we worry about in these situations is brain damage caused by a lack of oxygen to the brain, and the swelling of the throat affecting breathing. We are going to give the anti-inflammatories some time to work, and then will evaluate him again, but right now it looks like he should make a full recovery."

"Can I see them?"

"Your daughter asked the same thing, and I believe they are both in your husband's room." With the blanket still around her shoulders, Evelyn walked quickly to Mark's room. She was running by the time she got there. The lights were off, and it took a moment for her eyes to adjust to the dark room. Mark was in bed, the EKG line shining bright above him. At first, she couldn't find Julia. She was curled up next to her father in the hospital bed, her head resting on his shoulder. Mark's hand rested on the blanket he had pulled up over her, and his head was resting against Julia's, as if he'd kissed her forehead and fallen asleep. Pulling a chair up next to the bed, Evelyn laid her head on the bed, placing one of her hands across Mark's legs to Julia's, encircling them both. They were all together, and right now, that was all that mattered. Closing her eyes, the exhaustion was about to pull Evelyn to sleep when she felt a hand on her shoulder. It was Mark's other hand. He didn't not open his eyes but gave her a half grin and a squeeze on her shoulder before falling asleep.

<h1 style="text-align:center">41</h1>

"What are you doing? I thought you would be at the hospital with Mark." Evelyn had been checking the small boat to see if she had enough gas to get to the island and back. She nearly jumped into the water when Meg spoke from behind her.

"Jesus Meg! I don't need any more surprises after last night." Meg smiled sympathetically.

"Sorry. I'm just surprised to see you out after yesterday. I thought you would be at the hospital taking it easy."

"I could say the same thing to you. Julia is there with him. How is Henry doing?"

"Good. I just talked to him. He's had breakfast and said it tasted terrible. They are treating him for a heart attack, so he is on a heart friendly diet. Where are you going?" Meg knew the answer to this. It was the same place she was going, but she wanted to know if it was for the same reason.

"To the island. I was going to grab our things. Needless to say, we will not be going back there." The two women looked at each other. Evelyn had told herself at least a hundred times this was the reason she was going back. It was a completely logical reason to go back to the island, unlike the real reason she wanted to go back, which made no sense at all. To see if there was anything left of the events of last night and to help convince herself that it really happened.

"Mind if I join you? I was heading there myself. I just need to see it one more time." For some reason, coming from Meg, it didn't sound as crazy as when Evelyn said it to herself. She was glad for the company. There was no telling what she would find when she got over there.

"Of course, come on." Meg hopped in, and the women made their way over to the island. The scene could not be more different. The sky was clear today, fluffy white clouds hanging high in the sky, and the water was calm. Evelyn had no trouble navigating her way, but even in the light of day, the island made her heart beat faster, and when the dock and the house came into view, Evelyn slowed the boat . They said nothing, but both were looking for any evidence of what happened the night before. Bringing the boat up slowly alongside the dock, Evelyn looked at Meg.

"Anything?" Meg shook her head 'no'. Evelyn had gone from doubting Meg's abilities to relying on them.

The breeze was blowing through the trees and everything seemed extraordinarily ordinary.

"Amazing isn't it?"

"Mmmm." The two women made their way up to the house. Evelyn half expected to see Eustice sitting on the couch waiting for them.

"He's not here, Evelyn. You can relax."

"He was dead before, and that didn't stop him." Meg went up stairs to get Julia's things, and Evelyn quickly packed up her and Mark's. They met on the front porch, both slightly out of breath from hauling the luggage down the stairs. Evelyn stopped and looked at the path that would take them back to the boat.

"You know what bothers me?" Evelyn asks.

"What?"

"Why now? Why did it all happen this week? According to all of you, this has been going on for years, so why did it all come to a head this week?" Evelyn sat down on top of one of the suitcases. She was at the top of the hill looking down at the dock. Everything was so calm, there was hardly a ripple in the water. Meg came up next to her and sat on another suitcase.

"I've been wondering the same thing. Spent half the night and all of this morning thinking about it." In truth, it had been one of the reasons she had wanted to come out to the island. "I mean there was energy in the house for the first time in years, but that doesn't explain everything. There had been construction going on in the house before that. Things happened, but nothing on this scale. Can I be perfectly honest with you?"

"I really don't know what you could tell me at this point that would surprise me. Not after what I saw last night."

"I think it was because there was a mother here."

"Why would that make a difference?"

"Eustice came because there was energy in the house and, not to put too fine a point on it, but there was a young girl here." A shiver went down Evelyn's spine. Worrying about living men and how they saw her daughter was bad enough. "I think the children had powers for the first time, and also, there was someone in the house their own age, something that would have been a novelty even when they were living. Eustice kept them so isolated."

"So, bringing Julia here was what stirred everything up?"

"I think it definitely got Eustice moving, and the kids. I'm not sure it's what brought Helen." Meg looked at her sideways.

"I'm not following you." If Evelyn was truthful with herself she thought she knew why, but she thought it might sound less nuts coming from Meg.

"That scene on the beach. Helen finally got her kids away from Eustice and sent Eustice to the sea, and she chose last night to do it. Do you remember the moment it happened?"

"I can honestly say, Meg, that I will never forget a single detail of last night no matter how long I live."

"Eustice looked like he was going to strike her. He was going after her and the children. We yelled 'No,' didn't we?"

"Yeah, and then she made the wind do that thing and blew him into the water."

"The wind came from both directions. Ours as well as hers. I think Helen needed the help of other mothers." Evelyn stared at her. "You're a mother, what do you do when you see a kid out on their own?"

"Look for the parents."

"If that child wandered into traffic, would you ignore it and wait for the parent to deal with it?"

"No, I'd get them out of harm's way."

"We yelled last night at a man who had killed more than one woman, who would have continued killing if he hadn't been killed, and we did it without thinking. We did it because he was going to harm those children. We did it because we are mothers. There is a power in that. Look at you last night. Hardly driven a boat before, and you not only drove a boat you weren't familiar with, but through a horrible storm and towards unknown danger because you knew your daughter and husband needed you. There's a power in that, and Helen harnessed it to get her kids free from Eustice at long last. I think that's why you had the dreams you did. She knew you would listen. I am almost convinced that she is the one I have felt out here but haven't been able to find. Eustice was so scary in life that they feared him even in death. Last night the children protected Mark. Helen couldn't watch while Eustice hurt Julia, and we couldn't watch him hurt those kids."

"Why the water? He just kind of disappeared. Was it because that was where he put her body?"

"Maybe, but I think it had more to do with the fact that Eustice couldn't swim. She placed him in his worst fear and watched him sink."

"I like her style."

"Justice if you ask me."

They both looked out over the water for a long time before Evelyn said, "It is very humbling to get to this age and realize you know so little about the world."

"Makes you wonder what else we may not know." Meg answered. Evelyn got up and picked up the suitcase again.

"I'm happy to wait a few more years before finding out, if that's all right?" Evelyn said pushing one suitcase in front of her and dragging the other one behind her. Meg smiled broadly as she flung Julia's bag over her shoulder.

"How many books did she bring? Good Lord."

42

"How are you feeling?"

"Like someone tried to kill me by squeezing my throat. How's the sheriff?" Mark whispered. His voice was dry, and he had to work hard to make himself heard.

"Fine, it wasn't a heart attack, but Meg says they are treating it like it was since they can't figure out what it was."

"When am I getting out of here?"

"I spoke to the doctor, and they are thinking tomorrow as long as you continue to improve."

"How is Julia?"

"She was in here earlier, wasn't she?"

"You know what I mean. How is she?" Evelyn did know what he meant, and the truth was she didn't know. She didn't even know how she felt.

"She's quiet. I think we are all still processing what happened last night. I went over this morning and got our things."

"You went back there by yourself?" Mark was up on his elbows and trying to yell, but his voice wouldn't go farther than a whisper.

"I ran into Meg on the dock, so she went with me. They aren't there anymore anyway. The whole place feels different. I can't tell if it's just because we know what happened there or what, but it actually seems heavier, like the island and the house were pretending that there was nothing wrong, and now there isn't any point."

"I wish you hadn't gone back."

"We needed our things." Evelyn said, shrugging.

"Where are we going to stay?" Mark asked. He didn't really care as long as it wasn't that house.

"I'm at a B&B until you get out of here, and then I guess we will go home." Mark leaned back and looked grumpy. "What?"

"This is our vacation, and so far, I feel like it hasn't really been one. We've uncovered a body and a family of demented ghosts. We need a vacation more now than when we got here."

"Can't argue with that. Where do you want to go?"

"Can't we stay here? Surely the rental company will give us a refund after last night." Evelyn was too tired to think about going around with the rental company at the moment. "I'll look into it." Mark had a horrible bruise that took up almost the entirety of his neck. He caught her looking at it, and his hand went to it.

"He wanted Julia." They locked eyes. "I was prepared to protect her until I took my last breath. You always say that about your kids, but I would have Evvy. Last night was the worst night of my life. I almost died, but I can't help but feel pleased with myself. I know what I'm made of now, and I'm not disappointed." He grabbed her hand, tears welling up in her eyes. She had come very close to losing him. "I was really glad to see that police boat, though."

"I've never been so scared in my life." She said through

sobs. "I didn't know what I was going to find when I got there. I can't say I'm as pleased with myself as you are, though. I saw you were in a bad way, but my first thought was getting Julia out of there. I was worried about you, but I don't think I took a breath until she was on that boat." He squeezed her hand because the tears were running down her face now.

"I know, love. I wouldn't have had it any other way though."

Before she left the hospital, Evelyn went down the hall to see how the sheriff was doing. Meg and she had left the docks together, and after stashing the luggage at the B&B, had walked to the hospital together, only parting when Meg went to the sheriff's room. Meg was sitting in the chair next to the sheriff's bed. They were both smiling.

"Glad to see you doing so well." Evelyn said.

"Glad to be alive and feeling surprisingly well, all things considered. How's Mark?"

"Feeling much the same way actually. They are probably going to let him out tomorrow. What about you?"

"I'm trying to talk them into letting me out today. They want to run more tests to try and figure out what happened, but we all know they aren't going to find anything."

"You still get to take it easy for a while." Meg reminded him. "Your heart went through some trauma yesterday regardless of whether they can find anything or not." The sheriff's face went serious for a split second before the smile returned.

"How is Julia?" He asked, obviously no longer wanting the attention to be on him.

"All right, all things considered. She's asleep in the room, and Twain is standing guard."

"Meg said you went back to the island today."

"Yeah, just before coming here actually. She helped me get our stuff."

"I haven't decided if that was practical or stupid."

"Let's go with practical then." Evelyn said.

"I guess you guys are going to go back home now? Can't say that I blame you."

"Mark wants to stay. He says we need a vacation more now than ever."

"I would agree with that. Is there a problem with staying?" Meg asked.

"I'm sure the rental company would give us a refund if I could figure out how to explain to them what happened. If we had the money, I would more than gladly stay. Anyway, I better get back to Julia. Glad to see you doing so well Sheriff. Thank you for all your help last night."

Evelyn went back to check on Julia. They got dinner together and then went back to the hospital to be with Mark. Evelyn's phone rang.

"Hello?"

"Evelyn, it's Meg. Are you at the hospital?"

"Yeah, why?"

"Henry's deputy just called. The house is on fire."

"What house?"

"The one on the island. He just heard the call go out on the radio. Someone reported seeing flames and called the fire department."

"How did it happen?"

"No idea, but you should be able to get your refund from the rental company now. You might be able to see the flames if you look out the window. They are going to let it burn, not much choice, actually, since they can't get the trucks over there."

"What is it?" Mark asked.

"The rental house is on fire. That was Meg. They are going to have to let it burn because they can't get the fire trucks over there." Evelyn got up and went to the window. It wasn't hard to figure out where the house was. A soft orange light was coming from that direction.

"What caused it?" Julia asked standing behind her.

"They don't know yet."

"Good thing we got our stuff out of there today then." Mark said. He had gotten out of his bed and was watching as well. It seemed fitting to Evelyn that the house no longer stood. She did feel that buildings somehow remembered what had happened within their walls. Like when old churches are converted to loft apartments. They somehow always still feel church like. Or court houses. She remembered the first time she went to D.C. and walked through the capitol building. She could feel all the history that had gone on there. Too much had happened in that house for it to ever be a normal house again. Watching it burn seemed like watching the final chapter be written. There would be no more to tell now.

43

Evelyn was surprised to see such a large group of people gathered, but perhaps she shouldn't have been. The recovery of Helen's body and the burning of the house shortly thereafter had gotten a lot of coverage in the local papers. The sheriff had told her Helen had no family they were aware of. She had expected it to be herself and maybe a few other people, but there was a sizable crowd standing out in front of the small church. The sheriff was there looking very smart in his dress uniform, and a number of other officers were also there. Seeing Evelyn's questioning look, he offered, "Helen was a victim of Eustice as much as any other. The town has come to give her a good send off. We didn't forget about her. Good to see you, Mark." And the sheriff offered his hand.

"And you, Sheriff."

"There is a seat for your family in one of the front pews, Evelyn."

"That will be reserved for her friends, surely."

"There were few of those. Eustice made sure of that. You found her body. She seemed to want you to find her body. I'm sure she won't mind."

Because of the circumstances, Helen having been dead for so many years and being isolated for years before that, the service was rather generic. There were no stories, no remembrances. It seemed no one really knew enough about her to offer any specifics. This more than anything brought the tears to Evelyn who, to her great surprise, found herself standing at the front of the church. All eyes on her. The minister looked confused, but he stopped talking and gave her the floor.

"None of you know me. We rented the house on the island recently. I didn't know anything about Helen, or her family, until we got here. I think the one thing that could be said about Helen was, she loved her kids. I think all the parents here can imagine what she must have gone through trying to protect her children from their own father. Especially as isolated as she was. The fear that must have absolutely consumed her on a daily basis wondering what was going to happen next. We don't know if she knew what Eustice really was, we think she knew about the killings and that may be one of the reasons she was killed." Evelyn looked at the sheriff. How was she going to say what she wanted without saying how she knew what she knew. "Out of all Eustice's victims, Helen may be the most tragic. As a mother, I know what I fear most in the world is leaving my daughter. It isn't the death itself that I fear. It's leaving her. Who will protect her? Who will love her like I love her? With Helen, I can only imagine these feelings were amplified by the environment they were living in. She had to wonder what would happen to her children if she wasn't there to protect them. Helen Sinclair was a mother, and I truly hope that she can now find some peace with her children. I can only hope that the eternity they will now have together can in some way make up for the years they spent apart. Thank you." There was sporadic clapping as she took her seat again.

"Good job honey." Mark whispered to her.

"She would have loved that." Meg said, on her other side. Evelyn worried what the town thought about a tourist speaking at the funeral of one of their own, but she felt better for having said it. For a week Evelyn had spent every night feeling the fear Helen felt. It had not been for herself, it had been for her kids. Accused of leaving them to deal with their father on their own, Evelyn thought it needed to be stated clearly that the last thing Helen had wanted was to leave her children.

At the graveside, Evelyn watched as the coffin was lowered down into the earth. She noticed with joy that there were three names on the headstones Helen, Victoria, and Gerald . The minister uttered the words 'rest in peace' and a sob escaped from Evelyn. She hadn't even known it was there. She stepped away from the crowd, not wanting to be heard. The sheriff came up beside her. "You all right?" The tears kept coming, and at first Evelyn tried to hold them back, embarrassed by her emotion. 'Cry for her, someone should.' She told herself and the tears flowed freely. She took the sheriff's offered shoulder and said, "Thank you."

"For what?"

"For giving her back her children." And she looked at the headstones. He followed her line of sight.

"Well, of course."

"All she wanted was for them to be safe. She couldn't be with them safely in life. Here, he can't touch them."

"She was a good mother. Lord knows what she had to put up with out there all by herself. Come on, let's go raise a glass in her memory." His arm still strong over her shoulder, the sheriff turned her back towards the car. Mark and Julia were already there. Mark had been released from the hospital just that morning and still wasn't back to his normal self. "We are going to go raise a glass to Helen." The sheriff said, "Care to join us?"

"I think I'm going to take them back to the room. I'll meet you there." Evelyn said, looking at Mark who raised his hand.

"I have needed a beer for two days now. Doc said there was no reason I couldn't have just one."

"I want to come too, Mom." Julia said. She looked so grown up now. That night had taken her from teenager to adult. Evelyn nodded her head and got into the car. Meg met them at the bar, and together they all raised a glass.

"To Helen. May you find the peace you deserve." Meg said, raising her glass.

"Did you ever find out what caused the fire at the house?" Evelyn asked.

"Lightning, according to the fire marshall." The shrimp answered.

"There wasn't a storm that night."

"A storm no, but witnesses saw lightning off in the distance not far from the island. Fire marshall was even able to pinpoint where the lightning hit the building. Good news for you, though, because now you can get your money back on what has to be the worst holiday beach house ever rented."

"It was good news, actually. They called this morning to let us know we would be getting a full refund."

"Good news, that means you can stick around and have a proper vacation. We are determined to prove to you there is more to this town than death, murder, and the undead." Meg said smiling, but Evelyn did not return her smile. She had been wanting to avoid telling them, but to say nothing now would be too close to lying.

"We won't be able to stay, actually. Mark and I paid for Helen's head stone, and, as you know, they are not cheap. We leave in the morning to go back home and salvage what is left of the summer." Meg's face fell, and the sheriff, who always looked a little grumpy, looked grumpier.

"You paid for her headstone?" Meg asked.

"It's ridiculous, I know. But I'm the one who had the dreams that led to the discovery of her body. I didn't know her in life, but I feel like I got to know her in her last moments, and I couldn't bear the thought of her being put in the ground without a marker. It seemed like just what Eustice would want." Tears started to well up in her eyes again. She squeezed Mark's arm. "There will now be a head stone stating her name, when she was born, when she died, and that she was a loving mother. I know nothing about Helen, but I know that. She was a loving mother."

"To loving mothers." The sheriff raised his glass and then drank the contents.

44

The next morning, Henry and Meg were at the B&B to see them off. "I can't help but think you are going to give a sigh of relief when you see us drive off." Evelyn said to the both of them.

"Please, this town needed to be shaken up. I'm just sorry you aren't going to stay and let us show you what a great town this place is."

"We'll be back." Mark said, bringing one of the cases out of the room.

"Is that a promise?" The sheriff asked.

"A guarantee. If I know my wife, there is a book about to be written, and it is our custom to take a trip after each book. We have already agreed we are coming back here."

"Plus, they have the coolest book shop here." Julia piped up. She was smiling, which was good to see. "Do you sell online Meg? My friends are asking."

"I'm not, but I will look into it, Honey. I have to keep you and your friends supplied with books." Meg gave the teenager a hug. Julia was a full head taller than Meg.

"And you have to come back for a reading as soon as you get that book out." Meg said, giving Evelyn a hug.

"You can count on that. After all, it is going to have some characters I think you will recognize. You don't mind do you?"

"Mind what, if you write about this? Why would I?"

"It's your town, it's your lives. I've never written non-fiction before. We'll see how it goes."

"Oh, I think you are still going to have to list it as fiction. No one is going to believe this really happened. I look forward to selling it."

"Make sure you change names to protect the identity of the innocent." The sheriff added.

"Don't worry, Henry, I'll make sure no one can trace it back to you. I'm really going to miss you guys."

"Well, friend us on Facebook . Call me when you get home and get back here as soon as you can." Meg said, giving Evelyn a hug.

"That sounds like a plan." Evelyn said.

"Honey, we better go if we are going to get there on time." Mark added. With one more round of hugs, they piled into the car, rolling down the window so Twain could stick his head out. With waves, Meg and Henry stood and watched as the family pulled out of the parking lot and joined the main road out of town. Twain barked, his blonde hair blowing in the wind, and then they were gone. They both let out a long sigh.

"I'm going to miss them." Meg said.

"Miss them? They were nice, but they were nothing but trouble the entire time they were here. I for one will be getting a good night's rest tonight." They turned to walk back to the shop.

"I would have thought you of all people would have been grateful for what they did when they were here. You solved a mystery that had been bothering you for years now."

"I do feel better. I knew Helen hadn't run away from her kids. That turned-up grave always bothered me too." He was kicking rocks along the road as they walked.

"Not to mention Eustice has been put to rest at last and forever."

"Yeah, the whole town feels lighter now."

"Well then...what's the problem?" The sheriff gave her a sideways glance before continuing to kick rocks.

"Meg, when you first came to me and told me that you were speaking to the dead, I thought you had snapped. I didn't say anything because you seemed better. You were able to function, which was a damned sight better than what you had been. Who cared if you now thought you could speak to the dead?"

"You thought I was crazy?" The sheriff nodded. " Imagine waking up one day having had a great conversation with your husband, but he's dead. Scared the crap out of me." Meg said, without looking at him. Henry stopped walking.

"Did it?"

"Of course it did. All these other people started showing up, wanting to talk to me. All of them deader than the last."

"Why didn't you get help?" Meg looked him in the eye.

"Because I couldn't give them up, Henry. I didn't give a damn if I had to sort through the problems of every dead person there was if it let me see my boys." Meg choked up talking about them for the first time in a long time. Henry reached out for her arm.

"Well, after the events of the last week, I can't deny what you are. I'm sorry I ever doubted you, but I can't deny it any further. What I can't explain is how a woman like Evelyn came here having never communicated with the dead before and then helps find a dead woman's body through dreams she had."

"Oh, I think Evelyn is going to find that ability was there all along. Helen chose her because she was a mother, but Evelyn was able to hear her. I think Evelyn is going to find she can communicate with the other side more than she thought."

"You don't think things will go back to normal now that she's gone?"

"Probably not."

"I think she's going to be disappointed to hear that."

"Probably not as much as you would think."

They were driving the windy roads that connected the town to the city. From there, they would get on the interstate that would take them home. The road was lined with pine trees, and Evelyn leaned her head back and watched the tops of the trees pass over the sun roof backed by a clear blue sky. Twain had found a way to lay down and rest his head on the edge of the open window so he could nap and sniff the fresh air all at the same time. Julia was reading a book, her headphones in place. So they hadn't managed to get her away from the headphones. Oh well. Evelyn was just about to close her eyes when Julia said from the back seat, "I love you too."

"What?" Evelyn turned to look at her daughter who pulled an ear bud out.

"What?"

"You said you loved me too."

"Yeah, didn't you say 'I love you'?"

"No. I do love you, but I didn't say it right then." Julia shook her head.

"I heard someone say 'I love you' clear as day." The thought occurred to Julia just then that she wouldn't have been able to hear her mother say those words clear as day with her earbuds in.

"Mom, have you changed your soap?" Julia said, feeling a bit strange. Evelyn knew why her daughter was asking. She could smell it too.

"No, I haven't."

"The car smells like Grams."

"Lavender. You're right. The car smells of lavender." Twain started wagging his tail so hard in the back seat it was making a thumping sound on the seat. His standard greeting. Julia and Evelyn looked at each other, knowing they were having the same thought but not putting it into words.

"I don't smell anything." Mark piped up from the driver's seat. It seemed life was going to go back to normal for at least one of them.

Other works by K. Patteson:

Ross and Jack Series:

Trouble On The Water
Book 1
ISBN: 978-0-578-67787-3

www.ingramcontent.com/pod-product-compliance
Lightning Source LLC
Chambersburg PA
CBHW061918130726
47908CB00017B/2078